PENGUIN BOOKS

FULL
DISCLOSURE

FULL DISCLOSURE

CAMRYN GARRETT

PENGUIN BOOKS

PENGUIN BOOKS

UK | USA | Canada | Ireland | Australia
India | New Zealand | South Africa

Penguin Books is part of the Penguin Random House group of companies whose
addresses can be found at global.penguinrandomhouse.com.

www.penguin.co.uk
www.puffin.co.uk
www.ladybird.co.uk

Published in Great Britain by Penguin Books 2019
Published in the United States by Alfred A. Knopf, an imprint of
Random House Children's Books, a division of Penguin Random House LLC,
New York 2019
001

Text copyright © Camryn Garrett, 2019
Jacket photograph copyright © Theodore Samuels, 2019

The moral right of the author has been asserted

Set in 9.98 pt Berling LT Std

Printed and bound in Great Britain by Clays Ltd, Elcograf S.p.A.

A CIP catalogue record for this book is available from the British Library

ISBN: 978-0-241-36706-3

All correspondence to:
Penguin Books
Penguin Random House Children's
80 Strand, London WC2R 0RL

For anyone touched by the AIDS crisis.

And for Mom, always.

CHAPTER 1

As much as I've tried to convince him otherwise, my father still thinks he needs to accompany me to my first gynecologist appointment. To him, it's an important rite of passage.

"I'm sure Tía Camila would've taken me," I say, glancing out the car window. It's bad enough that we're going to this appointment *together*, but it's also uncomfortably close to the hospital where he works, which means we're going to run into at *least* three of his patients. "She likes doing this sort of stuff, and we could've worked it around her business trips."

"Well, you're *my* daughter," he says, pulling into a parking spot. "And this is the sort of thing parents live for."

"Somehow I doubt that."

Dad has patches of gray sneaking into his black hair, and there's an indent in the tan skin of his nose where his glasses rest. When he isn't wearing a lab coat, he dresses in old-man clothes like sweater vests and khakis. I wish his lack of fashion sense were the most embarrassing thing about him, but it isn't.

Inside, he actually pulls out a clipboard with *questions* to ask the doctor. I might just die. The waiting room feels too small and smells like cheap air freshener.

He tucks the clipboard by his side, looking down at a questionnaire from the secretary.

"When was your last menstrual cycle?"

"*Dad.*"

"These are normal questions."

"Just . . ." I take the questionnaire from him. "I'll figure this stuff out."

"I ask my patients these sorts of questions all the time, you know. It doesn't have to be awkward."

"But I'm your *kid*. That makes it weirder."

I fly through the questions, and I'm mostly honest. He's already filled out the parts that take the most time—my medical background, especially—so I bring the form back up to the lady at the desk. When I return, Dad's pulled out the clipboard he brought from home, reviewing his questions.

"There's really no reason for you to be nervous, Simone," he says, patting my leg. His glasses keep sliding down his nose. If he were my doctor, I wouldn't be able to take him seriously. "A lot of the women I see are nervous for their first appointments."

"I'm not a woman." My legs bounce up and down. "I'm, like, twelve."

"You're seventeen. Most girls have their first appointment when they're fifteen, but it's more of a formality. You aren't even—"

"Sexually active. I know. But we both know I'm not having sex."

A woman with a gigantic pregnant belly glares at me. I don't know why she seems irritated. She'll be *lucky* if her kid ends up anything like me. I've made it to seventeen without dying, first of all, which I'm not sure my parents even expected.

"So," he says. "Why were you so adamant about making this appointment now?"

I bite my lip. Technically, I don't need to see a gynecologist. I'm not dating anyone. My chances of losing my virginity haven't magically increased recently. But Dr. Khan, my HIV doctor, recommended that I see a gynecologist if I have questions, and, well, I do.

I can't exactly tell my dad the other part of the truth—that I want to know more about sex because of a hot guy at school. There's nothing going on between us, but still. I can hope, can't I?

"It's not bad that you wanted to come," he says, tugging me out of my thoughts. "I just want to know what struck your interest."

"Um. I'm just—you know," I say. "Curious and a little nervous. I want to ask questions, like I told you. I feel like I don't know anything, and Dr. Khan said this would be a good idea."

"You'll have the chance to ask questions," he says. "I promise. I've spoken to Dr. Walker tons of times. She's very good at what she does, and I figured seeing a woman would make you more comfortable."

"Simone Garcia-Hampton?"

The nurse seems nice enough, and I'm grateful that she doesn't make any chitchat with my dad right away. I get up, walking stiffly through the door. Dad presses a hand against my back, guiding me behind the nurse.

"It's been a long time since I've seen you, Dr. Garcia," she says, flashing my father a smile as we enter the examination room. Since she doesn't say anything to me, I just hop up on the table without a word. "How have things been over at St. Mary's?"

"Excellent," Dad says, smiling back. "And how is little Jason?"

I guess I wasn't spared the chitchat after all. It seems like everyone working in the medical field has seen Dad at the hospital or at a doctor's appointment—or he has delivered one of their children.

"Getting bigger every day," she says, flipping through my file. "Okay, Simone. Dr. Walker is going to come in and do a breast exam and check a bunch of other things. We aren't going to do a vaginal exam today, though."

I breathe a sigh of relief. "Thank Go—"

"Goodness," Dad says, giving me a pointed look. "You're thanking goodness, aren't you?"

"Yeah," I say, tucking a short strand of hair behind my ear. Dad is supposed to be a *lapsed* Catholic, but he's more religious than he wants to admit. "I was going to say goodness. Gosh, don't you know me at all?"

The nurse smiles as she does all the normal things, like taking my blood pressure and checking my heartbeat. She asks me about my period and sexual activity, and I try to ignore Dad, standing at my side.

"It's nice to see such a close relationship between father and daughter," she says, holding her clipboard to her chest. "My daughter is attached to my hip. I *wish* I could leave her alone with her father."

"Well, I don't have a mom," I say, shrugging. "So I don't have much of a choice."

Dad gives me another one of his *glances*, but seeing this lady's face is worth it. It gets all red and blotchy, like she's just kicked a puppy by mistake, and she backs toward the door with big, slow steps.

4

"I'm so sorry," she says, shaking her head. "Here—change into this gown and make sure to take off your bra. Dr. Walker will be in to see you soon."

"Simone, that was rude," Dad says as soon as the door shuts. "It's not her fault she doesn't know our family history."

He makes it sound so *formal*. People get confused about our family situation, and I guess I can see why. For one, I don't look like his kid. Even though his skin is the color of darkened sand, it's clear that I'm black, several shades darker than him. I'm sure people assume I take after my mother, especially when they see the ring on Dad's left hand. Dad isn't really *out*. I don't think he tells anyone about Pops, not unless he has to. On the other hand, Pops flaunts his ring to everyone within a ten-mile radius. They're different that way. I just wish the world didn't spend so much time making Dad feel like he has to hide.

"But she shouldn't just make assumptions," I say, stepping behind a curtain and stripping off my clothes. "You know what Pops says: when you assume, you make an *ass* out of you and me."

"I know. It gets worse each time I hear it." He sighs. "Do you have some questions in mind for the doctor?"

"I'm gonna ask her if I can have sex." I pull the gown over my head, shielding myself from the awkwardness that's probably all over his face right now. "And about tearing my hymen. Also about pregnancy."

"Oddly enough, I don't find this funny."

"That's because it isn't." I pull at the edges of the gown before drawing back the curtain and wagging a finger at him. "Sex is never funny, especially when you're me."

His face softens. "Simone—"

5

"Ah, the famous Simone!" A tall white lady with bright red hair and a lab coat swings into the room. "I've heard so much about you from your father. The last time I saw you, you were barely big enough to stand!"

Dr. Walker knows me, but I don't remember her at all. I give a tight smile. Somehow, I doubt she's the great family friend she presents herself to be. I guess it doesn't matter. It's not like I'm looking to be her best friend. I just need her to answer my questions.

"So, Simone," she says, folding her hands. "The reason why Dr. Khan referred you is because I've had other patients with your condition, and I have experience in this field. I want you to know that you can ask me any questions you might have, and I'll try my hardest to answer."

Damn. She gets straight to the point.

"Let's say I want to have sex." I try to mirror her stance on the exam table, placing one leg over the other. My paper gown crinkles as it moves. "Are condoms enough? Do I have to use them if I'm having sex with a girl?"

"Well, there are internal condoms and dental dams if you have sex with someone with a vagina," she says, leaning back on the stool. I have to give her credit; she doesn't seem fazed at all. "But you have to keep in mind that the virus is acquired through an exchange of certain bodily fluids, like blood or semen."

"Wait a minute," Dad says. "Simone, you know that the best way to stay safe is by remaining abstinent. We've spoken about this, honey."

My cheeks heat up. It's another reason why I didn't want him here—I should be able to ask my questions and get answers

without a filter. The worst part is that I *know* he's right: abstinence is the only way to be absolutely sure of preventing HIV
acquisition. I've had that pounded into my brain ever since I
turned thirteen. By now, it's like a reflex.

But that doesn't mean I can't *want* sex. Lately, it keeps creep-
ing into the back of my mind. I'm not sitting around, looking for
people to have sex with, but I *want* it. I want to look at someone
and love them the way other people are able to.

I'd like to know more.

"I *know*," I say, playing with the wrinkled edges of my gown.
"But I won't be a virgin forever. And I'd like to have some idea of
how protection works for me, since my partner probably won't."

Dad shakes his head, groaning. I turn back to Dr. Walker.

"I've tried to google this stuff," I say. "But I get different answers each time."

I know a lot about HIV—including the U=U rule. If someone's viral load, the level of HIV in the blood, is *undetectable*, the
virus is *untransmittable*. In other words, they can't transmit HIV
to someone else. Undetectable = Untransmittable. It doesn't do
much to help me now, though.

"That makes a lot of sense, Simone," Dr. Walker says, placing
her hands on her knees. "And I want you to know that sex is a real
possibility for you when you're ready, all right? You can speak to
your other doctors if you want a second opinion."

I nod. I can't really see myself asking Dr. Khan about sex,
though—she's been seeing me since I was a baby, so she's practically family at this point.

"The best time to have sex would be when your viral load
has been undetectable for at least six months," she says, glancing

down at my file. "I'm not sure if that's the case for you. Either way, it's important that you continue to take your medication every day, at the right times."

I press my lips together. Dr. Khan had to switch me to a new medication because I'd developed resistance to the old one. The last time I saw her, the virus was still detectable in my blood.

"It's also important to take note of the types of sex and the risks that come along with them. Anal sex has the highest rate of transmitting HIV, while oral sex has the lowest rate."

A glance to the side reveals Dad's face, redder than I've ever seen it. He coughs into his elbow, like there's something caught in his throat. I would tease him, but I don't want him to think I'm being immature. I want him to *know* that I've already researched this. I never skip my pills and always cover open wounds with Band-Aids. I'm responsible about my illness.

"Like you said, you'd use condoms, but it's important to make sure they're made of latex or polyurethane," she says, tapping against her folder. "I suppose it could be easier if you're having relations with an HIV-positive partner, but you should take precautions regardless."

"Yeah, I've heard that." I scratch the back of my head. There's one person I keep thinking about, someone with dark skin and a nice smile. "But what if my partner doesn't have HIV? And my viral load is detectable?"

"Simone—" Dad starts.

"What?" I ask, raising a brow. "You don't want me to know? I'll be eighteen next year, Dad. Like you said, I'm not twelve anymore."

HIV medication is weird. Sometimes there are side effects. If

8

you skip it too often, the virus can develop a resistance over time. Maybe this won't be the last time I have to switch medications and start over. Maybe I'll have a partner who doesn't have HIV. Am I banned from having sex with them until my viral load is undetectable again? Or is there another way?

Dr. Walker clears her throat, and I turn back to her. She has this gentle look on her face, like she's speaking to little petting-zoo animals. I'm sure that other patients show up with over-protective dads all the time. She's probably had a version of this conversation before, just less intense.

"That would be a sero-diverse relationship," she says. "There are medications that an HIV-negative person could take in order to prevent transmission; that's something you should discuss more with an HIV specialist. While I'm glad we're talking about this, I really want to stress how important it is to disclose your status *before* anything sexual happens."

"I know." I stare down at my hands. "I've heard about that, too."

In the state of California, there used to be a law saying I could get thrown in jail for having condomless sex without disclosing. It's different now; if I'm undetectable and get the other person to wear a condom, I have a defense. It's just that the law makes things *more real*. It reminds me that I'm different from everyone else.

Pops and I make fun of all the weird ways people think the virus can be acquired—kissing cheeks, touching hands, sharing sodas. But having sex with someone is real. Everyone knows that sex puts you at risk for STDs, but I doubt anyone I go to school with is expecting to deal with HIV. Whenever I imagine what it would be like to tell someone I like, the scene ends with them walking out the door.

"Simone?"

I blink up at Dr. Walker. She's giving me a sad smile, like she can tell what I'm thinking. Part of me wants to hug her.

"Do you have any more questions?"

I shake my head, and she pats my hand.

"Lean back for me, sweetie. We're going to start your breast exam."

CHAPTER 2

My parents gave up on driving me to school ages ago, most likely because I wait until the last possible moment to wake up and get ready. Today's different. Waking up late would mean letting Lydia down.

It's weird to hear Dad pulling out of the driveway as he heads for the hospital. Pops is in the kitchen, making coffee. I guess there's a lot I miss while I'm asleep.

"You're up early." Pops stirs his coffee. He always takes it black. "Are the girls up to something?"

I swallow, sliding past him and the kitchen island. I can tell Pops anything, but the line blurs when it comes to things that are happening to my friends. If Lydia doesn't want her parents to know where we're going, I doubt she'd want *my* parents to know.

"We have to run an errand," I say instead, reaching for a mug in the cupboard. "And we can't go after school, because I have play rehearsal."

"You all need to go together to run this errand?"

I shrug, stealing the coffeepot and pouring a liberal amount into my cup. There's sleep in my eyes, but I can still see his De La Soul shirt clearly—which he wears all the time even though the only students who understand the reference are black,

11

like us. Sometimes I wish I went to the public school where he works, but it's thirty minutes away. Sacred Heart is closer, not as conservative as my old school, and doesn't require uniforms. Even better, no one *knows* me at Sacred Heart, not the way they did at my old school.

Our Lady of Lourdes had only a hundred girls, and we all lived in the same dorm. It meant we were closer than normal classmates. I never minded—until they found out I was positive.

"Simone," Pops says, placing his coffee on the counter. "If something were going on, you'd tell me. Right?"

I sigh. "It's something Lydia doesn't want to tell her parents about. Not now, anyway. We just have to make a stop."

He stares at me for an extra beat.

"I swear," I say, resting my hand on his. "If she were in trouble, I'd tell you."

He grunts into his cup. I turn toward our medicine cabinet, satisfied. In order to keep my viral load down, I have to take a gigantic pill every morning. The alarm on my phone is probably going off, but I don't need it most days. Taking my meds is like clockwork at this point.

I feel Pops's eyes on me as I toss back the pill. He and Dad used to give me stickers for every day I remembered to take it all by myself. If I went a month without missing, they'd get me a prize. I guess my prize is my health now. Definitely not as fun as going to Chuck E. Cheese's.

The doorbell rings, and I jump, almost spilling my coffee. Lydia's on the porch, dark hair tucked behind her ears and face clear of makeup.

"Hey," she says as I open the door. "You ready to go? Claudia's waiting in the car."

"Right." I pause, looking her up and down. She looks paler than usual. "She made you come get me?"

"No, no. I wanted to."

I squint at her.

"You're my friend, Simone," she says, shaking her head. "I'm allowed to want to see you."

"But you're nervous," I say, guessing. "Otherwise, you would've just waited outside."

"A little," she says. "But it's better because of you guys."

As if to prove it, she wraps her arms around me in a hug.

"Aw, Lydia," I say, face in her shoulder. "You're too much."

Really, though, I love her.

"I just have to get my bag," I say, pulling back after a minute. "You should come in."

She nods, following me. Her bag is decorated with different pins—our school logo, characters from *The Lego Movie*, and *I Love Taiwan* pins from her trip to visit family last summer.

"Hi, Lydia," Pops says as I grab my bag off the counter. "How are you?"

"I'm good, thanks." She flashes a smile. "Ready to get to school."

I snort into my arm. Lydia actually *likes* school, something I'll never understand.

"And your parents?"

"They're fine." She rocks back on her heels. "Busy, as usual."

Her parents, Mr. and Mrs. Wu, want her to get good grades, but they aren't annoying about it the way Claudia's parents are.

They never painted multiplication tables on her bedroom wall or forced her to go to math camp, but they do check her progress reports as soon as they're sent home. The most my parents have ever done is ask if I need help from a tutor, and that's when I still went to boarding school. I can't picture them monitoring my computer time or peering over my shoulder every few minutes, but hey, different strokes.

Pops gives me a quick peck on the cheek, waving at Lydia as she drags me toward the door.

"Good luck today, girls," he calls. "Text me once you get to school."

The door slams behind us.

Claudia drives an old blue Ford Bronco, but I never sit in the front. I'm still not sure how Lydia is brave enough to do it, especially today. Whenever I get in the car with her, Claudia alternates between driving like she's in *The Fast and the Furious* and driving like she has a flat tire.

"I'm surprised you still have your license," I say, sliding into the center of the back seat. "Don't you have a ton of tickets?"

"Oh, shut up," she says, hands resting on the wheel. "If you think I'm so horrible, *you* can drive. Believe me, it's not as easy as I make it look. Go take your driver's test and find out."

I could think of a witty comment to throw back at her, but I won't. She's being nicer than usual to Lydia today, which means all her snark needs to end up *somewhere*. I'm sure it'll even out once we get this over with.

The car starts moving right after we buckle up. The gentle movement pulls at my eyelids. I'm so close to sleep, despite the coffee. The silence doesn't do much to help.

"You're just going to get some pills," Claudia says, turning to Lydia. "Come on, it's no big deal."

I blink my eyes open. I can see Claudia's face—full of concern, unusually soft—but I can't see Lydia's. I don't get why she's so nervous.

"I just feel like a liar," she says. "You should've seen my mom the other day. She wanted to talk about *feelings* and *changes*, and I told her I'm not having sex. Now I'm going to get birth control without telling her. Does that make me horrible?"

"I don't think so," I say, shrugging. "Do you *want* to talk to her about banging Ian Waters?"

"First of all, ew." Claudia glances up at me in the mirror. "And second, no one says *bang* anymore."

"I do."

She snorts.

The clinic is about fifteen minutes away, and we spend the rest of the ride in silence. Lydia's parents both work in finance, so she doesn't have to worry about seeing any family friends working there. All she has to do is go in, pay for the pills, and come back out.

Claudia pulls into a parking space. There are about six other cars here, even though it's early in the morning. The faded pink lettering near the heavy metal doors seems like something out of a movie.

I click off my seat belt, leaning forward so that I can see Lydia's face.

"Do you want us to come in with you?" I ask. It's so odd to see her without her signature smoky eye on. "Because we will, if you want us to. We can all walk in together."

Lydia shakes her head, taking off her seat belt.

"No. People might not recognize *me*, but they'll recognize *us* if we're together."

It's more like they'll recognize Claudia and Lydia. They've been friends for ages, going to the same school and playdates at each other's houses.

"There are confidentiality laws," Claudia says, killing the engine.

"Yeah," I say. "The nurses and the doctors can't tell anyone without your permission. It's going to be fine."

"What if we're late to class?"

Claudia and I scoff, the sounds overlapping.

"It doesn't matter," I say. "If anything, we can tell your parents that you were helping me with something family-related. You can tell them that I got sick, if you want."

It would be weird to lie to Mrs. Wu. I've only been to her house once, for a sleepover back in September, and she made pancakes for breakfast when we woke up. But I wouldn't mind doing it for Lydia.

"Ugh," Lydia says, rubbing her arms. "All the lies."

"I feel like that's a vital part of the whole teen-rebellion thing," Claudia offers. "And, like . . . Eventually, your parents will just assume you're on birth control, so you won't have to have some big discussion. It's not like they're *my* parents, you know?"

"I know," Lydia says. "Okay. I'll be right back."

She pushes herself out of the car, slamming the door shut behind her. I guess I could move to the front passenger seat, but I stay in the back, pulling my legs to my chest.

"This is weird," I say, piercing the silence. "I never thought

16

I'd come here. I figured I wouldn't have any reason to even *think* about sex."

"Please," Claudia says. "You think about sex more than anyone I know. What are you talking about?"

Ugh. Claudia and Lydia are the first—and best—friends I've made at Sacred Heart. Part of me, something deep in my stomach, feels like I should be able to tell them that I'm HIV positive.

"I don't know." I push my hair back. "Just because I *think* about it doesn't mean it'll happen." I leave my other thought unsaid: *Just because I think about a particular guy all the time doesn't mean anything will happen.*

She turns, raising a dark brow at me. Her hair is short, a bob cut that hasn't grown an inch since the first day I met her, and she has the same tan skin as my dad.

"Do you wanna tell me something, kid?"

I scrunch my lips together. Claudia Perez is not the type of person I want to keep secrets from, but this is *secret*. The biggest one I've got. I don't think she would tell, but I don't actually *know*.

"*Simone*," Claudia presses. "What's up?"

"I just . . ." I look down. Study sheets litter the floor, and I crush them under my feet. "I just can't picture anyone wanting to do it with *me*."

"Why not?" Her voice is sharp. "I'd have sex with you, if I were into it. You're awesome."

I laugh, despite myself. "Do you know how *weird* you sound?"

"Well, who cares?" She shifts again, giving me a half smile. "Why wouldn't someone want to *bang* you?"

I'm not sure what to say. Lydia opens the passenger door, sliding in. Her face is flushed, and there's a small white bag in her hand. We wait in silence for her to say something.

"She was the nicest lady ever," Lydia finally says, heaving a sigh. "I don't know why I was so worried. She was nice on the phone, too, and answered all my questions."

I squeeze her shoulder. "I'm so proud of you, babe."

"Yuppp." Claudia smacks her hands against the steering wheel like it's a drum. "Lydia's the best."

I can't tell if Lydia's flushed or if she's blushing. Claudia pulls out of the parking lot, heading toward our school.

"I just took it," Lydia says after a moment. "So I have to take it this time every day. I think it'll be fine."

"How do you feel?" Claudia asks before I can. "Better?"

"Definitely," Lydia says, letting out another big breath. "Ian and I are starting to—you know, take more steps, so I'm glad I'm prepared. I thought I'd feel worse about lying to my parents, though."

"I think that's normal," I say, leaning back in my seat. Memories of my appointment with Dr. Walker make me wish I lied to my parents more often. "Sometimes you need your little secrets."

"You guys are great," Lydia says. Claudia doesn't take her eyes off the road, but I smile at her, even though she can't see me. "And I love you lots. I know that you didn't have to wake up so early before school—"

"That was Simone's problem," Claudia interrupts. "Not mine. I'm always awake."

"Okay, but I already have an issue with waking up before

18

nine," I say. "It's not my fault that I feel more awake at night. The American Academy of Pediatrics—"

"—says that kids shouldn't be up so early," Lydia finishes, laughter in her voice. "We *know*. You only say it every single morning. I could probably recite the study in my sleep."

There are already a bunch of cars in the school parking lot. It's a large brick building that could be a firehouse or a nunnery from the fifties, but just happens to be a center for learning. Claudia's eighteen-year-old Bronco couldn't look more different than the sleek silver cars beside it.

"Come on, guys," she says, pulling out her keys. "I still need to go to my locker. There's a project I shoved in there. Lydia, you're responsible and I love you. Tell Simone that she'll have sex one day with the right person."

I flip my middle finger at her. She just flashes a smile. I try to follow her into the building, pushing past the cool burst of fall air outside, but Lydia immediately hooks arms with me.

"What's this about sex?" Up close, she doesn't look as clammy as she did earlier. "It's fun. You should try it."

"I thought you guys weren't there yet?"

"Well, there are different tiers."

"It's not the issue of *having* sex," Claudia says, stopping at her wide blue locker. I lean against the others as she fiddles with her combination. "She doesn't think she could find anyone to do it with her."

"What?" Lydia glances at me. "Why not?"

"You know, I don't really think I need to use my locker," I say, pulling at our interlocked arms. She doesn't let go. "Seriously, I'm not kidding. I put all the important stuff in my bag. I think the only thing I left in there is my orientation packet."

"I used my locker, like, once before today," Claudia offers, locker door swinging open. "But it's different. You've only been here, what, two months? I've been here three years."

"Wait a minute," Lydia says, holding up her hands. "Who cares about lockers? Simone, anyone would be lucky to have you. This is ridiculous."

This is the Lydia I know.

I know they're both speaking the truth—I *am* pretty awesome. Two months ago, I didn't even care about finding a boyfriend or having sex or anything like that. I just wanted to focus on integrating into a new place. Now I'm student director of the school musical and know how to find at least half of my classes.

"Maybe the patriarchy is killing my brain cells." I thump my fingers against my thigh. "Because I sound like I have no self-confidence at all. I'm an awesome bitch."

"Obviously," Lydia says. "It's common knowledge."

"There's no reason for anyone to be a dick to you, dude," Claudia says, holding her poster board against her chest. "If anyone is, tell me so I can kick their ass."

"Then get your legs ready," I say. "Because everyone is a dick. All guys our age, anyway."

"I resent that," Lydia says. "Ian is cute *and* sweet."

Claudia and I give her a pointed look. Lydia folds her arms, huffing.

"Well, no one is perfect. What about that kid from Drama you like?" Lydia says, wisely diverting attention from her boyfriend.

It doesn't make any sense to compare Ian, president of the

Mock Trial team, to *Miles Austin*. For one thing, I'm fairly certain that Miles is the only black lacrosse player in existence. Somehow, he manages to fit in with the other members of the team, with their clothes from J.Crew and Vineyard Vines. I'm sure the company he keeps says tons about him. None of it is attractive. But, for some reason, Miles still is.

"Well, he's not a jerk," I say, counting on my fingers. "He can lift really heavy things like it's no big deal. He's fun to talk to. He has a nice ass."

"I'm so glad I'm not attracted to boys," Claudia says, pulling her backpack onto her shoulders. I grab her rolled-up poster board, tucking it under my arm. "It sounds exhausting."

"Maybe you should actually *do* something about your crush." The look Lydia gives me is dripping with pity. "If you like someone, you're supposed to tell them, Simone."

I hold back a groan. Maybe I would say something if I were completely sure that Miles likes girls. Whenever I see him at rehearsal, he asks me about another musical. I've never met a straight guy who cares about musicals.

I know that stuff like the way he dresses and how he talks doesn't make him gay. But I still have this *feeling*. Maybe it's the musicals. Maybe it's the fact that he's always nice to everyone. Maybe it's because I've never seen him with a girl. *Ugh*. If only I'd gone to a coed boarding school, then I'd know how to deal with this shit.

"It's just not that simple," I say, lowering my voice. "You guys make everything seem easy."

When I'm around Claudia and Lydia, I feel cool. But feeling cool isn't enough. There's no reason for Miles to say more than a few words to me. I'm mostly fine with it; I don't care about chasing after a boy. It's just that part of me aches when I see him. There's a reason why everyone is drawn to him—during the rehearsals, in the halls—but I can't exactly say what it is. He just exists, and that's enough. I wish I could do that, too.

CHAPTER 3

After the last bell of the day rings, I head toward the auditorium for rehearsal. I can't tell if I'm into theater because of Lin-Manuel Miranda, like everyone else, or because I actually like it. Probably a combination of both. If I didn't enjoy it, I don't think I'd be able to spend two hours after school every day working on this musical.

"All right, come together, everyone," Ms. Klein says. During school hours, she teaches chemistry, so she's not exactly a theater expert, though I've been trying not to judge. She continues, "I think we're doing fine, mostly. *Rent* is a difficult show to do at a high school level, and I'm proud of how far we've come already."

The members of the cast and crew gather around her in a weird half circle. Mr. Palumbo stands beside her with his hands folded. He's a small man with a big belly and bald head. I feel like he has more command of the room than Ms. Klein, even though he isn't speaking. He catches my eye and winks.

Mr. Palumbo is probably the coolest teacher I've ever had. I'm in his music class, but during my first few days here, he let me hang out in his room during my study hall period. Most student directors get chosen after doing school shows for a while, but he chose me after a rousing debate about a potential film adaptation of *Wicked*. Now here we are.

"We have to keep in mind that the premiere isn't too far from now," Ms. Klein continues. Her eyes lock on me, and I look away. Back at my old school, I was a member of the backstage crew, but I never directed anything. Ms. Klein's not the only one who can tell that I don't know what I'm doing. "We have just over five weeks to make this show the best it can be."

Laila, a senior who plays Mimi, leans against me. She hugged me on the first day of rehearsal, and didn't glare at me behind Palumbo's back like some of the other cast members. I'm not sure if I'm allowed to pick favorites, but she's definitely mine.

"That's more than enough time to nail the finishing touches," Mr. Palumbo says. "So I don't want any of you to worry."

"But we have to remember that the audience isn't expecting much from us," Ms. Klein says, shaking her clasped hands. "And we want to blow them away, don't we? We want to show all of those parents who didn't want us to do this show that you are capable of handling the subject matter, that we're capable of going above and beyond."

"There also isn't any pressure," Mr. Palumbo says, glancing at Ms. Klein. The auditorium, which is normally filled with music from the pit, singing from the stage, and whispering from the crew, is oddly silent. "The most important thing is that you all learn more about what the theater process is like, to see if this is something you want to do beyond high school. And if it isn't, that's okay! I'm a teacher, but I do this for fun. Some of us just love theater."

Ms. Klein glances at him out of the corner of her eye. I love his real life subtweeting. She's never called him on it directly, but I'm waiting for the moment where one of them blows up.

I'm not sure how Ms. Klein would react if I said I'm just doing this for fun. Maybe she'd strangle me. Really, though, what does she expect? I love musicals, but making a career out of them is a huge risk. I'm not sure if I'm talented enough for that.

"It's also important that we have the best chance of winning something at the High School Theater Awards," Ms. Klein says, smiling without any teeth.

At the mention of awards, a low rumble spreads throughout the crowd. Everyone whispers at the same time.

Laila sighs against me. "I swear, that's all she ever talks about."

"Well," I say, leaning down to whisper in her ear, "awards will make her look good."

"But winning isn't everything," Mr. Palumbo says, taking a step forward. "I want you all to remember that *Rent* is an amazing play for so many reasons, one of them being how connected we are to the humanity of each of the characters. If there's anything I want you to take away from this experience, it's that."

"Yes," Ms. Klein says, lips pressed together. "The musical is well known for its subject matter, but especially for the music. I suppose the characters are also important."

They lapse into silence. Someone coughs.

"Can we start rehearsal now?" Eric, another one of our leads, calls out. He has an Afro that's longer than mine, and I resent him for it. "Because I have to be home at five, and I can't keep being late."

"Well, does our student director have any words of encouragement?" Mr. Palumbo asks, gesturing toward me. "Simone is more articulate than I am, so I'm sure she'll have something amazing to say."

Wow, no pressure at all. Thanks, dude.

"Uh, yeah." I take a step forward, Laila sliding away from me. I feel naked in the absence of an ally. I can't read all the faces, but I don't think I have many fans around here. Most of my notes on rehearsals are negative, unlike Mr. Palumbo, who makes everything sound like a compliment. "I think we're honestly doing great so far. I know that things are starting to get tight because other sports and clubs are going on, but I have to thank you guys for staying dedicated."

All I'm getting are blank stares. Eric leans over to whisper something in the ear of Claire, an ensemble member. She giggles. I cough.

"The show isn't going to be perfect when we do it on opening night," I say, rubbing the back of my neck. "I don't even think Broadway shows are perfect. They do hundreds of shows, and there are notes for every performance. So don't worry about perfection. Just try to make everyone in the audience cry."

A few laughs echo against the walls of the auditorium. Back at my old school, all the plays took place in the cafeteria. Here, the auditorium is dedicated solely to Drama Club. I love everything about it—the stairs that lead up to the stage and the heavy red curtains that frame it. The old, heavy smell of mothballs, the fresh wood shavings and open paint cans from backstage. The vastness, the way the room continues on, like walls can't stop it. Whenever Laila or Eric sings, I can feel it echoing in my chest.

"Damn straight," Rocco, who is playing Angel, hollers. "Let's do this!"

"Okay, cast members get ten minutes to go over their lines," Ms. Klein says. "*Exactly* ten minutes. We're going to run the entire show, so I want you to pay attention to how often you're looking at the script."

Mr. Palumbo glances at her, but instead of saying anything, turns his attention to the rest of the students.

"If you're ensemble, come over to the choir room with me," he says. "We're going to focus on nailing the first few songs."

I resist the urge to sigh. That means I'm going to be left alone with Ms. Klein. I try not to pout as he leads a large chunk of the company out of the auditorium. It's not even like I can work with the cast on my own terms, since Ms. Klein just gave them something to do. Maybe I'll watch their performances with her and try to give some pointers of my own.

As the actors take their places, I shoot Pops a picture of D.W. from *Arthur* without any context. He loves things like that, even though I don't think he understands them. He doesn't answer right away, which means he's probably doing something important—maybe grading assignments. I flick through my other apps—Facebook, Instagram—but it's the same stuff I saw at lunch. The algorithms are the worst. I feel like I'm running in circles all day.

Sometimes Twitter can be pretty interesting. It wasn't such a big deal at my old school, but it feels like everyone here has an account. It's great for news—breakups, college announcements, or just drama in general. The backstage crew runs the Drama Department's account, which is super interesting because of a certain someone I'm trying not to look at.

"What about crew?" a freshman named Lily calls from the stage. "What do *we* do?"

"Jesse is in charge of you," I say, shoving my phone in my pocket. "Ask him what he needs help with. If you can't find him, I'll try to get something for you."

Lily nods before scampering backstage. I turn my attention to the rest of the backstage crew kids. Most of them are focused on painting set pieces like tables and chairs so they look like they came from the same place. It doesn't take long for my eyes to focus on one kid in particular.

Miles is bent over this wooden frame taller than me, but I can see everything: the tendons in his arms, the crease of muscle in his legs, and the curve of his ass. I know, I know—I guess I shouldn't be looking at that. It's just hard *not* to. I'm not used to seeing guys all over the place. It was different at my old school. There were tons of pretty girls, but I'd known them for ages and didn't think to check them out.

Here? I'm not sure where I should look. It's sensory overload with all the girls *and* boys without uniforms. All I know is that Miles's ass is a pretty nice place to rest my eyes.

"Hey, Simone. What's the play of the day?"

I blink. He's looking at me now, a smile on his face. Maybe he didn't see me staring.

"They're musicals, not plays," I say, crossing my arms over my chest. "We've been doing this a month, Miles. Come on. Don't tell me my musical intervention hasn't made any difference."

"Fine, what's the *musical* of the day?" he amends, turning toward me. I forget to breathe for a second, but it's super quick, so it doesn't count. "What was it last time? *Cats*?"

"*Ugh*, no way," I groan, climbing up on the stage and plopping down next to him. He slides down so that he's sitting next to me. His knee, so much bigger than mine, rests against me. I glance up at his face, but he doesn't seem to notice. It's not that his touch is surprising, exactly. It's the warmth of another human, close enough to share, that startles me. "Don't talk about *Cats* with me. That show is terrifying."

He smiles wider, showing a flash of white teeth. I blink extra fast.

"You can't be *afraid* of *Cats*. I don't believe you." He shakes his head. "Your favorite musical is about a guy who cuts people up and bakes them into pies."

"Because it's amazing, obviously." I roll my eyes. "The actors in *Cats* are just creepy as hell, you know? Rolling all over the stage in their weird-ass costumes and trying to slither into the audience and hump your leg. I'm not into that. Keep the acting onstage."

"I don't know." He shrugs. Again, his skin rubs against mine. It's barely there, but I notice it. I can't help but notice. "That sounds cool. Like you're part of the art."

"Well, it's not." I shudder, remembering the time Dad and Pops took me to see the show. We see something on Broadway every summer when we visit my half-brother, Dave, but that summer was disappointing, to say the least. "Trust me on that. If the actors *have* to come into the audience, they should just do it like *The Lion King*. It's a thousand times better."

"You're shitting on something that Webber guy wrote?" He gives a dramatic gasp. "Wait, wait, wait. Have we shifted into an alternate universe?"

29

"Oh, shut up," I say as he collapses into laughter. "Don't get me wrong; all the music in *Cats* is amazing. I'd just rather pay attention to what's happening onstage without being distracted by a grown adult humping my leg."

He's staring openly at my face, smiling. Miles smiles more than anyone else I know. I wouldn't say his face lights up, exactly, because it's always bright. It makes it too easy to pretend he's into me.

Maybe this would be easier if he were a jerk. I figured he'd give me a hard time when he first showed up, but he hasn't done anything horrible since he joined the crew. He doesn't fool around with anyone in the prop closet and is always looking for extra work to do. I guess the only shitty thing he's done is walk around being a regular person instead of making out with me against a wall.

"So." He's moved closer to me while I wasn't paying attention. When he speaks, I feel his breath against my cheek. "If *Cats* isn't the musical of the day, what is?"

"Right." I scoot over a bit. His mouth twitches. "Uh, I love *Aida*. It's about this Nubian princess who is taken as a slave and then falls for Radames, the captain of the Egyptian Guard."

"Wow." He blinks. "Is it Webber?"

"*No*," I say. "It's Elton John, actually."

"Just Elton John?" He raises a brow. "Are you sure?"

"I mean . . . there's Tim Rice," I say, trying not to smile. "And he collaborated with Webber on stuff like *Evita*."

"Of course." He shakes his head. "You're in *love* with Webber."

"It's *not* Webber!" I nudge his shoulder. "Webber and Tim

Rice are two *completely* different people!" He starts shaking his head, but I go on. "It doesn't really count. Plus, I love *Sweeney Todd* and that's Sondheim."

"*Sure*, okay." He smacks his hands against his jeans, shaking his head like an old man. "Come on, Simone. You can say whatever you want, but I know you by now."

There's this stupid fluttering in my chest. All I can think about is kissing him and how I can't do that if he doesn't like girls.

I resist the urge to run a hand through my hair. Lydia would know what to say. What *would* Lydia say?

"*Anyways*." I swallow. "I was just thinking . . . You know, my friends are the co-presidents of the GSA. Are you gonna be at the meeting later today?"

"Uh." His brows furrow. "Should I be?"

"Well, I mean . . ." My voice trails off. Trying to *relate* and be *understanding* is overrated. "I've been to a few meetings before. It's cool to be around a bunch of other people who are like you. I just figured that you would want—"

"Wait," he says. "What do you mean by 'people like me'?"

Oh God. He's really going to make me spell it out.

"You know," I say. "It's the Gay-Straight Alliance. Other gay guys are there. I mean, there are straight people, too, but I promise queer people are accurately represented and—"

"Simone." His hand, very delicately, rests on my shoulder. I glance at his face. He looks like he's fighting back a smirk— Why is he laughing? "I—I think you've got it wrong."

It takes a second for his words to register.

"Oh," I say. "You're . . . *not* gay."

He shakes his head. "I'm not gay."

But the *musicals*. Miles *always* wants to talk about musicals. Every rehearsal, he manages to find me, always asking about the musical of the day and wanting me to elaborate . . .

Wait. He always *asks*, but he didn't even know who wrote *Aida*. I had to tell him. Just like I had to tell him about *Rent* and *Cabaret* and *Fiddler on the Roof*.

Oh.

Everything has gone silent. Then, the only thing I hear is Miles's quiet laughter in my ear. My cheeks flush. How did I think he was gay? My parents are gay, or at least queer. I should be able to figure this stuff out. It's annoying as hell when people make assumptions about me, and somehow I've ended up doing exactly the same thing with Miles.

But this isn't a bad thing. This isn't a bad thing at *all*. Before I can stop it, I'm smiling. It's not a normal smile, either. I'm smiling one of those stupid openmouthed smiles that shows all my teeth. I scoot back, pushing myself to my feet.

"*Oh*," I repeat. "That's—dude, that's awesome. That's fantastic. I mean, I love gay people, don't get me wrong. It's just—I'm glad you're not. Not gay, I mean. But not because I'm homophobic."

"Oh my God." Miles snorts, running a hand over his face. His shoulders shake with silent laughter. "Oh my *God*, Simone."

I force myself to drop the smile, pressing my lips tightly together. It doesn't do much to help. The corners of my mouth itch to turn up, even as my cheeks burn. I'm sure that his friends will hear about this later, since I've made a complete fool out of myself. If I'm lucky, they'll be the only other people laughing at me.

"Yeah, I just, uh . . ." There's nothing to lose now, so I plow forward. "Do you, like, um, like, you know—go out?"

His face goes blank. He might actually look *concerned* for me.

Oh God. I have no idea how normal people ask each other out, but I'm sure it's not supposed to be this humiliating. In my defense, I've never had to do it before. At this rate, I'll never be doing it again.

"All right," Ms. Klein says, clapping her hands. "We're starting!"

Thank *God*. I jump off the stage and bolt for the seats. I already know that there's no coming back from this.

CHAPTER 4

It's been thirty minutes and I still can't believe I did that. I could've just apologized for making assumptions about his sexuality. I could've just walked away and said bye, removing myself from the situation like a normal person. Hell, if I was going to make a fool of myself, I could've done it another time. Now I have to stay at rehearsal until five and try to avoid him at the same time. It's pretty hard to focus on literally *anything* else, because the scene keeps playing out in my memory.

Mr. Palumbo, now back from the choir room, claps his hands together, snapping me out of my embarrassing instant-replay loop. "That was amazing, guys. I think Simone's suggestions are really helping you bring the scene to life."

"Are you sure she doesn't have any more *notes*?" Eric asks, fixing me with a pointed stare. "She always does."

A few members of the ensemble turn to watch us. I bite back a groan. He couldn't have picked any other day to do this?

"Come on, Eric. It's Simone's job to provide notes. They aren't personal, remember?" Mr. Palumbo turns to me. "*Do* you have any notes?"

"Uh, no." I'm trying not to flush, but I doubt it's working. Thanks, Eric, for calling me out in front of everyone. "Not this time."

Rocco shuffles off the stage, Eric following behind. I'm not very close, but I still see Eric roll his eyes. Part of me can't blame him. I'm sure he can tell I wasn't paying attention. God, now I'm letting a *boy* distract me from the musical. Normal people get crushes without letting it go to their heads, or at least they're able to *act* like things are normal.

I've never been good at acting.

"Hey." Mr. Palumbo squeezes my shoulder. "You okay, champ?"

"Yeah," I say, unfolding my arms. "It's just an off day."

It's the understatement of the year, but if he thinks so, he doesn't say it. I've never been so glad that Ms. Klein left early.

"Come on, guys," I call, tucking my clipboard under my arm. Some of the kids onstage look over at me, but not all of them. "We're going to run the whole first act, with the sets and everything. Make sure that the crew is ready. I want to get notes for you so that we have them on Saturday."

Mr. Palumbo smiles at me. "That's the Simone I know."

"She didn't exactly run away."

Jesse comes out from behind the curtain, a pair of headphones resting around his neck. He has short, bushy brown hair and light brown skin. He has a habit of wearing all black at every rehearsal just to set an example for the other crew members. That's our crew chief: always taking this more seriously than everyone else combined.

Miles steps out next to him and I freeze. He glances at me, our eyes locking for a moment. I can't read his expression. I don't need to. He's probably telling Jesse all about what happened. I whirl around so I don't have to see the look on his face. I actually

35

like working with Jesse. If he heard about this, there's no way he'd take me seriously.

Come on, Simone, *think*. I could tell Miles I had a mild allergic reaction to the trail mix in the vending machine. *Or* I could blame it on my period, but that's, like, breaking the rules of feminism. I think.

"Hey, Simone."

I tense, turning my head slightly. It's just Jesse walking up behind me—thank *God*. Miles is nowhere in sight.

"Hey," I say, exhaling. I'm glad he's here, since thinking about the play is what I *should* be doing. "I don't know if you heard, but we're gonna run the whole first act. If you have your script, you might want to mark it up."

He nods, but his eyes linger on my face.

I cross my arms. "What?"

"Oh, nothing," he says, but there's a little smile on his face. "You just seem a bit stressed out."

Fuck. Miles told him. I hesitate for a moment before waving wildly toward the stage. Even though I just made an announcement, people are still lingering, like there's nothing to do. I like to leave the yelling to Ms. Klein, but watching them drag their heels makes me understand why she does it.

"Good point." He stares at my hands. "Are you sure there isn't anything else—boy trouble?"

My cheeks heat up again. Jesse is nice and everything, but we don't talk about anything besides the play. This seems like an awkward time to suddenly start being friends.

"Ugh," I groan, running a hand through my hair. "Did he tell you about it? *Already?* Look, it's not as bad as it sounds—"

"Tell me about what?" He shakes his head. "Miles just said you were having a rough day. You have that look about you—the boy-trouble look. I know I see it in the mirror all the time."

"Oh." Miles didn't tell him. I find myself smiling. "Boys suck, don't they?"

"Agreed," Jesse says. "And, for some reason, we still like them. It's the way of the world."

I might be wrong, but his eyes seem to linger on Rocco a little longer than they should. It's not like Rocco is a bad guy. It's just—they don't seem to go together. Then again, I don't think I match up with Miles, either. He's popular and good at talking to people, while I could make a career out of acting like a fool. It's nice to know I'm not the only one who's bad at this whole crush thing.

"We're gonna be eighty by the time this is finished," Jesse says, shifting his attention to the stage. "I think the other kids get worse every year. When I was a freshman, everything got done way ahead of time."

Most of the scenery is painted dark gray with a little bit of colorful graffiti spray painted on the sides. There's still a lot to do, but it doesn't look completely horrible.

"Oh, come on." I nudge his shoulder and he raises a brow. "It doesn't look *that* bad, dude. I'm sure you'll pull it together."

"Let's hope so." He folds his arms. "Otherwise, we're screwed."

"Your positivity is blinding." I shake my head, shoving my hands in my pockets. "Hey, we should talk more sometime. Maybe during lunch? You're really the only other student in, like, a leadership role."

"Sure. We can go over your notes," he says, pressing his lips

37

together in a smile. "But it might take more than a lunch period to get through all of them."

"I don't *mean* to have so many," I say. God, I hope I'm not blushing. "Palumbo just said to do what feels right, so I write down everything I'm thinking, and then I end up with pages and pages of notes. But I don't always expect Palumbo to agree with them. I keep thinking he'll tell me to shut up one of these days."

"Simone, it's fine." Jesse laughs, hands resting on his headphones. "I'm just teasing you."

Maybe he is, but it doesn't feel it. I'm sure Jesse isn't the only one who's noticed I'm new to this job.

"Hey, guys!"

Jesse and I turn at the voice. I almost jump backward when I see Miles standing at the door. My hands tense at my sides.

"What's up?" Jesse asks. I can't make my lips move.

"Principal Decker wants to see Simone." He glances at me for the briefest second. "She said right away. I think it's important."

Jesse turns to me expectantly. I just shrug. I've met the principal only once, and it was the day before I started here. She's nice enough. I can't think of any reason why she'd want to see me.

"Palumbo, I'll be right back," I call, jogging toward the doors. "Jesse, do me a favor and get the set for the next scene ready while I'm gone?"

I let the door slam behind me.

"Did she tell you what she wanted?" I ask Miles, switching my clipboard to my other hand. "Because, if it's something that'll take a while, I need to tell Palumbo—"

"Simone." There's a smile in his voice, and I snap my eyes

back to him. He bites his lip for a moment, something so quick I'm not sure I actually saw it. "The principal didn't actually need to talk to you. I just wanted to tell you something."

"What?" The flutters are back in my stomach again. I could handle the principal, but Miles alone? That's an entirely different beast. "What is it?"

He takes a step forward, and I press my back against the wall. I might be crushing someone's art project. He makes a noise, something like a soft snort. "You ran away."

I swallow. "I don't know what you're talking about."

I know *exactly* what he's talking about. I've only been replaying each excruciating detail over in my mind since it happened.

"You asked me a question," he says, lifting up my chin. "You left before I could answer."

He's touching my chin. *His fingers are touching my chin*, like in the movies I make fun of with my friends. I'm definitely not laughing now. They're soft, like he doesn't spend all his free time building sets and swinging lacrosse sticks. My heart is thumping.

"Really?" I say. Somehow, my voice is still working. "I figured— I don't know—that you wouldn't want to."

"How could you—" He stops himself, swallowing. "I want to. I definitely want to."

I'm either dreaming or high. Maybe both.

I wrap my arm around his neck, pulling him closer to me. He presses his lips against mine.

If I didn't have the wall for support, I'd be on the ground.

CHAPTER 5

Miles kissed me yesterday. Miles told me he wanted to go out with me yesterday, and then kissed me again. Miles kissed me, told me he wanted to go out with me, kissed me again, and now we're walking down the hallway together. I don't think this is real life. This must've been how Tracy from *Hairspray* felt when she finally got the guy. It's unreal.

Sure, we aren't holding hands or anything, but we're close enough that our shoulders are touching. And maybe people can't tell we kissed, but it doesn't really matter. I can't stop smiling. We're not even talking—I'm not sure what I can say without smiling like a creep—but I don't care. Being next to him is enough.

"I have to go to English," I say, slowing down my steps. "And that's upstairs."

He scowls like a little kid. I'm sure I look like a freaky clown who can't wipe off a smile.

"Don't worry," I say, patting his shoulder. God, who pats shoulders? Who do I think I am—Dr. Phil? "I'll see you at rehearsal later, right?"

"Yeah, I'm looking forward to the musical of the day." He bends down, pressing a kiss against my cheek. I have to *go*, but he takes his sweet time. Kissing him on the mouth is better, but I like the way my cheek tingles once he moves away. "I'll see you later, Simone."

I may or may not be staring at his ass while he walks down the hall. I watch until he fades into the crowd before finally turning toward the stairs. There are only a few minutes left until the bell.

Back at my old school, I couldn't walk down the hall without noticing at least five familiar faces. Here, it's pretty rare that I see someone I know. But today Eric is standing by the stairs, talking to someone. He glances up as I walk by, and I give him a big wave. The kid frowns so hard it looks like a sneer.

I blink, forcing myself up the stairs. Eric must *really* hate my notes.

• • •

"Oh my God, Simone, I have to know *everything*. Is he a good kisser? He just took you in the middle of the hallway and started making out with you? Just like that?"

Lydia is practically squealing as we walk down the hallway at the end of the day. Claudia rolls her eyes but doesn't say anything. I duck my head to hide my smile. It happened yesterday, but I can still feel the imprint of his lips on mine.

"Well, he called me out of rehearsal to see the principal," I say. This is the most cliché thing ever—me and my best friends squealing over a boy—but I don't care. "I swear to Cate Blanchett I thought I was going to melt right then and there."

"You are *such* a dramatic person," Claudia says, leaning against the wall of lockers. "I can't even handle you, *or* that boy. Why don't you date someone who actively avoids lacrosse, like a normal person? I think my brother is single."

My locker is in the same hall as Claudia's, which is probably the only reason why I was able to find it my first few weeks at Sacred Heart.

"You sound like a commercial," I say. "And anyway, isn't Julio, like, five years older than us?"

"Aren't you supposed to be looking for your welcome packet?" she mimics. "How did you forget who your guidance counselor is?"

"I don't *know*." How do I open the locker again? I spin to the left, right, and left again. It pops open on the first try. Claudia doesn't seem impressed. "My old school had us assigned according to last name. It's all messed up over here."

"It's not that complicated," Claudia says. "Here, let me do it."

"Don't listen to her." Lydia huffs. "Tell me what else happened!"

"He actually freaked me out a little bit with the principal thing," I say, tossing a pile of notes into the garbage. I've only been here a couple of months, but it's already a mess in here. "I thought something happened, like my parents needed me or something."

"Did you let him know he freaked you out?" Claudia asks, folding her arms. "Because I would've."

"I did," I say, but I feel like laughing. The kiss lasted maybe a minute or two, and here I am, still thinking about it. "But it was really good, Lydia. You were right—it's different when it's with someone you like. It's better. But listen, you have to promise not to talk about this at dinner Saturday night. My dads will never let it go."

42

"Say it isn't so," Claudia gasps. "You aren't telling us just to force your heteronormative agenda on us?

"I'm *not*," I protest, looking under a textbook. "I just—I *try* not to be so straight all the time."

I've only ever spoken to them about my crush on Miles. It would be weird to talk about Sarah now, like I'm backtracking, trying to present myself as a completely different person. Besides, Claudia likes making fun of me too much. Our whole relationship is built around making fun of each other. If she made fun of the way I used to feel about Sarah, I don't know if I could just brush it off.

"Oh, Mony. You sound so sad. I like boys, too," Lydia says. "Maybe you should consider the rest of your options."

I bite my lip. She's had multiple crushes on both girls *and* boys. It's not like that for me. I think girls—or people who look like girls—are pretty, but that doesn't always mean I have a crush. Besides, most of the people I'm attracted to are celebrities, and like Claudia said, those don't count.

The only person I was completely sure about was Sarah. It just doesn't feel like enough to make me think I'm bisexual like Lydia.

"Boys suck," Lydia continues. "And Ian doesn't know how to do a ton of stuff, like—"

"Damn," Claudia says. "I was just kidding. Poor Ian. If it helps, I'm not very good at going down on Emma, but I try because I love her."

I raise my eyebrows. Lydia cocks her head to the side.

"What?" Claudia says. "It's not like I'm incapable of having

43

sex. I just don't get into it, but I don't mind doing it if she wants—Look, it's complicated, okay?"

Sex comes after kissing, doesn't it? I don't know how any of this works, not really, since I haven't done anything more than go on a date. With the way Lydia talks about it, I figure she and her boyfriends started doing sex stuff right away. Even Claudia and her girlfriend are doing *things*. I might be getting ahead of myself, but I know I want to kiss Miles again. He can't get the virus from kissing, but I already know that *I* want more. What if he does, too?

"Guys." I grip my locker door, turning my body toward them. "What am I gonna do if we kiss again?"

"Enjoy it?" Lydia says, brows furrowed. "I don't understand. Didn't you *like* kissing him?"

"Yeah, of course," I say, trying to hold back a sigh. This would be easier if they *knew* why I'm so freaked out. "But what if he wants to have sex?"

Lydia cocks her head to the side. Claudia raises her brows. They both share a *look*.

"You literally kissed *once*, Simone," Claudia says slowly, like I might not understand. "It doesn't mean you're getting married."

"But what if—"

"I know what you mean," Lydia says carefully. "The kiss happened so fast, and now you're worried about what's gonna happen next. But sex is such a big step. I don't think you should worry about it so much until you know for sure where you guys are going with this. Does that make sense?"

That's the solution? Don't think about it? Maybe I *am* getting ahead of myself. Maybe nothing is going to happen after that kiss, even though I still feel wisps of it on my lips. A big part of me *hopes* there's more after this—even if it means I'll have to tell him the truth and risk the consequences.

"God, look at her," Claudia says, bringing me back to Earth. "She actually thinks they're getting married."

"I don't!"

"Simone," Lydia says. "You're kinda acting like it."

"I can't tell if you really like him or if you're just *really* horny," Claudia says. "Either way, you could use a good vibrator. We should all hit up a sex shop. I need to buy one for Emma, anyway."

"Don't you need ID?" Lydia asks. "We aren't old enough."

"We'll fake them." Claudia shrugs. "So, Saturday?"

"*Guys*," I moan. "You're not helping."

"Trust me," Claudia says, grinning. "A vibrator will do *wonders*."

I sigh, turning back to my locker. It's still a mess of papers that looks dangerously close to toppling to the ground. On my first day, it felt like *everyone* had something to give me: schedules, supply lists, rules, class syllabi. It's a mountain of white that makes me look like I just toss shit in here without a second glance. I scan the small space, keeping my eyes open for a blue folder. With this mess, I doubt there's a chance of me finding anything I need. A few stray papers float to the floor, and I bend to pick them up.

"Come on, Simone." Claudia squats down, grabbing some papers. "We're trying to help. I don't mean to sound bitchy. It's just—well, we know you don't have a lot of experience with this."

"Gee, thanks," I mutter, grabbing the remaining papers.

"See you later," Lydia says, touching my arm. "All right?"

"Yeah," I say. A folded piece of yellow paper sticks out of the stack. That's weird.

Lydia and Claudia walk down the hallway. I grab my welcome folder with one hand and unfold the note with the other.

It takes a few seconds to read. I go back and read it again. The words swirl in my head once, twice, three times, but they still don't register. I just hold the note in my shaking hands, blinking at the scribbled writing:

I know you have HIV. You have until Thanksgiving to stop hanging out with Miles. Or everyone else will know, too.

CHAPTER 6

"Simone, you'll get an infection if you keep biting your nails like that. I thought we talked about this, baby."

I yank my hand out of my mouth, but I don't look over at Pops. No doubt he can already tell that something's wrong. I haven't looked at him since we got in the car to go to St. Mary's Hospital. If I do, he might guess what I'm thinking. Sure, Pops wouldn't care about me having a crush on a boy, but the *note*? He and Dad would rip my school apart.

Maybe they *should* get involved. Whoever wrote that letter, they've definitely been watching me. How else would they know where my locker is? The question is, how long has it been going on? Since I started going to Sacred Heart a couple of months ago? Since Miles started working on the play? Since I kissed him yesterday?

And what if everyone finds out? No way. I can't deal with all of that again.

But if my parents go to the principal, she won't be the only one who finds out I'm positive. I'm sure another faculty member will overhear—the secretary, a security officer, maybe even a teacher. And sometimes kids work in the office for extra credit. One of *them* could hear, and then *they* could tell a bunch of people. By talking to the principal, my parents could out me to everyone.

And what if this is all a weird joke, something I'm blowing out of proportion? No, I can't tell my parents about this. I'll have to figure it out on my own.

I don't even know how I'm feeling about this whole thing. I figured I'd be angry or upset, but I'm just numb. Like what happened at Our Lady of Lourdes is going to happen all over again and I can't do anything to stop it. But I have to do *something*. If everyone finds out that I have HIV, I'll feel worse things than numbness.

"Something on your mind?" Pops makes a turn. "Excited to see your friends again?"

"They aren't my friends." I snort.

"I'm sure that's not true," he says, but doesn't meet my eyes. "Your dad and I think it's important that you have other kids to talk to."

"Other kids like *me*."

"Well, yes." He glances over. "You're not any different, baby, and you know that. But there are things that Claudia and Lydia don't understand, that your dad and I don't understand. You know what I mean."

"I don't really think about those things," I say, which isn't exactly a lie. "And no one actually *talks*. We sit around and give one-word answers until it's over."

Pops makes a sound, deep in his throat, as he pulls into a parking space. The hospital isn't very far from our house, making it easy for Dad to commute every morning. At least I have the comfort of knowing that no one from my old school will be here; it's too far to be convenient. Doctor's appointments were a pain when I still went to boarding school, but at least I got out of going to Group.

I've never thought about seeing kids from my new school here, but I probably should. It would explain how someone figured out that I'm positive. I just wish I didn't have to entertain the thought. Between Dad's job, Pops's volunteering, and my Group meetings, St. Mary's feels like *our* place. A creepy stalker shouldn't get to touch it.

"You seem cranky today." Pops glances at me. "Are you sure there's nothing you want to talk about?"

"I'm sure," I say. Instead of looking at his face, I stare at his shirt. Prince stares back at me in all his purple glory. "I just hate coming here."

"Aw, Mone." He places a hand on my shoulder. "It can't be that bad."

It actually *is* that bad. Every Wednesday, the support group is held in one of the conference rooms toward the back of the hospital building. I guess it's where doctors discuss things they can't talk about in the halls. Even though we're separated from the rest of the hospital, the antiseptic smell still seeps in. There are about ten of us, sitting in plastic chairs, arranged in a circle.

Julie, a recent college graduate who runs the meetings, pulls a rolling chair toward us. She's not positive, which makes her messages even more annoying since she can't exactly *relate*. But today she has donuts, so I might be more tolerant than usual.

"Hi, guys," she says, passing the box to the kid next to her. "How are you doing?"

Everyone responds at the same time, but it sounds like a half-baked mumble. I know that Julie tries—I'm pretty sure she bought those chocolate donuts with her own money—but I've never poured out my feelings before and I'm not about to start now.

Julie claps her hands together. "Right. Well, I brought a friend with me today."

She gestures toward the girl sitting in the chair next to her. She's black, with short, neat twists in her hair and a face that makes her look like she's always smiling. There's something familiar about her, but I could be confusing her with someone else.

"You might remember Alicia if you've been coming to meetings for a little while," she says, patting Alicia's hand. "She came here until she was too *old*."

The people next to me laugh half-heartedly, so I do the same. I think Alicia turned eighteen when I was thirteen or maybe fourteen, but I never thought I'd see her again. I figure most people graduate and decide to do something *cool*, not keep coming back to Group.

"Hi," Alicia says, waving. Now that I really look at her, she does seem older. There are bags under her eyes, lines where there weren't always. Somehow, she still looks happy. "I can't believe there are so many familiar faces here—and so many new ones!"

I'm pretty sure she's talking about Jack and Brie. They're the ones I see most around here, probably forced to come every week like me. It's hard to be negative around Jack, who flashes dimples and pearly white teeth when he smiles, so I tend not to look at him. Brie, on the other hand, always slumps in her chair. I think her bangs are so long because she uses them to hide. I know random facts about them—Brie is on some sort of dance team and Jack golfs like an old man—but we're not friends.

"I guess I'll just tell you guys a little bit about myself," Alicia says, tucking a twist of hair behind her ear. "Uh, I'm in my early twenties. My husband and I welcomed our son last year, and he's the cutest baby in the world. I'm also in the process of getting my master's degree in education."

There's some lukewarm applause from the group, but my hands sting from how loudly I clap. Maybe it sounds horrible, but I don't expect much from the kids who come to this support group. I've never seen any of them after they leave, so I don't *know* if they live or die or do anything else. But I know that Alicia has been living. What's even *more* interesting is the fact that she has a husband—and a baby.

My parents haven't actually sat down and told me that those things will never happen for me. It's just something I've figured out on my own. I wonder if I could ask Alicia what it's like, to know that someone wants to be with her enough that they don't *care* about the virus. It seems creepy to ask, but I still wonder.

I don't know who would want to date me after they found out. I guess it would be easier to date someone else who's positive, but it's not like I'm going to find one of them *here*.

The only cute guy in the group is Ralph, but I went on *one* date with him and realized he's the most annoying person I've ever met. He felt the need to explain *everything* to me—how Wi-Fi works, how commercials work, how the library works—like I wasn't an actual person with the ability to access Google. If that wasn't bad enough, he kissed like a slobbering dog. Today, he's sitting across from Alicia, arms crossed sullenly. What, does he think he's here to judge Alicia's performance? Ugh, I can't stand him.

"I asked Alicia to come back here because I wanted to show you guys how bright your lives can be," Julie says, leaning forward in that earnest way of hers. "I know that I tell you guys this every week, but HIV isn't a death sentence. You just—"

"Have to take your meds," we say, almost in unison.

"I don't want to sound like a mom," Alicia says, laughter in her voice. "But it's really important. I almost don't even think about it. You just take them at the same time every day, like with any other medication, you know?"

All I can think about is the birth control pills Lydia just started taking.

"I used to have a friend I met in support group," she says, her face falling a bit. "We hit eighteen, and he decided he wasn't going to take his pills anymore. He said he was feeling fine and didn't need them."

The room is silent. We all know what that leads to.

"He got pneumonia, and couldn't breathe without a tube in his mouth," she says, staring at the floor in front of her. "Something happened with his eyes after he stopped getting enough oxygen. He was surrounded by people he loved, but he wasn't able to tell. It took eight months for him to die."

I hate hearing about this. I know it's a real concern, but I'm not skipping my pills. Is it really necessary to suffer through the punishment of hearing this over and over?

"Sometimes horrible things happen," Alicia says. "But amazing, exciting things happen all the time. I do what I love every day and live with two people I love. I have my husband and my son and a job I love. I guess I'm saying that it isn't all doom and gloom. I'm here to prove that—you guys can ask me anything you want."

My hand shoots up before I can remember not to look desperate. Julie nods at me.

"So, like," I say. "This might be a little weird."

"That's fine." Alicia smiles. "I don't mind weird."

"Okay," I say. "Um, was it hard to, like . . . uh, conceive your son?"

The only person looking at me like I'm weird is Ralph. I count that as a win.

"Oh no," Alicia says, sitting back in her chair. "You know U equals U, right?"

I nod. I'm pretty sure everyone here knows it. If only the "undetectable" part of the equation still applied to me.

"So we actually got pregnant the natural way," she says. "My viral load was—has been—undetectable, and my husband was just more comfortable doing things that way."

"Wait," I say. "Seriously? No, like, fertility treatments or anything?"

"Nope." She shakes her head. "It was pretty easy."

Wow. My back slumps against my chair. I always assumed I'd have to have someone's help if I wanted kids. I didn't realize U=U applied to that, too. My mind is officially blown.

"Well," Julie says, "I'm sure you all have other questions, but we can get to those in a little bit. I think Simone's question is a great way to shift to our topic of the day: relationships."

More silence. I can't read Brie's expression with her eyes hidden behind her bangs. Jack stares down at his lap. Ralph is cracking his knuckles. A few of the thirteen-year-olds stare at Alicia with wide eyes, but I can't tell what anyone is thinking. Do they have the same worries as me?

"I want you to know that relationships are completely possible," Julie continues. "There just may be some challenges. Maybe some of you have already experienced this."

"Oh, *totally*," Brie announces, tossing her hair back. The sight of her bright hazel eyes almost makes me jump. "Whether it's a kiss or sex, you're screwed. If you tell someone *before* anything happens, they might just leave you and start telling other people."

I flinch. She's right, but *still*.

"And if they leave you, the process starts all over again with another person," she continues, counting each step on her fingers. "So if I wanna have sex with five guys and tell all of them that I have HIV, that's five extra people knowing who didn't know before, and I don't even get laid."

I haven't *ever* gotten laid, and a random creep just left me a threatening note in my locker.

"Tell me about it." Jack's voice startles me. He isn't yelling, exactly, but it's the loudest I've ever heard him speak. "And if you wait until after to tell them, they'd sic an angry mob on you."

Brie laughs, ducking her face like she's embarrassed. Jack's cheeks are tinted pink. Ralph rolls his eyes.

"Well, people are entitled to their reactions and feelings," Julie offers. "It's important to make sure that they're aware of your status before *anything* sexual happens, even if it's difficult to talk about. It's normal for them to be confused. The news could come as a shock."

"It shouldn't," I mumble, staring at my lap. My donut is still in my hand, uneaten. "It's not a big deal. They aren't living with it. There's such a small chance that they'd get it."

"But the chance of exposure is still there," Julie says. "It's not so simple."

"What chance?" I say, leaning forward. "If it's undetectable, it's untransmittable. Didn't we literally talk about this last week?"

"Simone—"

"Like, if I go into a situation where there might be sex, I'll have five condoms if it'll make the other person feel better," I continue. "And I'll have an undetectable viral load. If that's not enough, they can take those extra pills."

"Don't be so dramatic," Ralph says, cracking his knuckles and looking bored. "If someone doesn't want to have sex with you, there's no need for you to try to convince them. It just comes across as pathetic."

"That's not anything close to what I said." I'm pretty sure my eye is twitching. "I'm just saying that I'll be prepared if I want to have sex. That doesn't mean I'm going to beg for it."

Ralph narrows his eyes at me. I wish I could say he's just acting like this because he's having a bad day, but being a jerk is his most consistent character trait.

"She's right," Brie says, snapping me out of our little staring match. "We're prepared because we have to be."

Alicia laughs, startling me.

"I love it here," she says. "You guys are great. So *smart*. I wish I had been like this."

Julie clears her throat. Her face is red, but I don't feel bad like I normally would. Nothing I said was *wrong.* I take a bite of my donut.

"Okay," she says, voice steady. "We're going to talk about safe sex now. Okay?"

I lean back in my chair, arms folded. This is probably the best group meeting I've been to, and it's because Julie hasn't dominated the conversation. I'm glad she tries, but she just doesn't know what it's like. The other kids do. Even if they aren't my friends, they *get* it. Maybe Pops is right—I'll just never admit it.

By the end of the meeting, most kids are lingering around on phones, waiting for parents to pick them up. Only a few lucky souls are able to drive themselves home.

"So. Are you still into musicals?"

I cringe at Ralph's voice before slowly turning. His arms are folded and there's something stiff about his posture, like he's a teacher ready to call me out for violating the dress code.

"Yeah." I shove my hands in my pockets. Hopefully, one-word answers will discourage him.

"We should hang out sometime."

"No."

"Why not?" His mouth twists. "We've had fun together before."

"Having pneumonia was more fun than listening to you talk through *Mad Max.*" I take out my phone. My parents need to come *now.* "It's not happening, Ralph."

"Why do you have to be such a bitch about it?" He steps closer, almost cornering me against the wall. "It was just a question. Maybe you wouldn't have so much trouble finding someone to have sex with you if you learned how to be nicer."

"What does that even mean?" I snap. If Julie were still here, she'd be trying to mediate, but it's just us and a few wide-eyed kids. "I'm only a bitch to *you* because you ask for it."

My phone beeps. I don't even read the message. As soon as I see Dad's name, I turn on my heel and walk toward the door.

CHAPTER 7

There are a few secrets I won't share with just anyone. One is the fact that I have HIV, obviously. But there's also the fact that I didn't know how to masturbate until one of my old friends taught me. She took me into her room, with Sarah trailing behind. We locked the door—against the rules at Our Lady of Lourdes—and she pulled up pictures of the guys from *The Vampire Diaries* on Tumblr. Then I lay down on her bed, with a blanket over me, and she talked me through it.

It's embarrassing as hell, but hey, it was eighth grade. Can you blame me?

It's a little different now, mostly because of the viewing material. Claudia laughed when I told her, but I like to look at pictures of old white guys from their prime years. Say whatever you want about me, but Bruce Willis, Harrison Ford, and Richard Gere weren't bad-looking at all. Sometimes Cate Blanchett is thrown into the mix, but Claudia says it doesn't count.

"She's *Cate Blanchett*," Claudia had said emphatically. And that was the last time I talked to *her* about possibly liking girls.

When I'm done this time, I stare up at my ceiling. Our house isn't wide, but it's tall and narrow, and my room is at the very top. Being so far away means that my parents can't hear me. At least, I think they can't. If they *can*, I'm grateful they've never mentioned it. After I finish, my brain is normally clear. It's like the moment right before I drift off to sleep, no worries at all. Right now, though, I can't stop thinking. It might be horrible, but I'm jealous of my friends.

Claudia's asexual, and I know she doesn't spend her mornings thinking about sex the way I do. On the other hand, Lydia fools around with her boyfriend when her parents aren't home. I have neither situation.

Last week, my health teacher made this long speech about how girls should spend their formative years discovering themselves and making close friends. Friendships, she said, are just as fulfilling as relationships. And I guess she's right. I'm so grateful to have found Lydia and Claudia. I love them *tons*, but not in a romantic way. Not having that makes me *lonely* in a way that's hard to describe.

I force myself to sit up. It's a Saturday, which means I'll have to be at rehearsal in an hour, where I'll see Miles. I thought the lonely feeling would go away after our first kiss, but it's just morphed into something else: longing. Knowing that there's a *chance* we could have sex almost makes it worse because I can't help but hope. Even if it means I'll have to tell him.

Most people are worried about contracting the virus. If I told Claudia and Lydia, they wouldn't have to worry about that, since we're not exactly going to be *exchanging* "fluids" any time soon. But it's different with Miles.

It doesn't help that now I have to figure out who wrote that stupid note. I don't even know the first place to start looking. At the freshmen in Drama Club? Eh, I doubt any of them have the patience to leave a note in my locker and wait for me to read it. Ms. Klein? Doubtful. She's a pain, but not *evil*. Who else could it be?

"Why does this have to be so complicated?" I ask out loud. The *Aida* poster on my wall just stares back at me.

Whatever I'm feeling—frustrated, horny—gets worse at rehearsal. It's like an itching inside that I can't scratch and it just makes me uncomfortable. *Rent* is a great musical, but watching it every day makes me think about the friends my parents only mention occasionally, the ones who died before I could meet them. Ignored because they were gay guys with AIDS.

The epidemic is scary in a way I can't fully wrap my head around, like a horror movie that sticks with me for hours after the ending credits, making my stomach flop and my knees shake. It doesn't seem real. The fact that it *is* real, that it happened, makes me want to grab the kids onstage, shake them, and ask, "Do you know how serious this is? This isn't just stuff someone made up for a musical, this is about actual *lives*."

It doesn't help that Ms. Klein is obsessed with perfecting "Seasons of Love" today, stopping and starting over and over again. Mr. Palumbo watches with his mouth set in a flat line. I decide to wander around backstage. I could pretend I'm checking on the crew, but it would be a waste of time. My eyes look onto Miles as soon as I'm past the curtain.

He's clad in a short-sleeve black shirt and dark jeans. As he folds his arms, the veins in his wrists ripple out. I swallow. If there were no one else around, I'd kiss him until he couldn't see straight.

He's pushing a towering set piece, one even taller than him, onto the stage. Once that's in place, he picks up two benches, one in each arm. Pieces of bright blue tape signal where he should put them down. Kids scurry in different directions so they don't get trampled. Set pieces aren't usually *that* heavy, since the crew builds them on their own out of cheap plywood and other lightweight materials, but they weigh enough that teams of two are usually needed to move each piece. Miles is the only one who does it by himself. It's totally hot, but I should probably talk to him about it. Everyone knows about his injury. I don't want him making it worse.

I clear my throat. "Can't believe Jesse has you moving everything all by yourself."

He drops the benches into position, glancing up at me with a smile. I want to kiss it off his face, right here, right now, in front of everybody.

"It's not that hard," he says, wiping his hands on his jeans. "Not as hard as remembering lines."

"Maybe because it takes brains to remember important details."

"Are you saying I don't have any brains?"

I give him a pointed look. It only lasts for a few seconds, since I can't help but smile.

"I'm hurt," he says, holding a hand over his chest. "I might not have brains, but I have tons of skill. You know what my job was on the lacrosse team?"

"Pushing people." I shrug. "You might've mentioned it once or twice."

"Yeah, well, that's because it's important."

He steps away from the set so that he's beside me. Whatever he's saying about lacrosse fades out of focus as I glance down at his hand. It's barely inches away from mine. He did that on purpose, right? We've kissed before. Holding hands is, like, on a lower tier than kissing. I can hold his hand.

"Simone?" His voice is close to my ear. "You still there?"

I grab his hand fast. I'm sure mine is sweaty and unpleasant, but he doesn't pull away. His fingers wrap around mine. I bite my lip to keep my smile from splitting my face.

This isn't anything *close* to staying away from Miles. I don't know if I can do that, honestly. I glance up, but not at Miles. I turn toward the backstage area. Kids are sweeping up wood shavings or painting the back wall. No one is paying attention to us. If the note-leaver were here, I'm sure their eyes would be glued to us. I guess this means they aren't.

"You know," Miles starts, his voice a stage whisper. "We missed the musical of the day yesterday *and* the day before."

That's because we'd *kissed* the day before.

"I didn't think it would last this long," I admit, watching as he swings our intertwined hands back and forth. If I saw anyone else standing like this, I would laugh at them. I feel a little bit like laughing right now, but the fact that we look ridiculous is only part of it. "It's not like you're actually *into* theater."

"I mean . . ." Miles pauses. "I don't *not* like it."

"Come on, Miles," I say, squeezing his hand. "You don't even know the difference between *Hairspray* and *Hair*."

"That's true," Miles says, glancing down at our hands. "But— I don't know. I've never met someone so serious about it until now."

It's not like I expect him to be an expert. Just because I'm wild about musicals and plays and everything that happens onstage doesn't mean he has to be. This is my *thing*. It's like musicals are a different language, one that's easier to speak than English. The only downside is that it can make communicating with the nonmusical crowd harder.

When I was little and always in the hospital, Dad and Pops watched *The Wiz* with me until I had all the songs memorized. The week leading up to my first day here, I listened to the *Dear Evan Hansen* album on repeat. Musicals are what keep me going when everything else feels pointless. Everyone needs something like that. "Well, yeah." I glance around as if to prove my point. "Joining Drama Club will do that to you."

"No, I mean, I like the way *you* talk about musicals." The intensity in his eyes presses me into my spot on the stage. "Jesse likes musicals a lot, too, but he doesn't talk about them the way you do. You get so excited. Your eyes light up and everything. I don't even know what you're talking about most of the time, but I want to listen because you're the one saying it."

My mouth twitches open, but nothing comes out. I've always figured he just listened because he's nice. And he *is*—this just seems like more than that.

"Was that weird?" He licks his lips. "Do you—"

He doesn't get to finish because Jesse's heavy footsteps cut him off.

"Miles," Jesse starts, out of breath, "I need you to move the— Oh, hey, Simone. I thought you were in the choir room with Palumbo."

The thing about Jesse is that it's impossible to be mad at him. I've never heard him talk shit about anyone, which seems unrealistic, because *everyone* talks shit at some point. If he were anyone else, I could snap at him so he would go away. Instead, I pull my hand from Miles's, ignoring the look he gives me.

"Yeah, we were just . . ." My voice trails off as I stick my hands in my pockets. What *were* we doing? Talking?

Miles turns to Jesse. "Do you need the apartment set moved again?"

"Yeah." Jesse nods. "You're the only one who can do it."

The two of them walk toward the curtain, and I lean against the wall. I can't even touch Miles's little speech. What can I say to him in response to that? *I like your ass?* He can't be all sweet and mushy while I just think about kissing him the whole time.

I take a deep breath, gathering courage, and run after them.

Miles turns at the last second. "Simone? What—"

I grab at his shirt. I'm hoping for a special kiss, one where he leans down and music swells in the background. Since this isn't a movie, he doesn't lower his head, and I end up with my face buried in his shirt.

"I was trying to"—I gesture vaguely with my other hand—"you know. Uh, have a moment."

Miles ducks his head. For a second, it looks like he's pissed, but then I see his shoulders shaking in silent laughter.

"Don't *laugh*." I let go of his shirt, taking a step back. "I'm not sure how to do this."

"Don't feel bad about it." His face softens. "We could hang out later, if you want. And have a *real* moment."

That could mean a million things—my brain keeps jumping to sex, and that thought triggers *the note*, and my stomach plunges—but I force the thoughts away.

"I wish I could, but I can't," I say, rocking back on my heels.

"I have to do something with my friends. We're gonna—well, we have to go do something. I swear that I'm not making it up."

No matter how cool Miles seems, I'm definitely not telling him that I'm spending my Saturday afternoon in a sex-toy store with my friends. It might freak him out. But honestly, I could use the space to figure out what the hell I'm going to do about this stupid note situation.

"Miles?" Jesse calls.

"I *guess* I believe you." Miles turns toward the sound of Jesse's voice. "Next time?"

I smile. I can't help it. "Definitely."

CHAPTER 8

Even when I'm on a train speeding away from everything, it's still hard to leave the note behind. I can't stop thinking about it. I'm sandwiched between Claudia and Lydia, but I'm not paying attention to what they're saying. I'm looking out the window. Who could've written it? Who would even *know* that I have HIV? They'd have to have seen me at the hospital, and I can't imagine another kid taking time out of their day to follow me there. Maybe they were already at St. Mary's visiting a sick relative or something.

"Hey, *Simone*. Earth to Simooooone."

The train is slowing to a stop, and Lydia squeezes my hand.

"Are you okay?" she asks. "You seem pretty out of it."

"She's probably thinking about the Pleasure Chest," Claudia says, nudging my shoulder. "Are you excited?"

"Totally." I jump on the distraction. "Hey, since this was your idea, shouldn't you buy me whatever I want?"

"Absolutely not," she laughs as we get off the train. "We're here to get one vibrator for you and one for my girlfriend, so both of you horny broads can *simmer down*."

Since Our Lady of Lourdes was two hours away from San Francisco, I never had much of a chance to explore the city with my old friends. I was never here long enough to see all the cool places and on holidays, I usually went to New York with my parents. Now I'm going to a place called the Pleasure Chest with my friends in the heart of a city that feels like a new world. I've never been so excited.

"What if I don't want to simmer down?" I say. "What if I want to get laid?"

"Oh man," Claudia says, shaking her head. "I'm afraid I can't help you with that."

"Oh my *God*," Lydia says. "I can't believe the two of you."

"What are you talking about?" I give her some serious side-eye. "We talk about sex all the time."

"It's different this time." She's actually wearing a trench coat, even though it's nowhere close to raining. "We're going to a store that sells dildos. Why can't we just buy a vibrator online, like normal people? They might not even let us in!"

"That's why we have fake IDs, Lydia," I say, banging my shoulder against hers. "Not to vote or drink, but to buy vibrators for our girlfriends."

Claudia nods. "It's the best way to use a fake."

Lydia huffs. "I can't take either of you anywhere."

Claudia raises a finger to her lips as we get closer to the store, passing a group of white people with dreads, big colorful row houses, and a Chinese food place. The Pleasure Chest doesn't have a lingerie display in the window, which is mildly disappointing, but I can see workers lingering around the front door. I always figured that there would only be women at sex stores, but it looks like there are guys, too. I guess they also need *toys*.

The thought makes me snicker. Lydia glares at me like she can read my mind. Claudia opens the door.

"Hi!" A perky blonde materializes in front of us. "Would you mind showing me some ID?"

Okay, that's kind of sudden. I thought Claudia was just being dramatic when she insisted on bringing the fake driver's licenses. I don't know how she got them and I didn't ask. Claudia always gets shit done. I don't need to know *how* she does it.

Lydia glances at me, panic in her eyes. I pat her pocket, reminding her of the ID there, before whipping out my own.

There's an awkward silence as the blond woman looks at our IDs, handing them back one by one. If she can tell they're fake, she doesn't say anything. Maybe she understands that girls under eighteen have needs, too.

"You're all set!" She smiles. "If you need any help, you can come find me—I'm Ashley—or anyone with a name tag."

Lydia promptly grabs our arms and steers us toward the back of the store.

"Do you even know where you're going?" I ask, a laugh in my throat. I don't know why she's so freaked out. It's not like this is the sex dungeon from *Fifty Shades* or anything. It actually looks like a regular store, like it could pass for a CVS, until you notice the gigantic dildos lining the walls. They come in all different colors—yellow, green, purple, blue—and they're lined up like a rainbow.

"I'm never doing this again," Lydia hisses. "So don't ever ask me to come back."

"Fine." Claudia shrugs, glancing down at a metal shelf full of sexy soaps. "Simone and I will just have all the fun. How big do you think a vibrator should be, Simone? And should it be charge-able or run on batteries?"

"I think being able to charge it would be very convenient," I say, glancing at the posters above my head. They list times for different sex education classes held here. "Hey, maybe we should come back for one of their upcoming workshops and learn the 'beginner booty basics'. I've always had questions about booties."

"*Guys*," Lydia whines. "Why can't we just google this stuff in my room?"

"That's not as fun," I say. "You just have to change your attitude." I turn down the next aisle, which is filled with color-ful posters. "Look! This one says *Give and you will receive*—I'm pretty sure that's from the Bible. You're not embarrassed of *God's word*, are you, Lyd?"

Claudia cackles, hooking arms with me. We walk closer to a pink display table in the corner. A black mannequin is dressed in a red leather outfit. Different pieces of lingerie are fanned out around it. When I step closer, I can see the mannequin's bedazzled nipples. I can't imagine anyone seriously buying this stuff. I'd never wear it in front of anyone, except maybe Claudia and Lydia as a joke.

"Why are we in the BDSM section?" Lydia asks. "We're supposed to be looking for a vibrator. It shouldn't take this long to find a vibrator in a sex store."

"Maybe we should check the queer section for that." Claudia grabs my hand. I blink in surprise as she drags me to another aisle. "Oh shit, look. An aphrodisiac cookbook! Maybe that would help you out with your lover boy, Simone."

"*Hey*," I protest. "It's feminist to be bad at cooking. Fighting against gender roles and stuff."

"No." Claudia gives me a blank stare. "Those things have nothing to do with each other."

"Guys, look at this." Lydia holds up a book called *The Virtuous Slut*. It takes all my effort not to snort out loud, especially since Ashley is eyeing us like we need help. "This looks like something Miranda Crossland would gift to me."

"Don't even mention her name in my presence," Claudia says, turning away. "I don't want to think about that bitch."

"She's the reason we met Simone, though." Lydia tosses an arm around my shoulder. "I'd let her call me a slut again if it meant you'd come to my rescue."

"Aw, Lydia." I rest my head on her shoulder. "I'm touched."

"Don't forget who was about to punch her for you!" Claudia calls. "I was totally going to do it."

I bet she would've, too. I barely knew them the day that Miranda Crossland called Lydia a slut in the cafeteria. There were tons of people around, and Miranda just *screamed* it out. It's bad enough to call someone a slut, but at least do it in private. Even *I* understood that.

I don't even know why she thought Lydia was a slut—maybe because she dates a lot of boys? I don't care—but I could tell she wasn't saying it in a friendly, joking way. She said it in a totally evil way.

Even now, I don't know what made me step in. It was still my first week at Sacred Heart, and I'd been trying to keep a low profile. But really, some things just aren't cool, and I knew how it felt to be taunted like that. Telling Miranda off didn't really stop her—it just made her call *me* a bitch—but whatever. It led me to my two best friends.

"Why are there so many different types of condoms?" Claudia asks, snapping me out of my thoughts. They're all piled into different clear bins the way taffy would be organized at a candy store. "I thought it was just different brands."

I frown. "Why the hell are they flavored?"

"I don't know." Lydia shrugs. "I guess for oral sex."

"Wait, what?" My head snaps in her direction. "They're supposed to wear condoms during blow jobs?"

"Um, *yeah*." Lydia manages to raise her eyebrows and give me her mom stare, even though her cheeks are red. "You're supposed to use condoms all the time, even during oral."

"Yeah . . ." My brows furrow. "I've never heard that before. That sounds fake."

"It's not," she says, shaking her head. "Simone, you seriously scare me."

That's definitely something I did *not* hear from Dr. Walker. How did she forget to tell me? It's times like these I wish I could talk to my doctor without my dad hovering around.

"Do I have to wear something?" I ask, rubbing the back of my neck. "Like . . . if someone wanted to go down on me?"

"They have these plastic things," Claudia says, waving her hand. "I forget what they're called. You hold them over your—"

"Dental dams," Lydia interrupts. "They might have some here."

"Don't bother," Claudia says, already wandering away. "Here's what you do: Get a condom. Cut off the ring and the tip. Make one horizontal cut. Then you've got a dental dam. Boom."

"Wow, Claudia. You're a genius."

"Yeah, yeah," she says, already distracted by a new shelf. "Emma showed me how to do it. Hey, do you think I should buy a strap-on?"

"I found the vibrators!" I call, walking over to a different section. "Oh, there are so many types."

I gaze openmouthed at the selection as the girls come over to see.

"G-spot, couples' action . . . ," I read, squinting at the labels. "Oh, *dual action*. Dude, I definitely recommend that one."

Claudia holds it up to the ceiling. It's pink and seems to sparkle in the light.

"So?" Lydia taps her foot. "Is it the one?"

"Definitely." Claudia grins. "This'll be perfect. She'll love it."

I go for a bullet vibrator. It's purple, small, and cheap. The two twenties in my back pocket will cover it.

Claudia turns toward the cash registers, ready to check out, but I grab her arm.

"Wait, guys," I say, staring at the two of them. "I probably don't even need to say this, but you have to *promise* you won't say anything about this when you come over later. My dads will never let it go."

I doubt they'd care if I buy a vibrator, since masturbating doesn't carry a risk to anyone. But it's not something I want to *share* with them. Anyway, I doubt they'll hear "sex-toy store" and think I bought a vibrator. They'll think I'm having sex and try to lock me in my room for the rest of my life.

"Trust me," Lydia says, holding up her hands. "I don't want my parents finding out about this, either."

72

"But why?" Claudia asks, glancing at me. "I thought your parents were super, like, liberated. I don't know."

She's not wrong. I don't mind talking to my parents about most stuff. Weed? Sure. Underage drinking? I'd get a lecture, but at least we would be able to laugh about it. Talking about sex doesn't make either of my parents laugh. I hate the way they deflate whenever the subject comes up, as if the idea depresses them.

Look, I get that most parents don't want to think about their kid engaging in sexual acts. But when it comes to my family, their general openness with everything else makes the awkwardness about sex even worse. If they had any other kid, a kid without HIV, I'm sure they'd leave condoms in the bathroom. Knowing that they can't—*won't*—do the same with me sucks.

"Yeah, they *are* cool," I say, scratching the back of my head. "But they're still parents."

• • •

Lydia shows us this random hippie coffee shop down the street from the Pleasure Chest. I've never been there before, but apparently it's cheap, and that's enough for me.

"How do kinks work, though?" I ask, stealing a sip from Lydia's cup. The Pleasure Chest has awakened my curiosity. "Like, do married people buy sex toys together? Do you talk about your kinks the first time you bang? What if you don't have sex until your wedding night and then find out that your spouse is into butt plugs?"

"I think that's why you should discuss sex before marriage,"

Claudia says, twirling her straw. "So you know that you're compatible and everything. You wouldn't want to marry someone who, like, wants you to dress up like a dog while you have sex. It helps you weed through the dating pool."

"Don't *kink-shame*," Lydia says, not looking at me as she takes her cup back.

"Wait, so what if you're having sex with Ian and he stops and asks you to wear a dog mask?" I ask, leaning forward. "Are you saying that you'd do it?"

"Hell no," Lydia scoffs. "I'm just saying that you shouldn't judge. Hopefully, Miles won't judge you when he finds out about your old-white-man fetish."

"It's not *that* weird," I say, even as Claudia laughs. "And it's not like I'd just randomly mention *Yeah, I love to look at pictures of Harrison Ford when I get off.*"

"Hey, you never know," Claudia says, leaning back in her chair. "Boys don't listen to anything, anyway. You could probably tell him that you're the Zodiac Killer and he wouldn't actually hear you."

"That's not true—"

"He's definitely not hearing anything after getting laid, though," Lydia agrees, pointing a finger at me. "So you could give him head or something and then share all your darkest secrets."

"*What?*" I shake my head, shoulders heaving with laughter. "Lydia, do you *hear* yourself sometimes?"

I turn to Claudia, but her face is red from laughing too much. I can't even blame her. It doesn't matter if Lydia is serious or not. She goes from being embarrassed about buying sex toys to providing explicit advice like it's not a big deal. I love her so much.

"Wait, wait," Claudia says, finally catching her breath. "If you're giving him head, he should do something for you. It's only fair."

"I'm not on the pill," I say. It's the truth, but not the main reason why I'm hesitant.

"So?" She wiggles her eyebrows. "You don't have to have, like, penetrative sex."

"Claudia," I say. "You sound like my doctor."

"I'm just saying you can figure it out," she says. "Who knows? Maybe Miles will want to return the favor."

I stare at her. "You think you're so clever, don't you?"

She grins.

"Maybe you can jerk off together," Lydia suggests. "That's kind of nice."

A woman walks past, glancing over at us. There aren't many people around—mostly senior citizens who probably can't hear what we're saying. It still feels sort of icky. There's a difference between talking about this in front of people who remind me of my grandparents and joking within the walls of the Pleasure Chest.

"*Guys*," I hiss. "We're in a public place."

"Old people have sex," Claudia says. "There's not an age limit on getting off."

I almost choke on my hot chocolate.

It's impossible to be around my friends and feel uncomfortable. I just met them this year, but I feel like I fit with them. I bought a vibrator with Claudia. Lydia let me sleep over at her house a week after I met her. They act like they can tell me anything. That means I should be able to do the same with them, right?

I don't want to tiptoe around it anymore. I want to tell them about the stupid letter I got and ask for their advice. I want to complain about my parents being weird about sex without blaming it on religion. I want to *talk* to them without worries, the way we talk about everything else.

I glance around the café. It's not like anyone from school is here. I force myself to take a breath.

"I need to tell you guys something." I run a hand through a portion of my hair. My hands get stuck on the short, kinky curls. "But you have to promise that you won't tell anyone else. Like ever."

"Um," Claudia says.

"I'm worried," Lydia says. "Should I be worried?"

"No," I say. Even though *I'm* worried. "It's just—something important."

"As long as you're not pregnant," Claudia says, waving a hand. "I promise not to tell."

"I'm the best secret keeper," Lydia adds. "You know that."

"Right." I rub my hands on my jeans. "Well, um. I have HIV."

I swipe my hand over my eyes so I don't have to look at them. My voice is a whisper, and part of me wonders if they can hear me.

"And," I say, "I just wanted you guys to know because you're my best friends and you're really important to me."

Silence. I slowly move my hand away. Claudia's eyebrows are raised. Lydia looks like she's going to cry.

"So you're sick?" Lydia asks, dropping her fork onto her plate. "Are you—do you—are you going to be okay?"

"Yeah, yeah, of course," I say, voice thick. She grabs my hand, giving it a squeeze. "I'm on medication and I go to the doctor all the time. It's pretty normal. Like, I'm not dying anytime soon, if that's what you mean."

"That's good," Claudia says, eyes roaming over me. "You don't look like you have it."

My brain almost short-circuits. "What does that mean?"

"No, it wasn't, like, an insult," she says, eyes wide. "I just mean—you don't look sick. You look normal. I don't know."

"Yeah," I say, rolling my eyes. "You obviously don't."

I don't know what I expected—not outright hatred, but not for her to say something so ridiculous, either. Claudia's smart. Part of me feels like she said it to bother me, but that isn't fair. I've lived with this forever, and she's probably never dealt with it until today. She's allowed not to know. Still, I twist in my seat. The air has shifted.

"Well," Claudia says after a moment. "I'm really glad you told us, Simone."

"Definitely," Lydia says, squeezing my hand again. "How—how'd you get it?"

"Why do you care?" I snap. The words come out like a reflex. Lydia just asked a question, but all I can think about is what Sarah asked when I told her: *How did you get it?* Like she was looking for some way to blame me. To find out if I'd been doing drugs or sleeping around.

"Oh, I just . . ." Lydia's voice trails off. "Never mind."

"Do your parents know?" Claudia asks.

"Yeah, of course." My brows furrow. "Why wouldn't they?"

"Well," Lydia says, mouth scrunching, "at the Pleasure Chest, you sort of made it sound like they're a little strict about sex. So if you told them about something like this—"

77

"*Oh*," I say. "No. No, no, no. It's not like that."

I shake my head, forcing myself to swallow. I guess I should've made this a little clearer.

Lydia blinks, glancing at Claudia. They seem to have a silent conversation. I hate it. I wish we could go back to before, when all three of us were talking together.

"My biological mom had it, so I was born with it," I say. "And I wanted to tell you guys sooner, but it's just that I told one of my friends at my old school and it didn't really work out."

"What do you mean?" Lydia asks. "Did she get mad?"

"She was just weird." I shrug, thinking back to when I first told Sarah my secret. How she recoiled like I'd just spat on her. How she called me selfish for keeping it to myself. How I knew that everything would change, right there, even before she left my room. "She told a bunch of people so, you know. That gave me some trust issues."

"What a bitch," Claudia says, leaning back in her chair. "What a *fucking* bitch."

"Yeah," I say, picking at the table. "Anyway, that's why my parents are so weird about sex. They don't want me to expose anyone."

"Oh," Claudia says. "That's . . . good, right?"

"I guess," I say. "But they're just—intense about it. Like, if I weren't positive, they'd probably be the type to leave condoms in the bathroom."

"I mean," she says. "You don't . . ."

She goes silent as I stare at her. She knows my parents. *I* know my parents. There's no point in trying to argue with me.

"I'm sorry about all the questions," Lydia says, rubbing her forehead. "I just—I don't really know anything about this."

"Yeah," Claudia says. "And I'm glad no one gave it to you. I mean, your mom did, but I was worried, like, you got assaulted or something."

"No." I shake my head. "Nothing like that."

We lapse into silence. I've known Claudia and Lydia since the beginning of the school year, and we've never had a silence this awkward. They didn't react *badly*, I guess, but this still feels painful.

"Well," I say, clearing my throat. "I guess now's the time to tell you about the letter."

They share a confused glance.

"Someone left a letter in my locker." I tap my fingers against my knees. "They said they would tell everyone I have HIV if I don't stop hanging out with Miles."

"What the fuck?" Claudia's voice is blunt. "They don't control who you can and cannot talk to. Fuck them."

"You don't get it, Claudia," I say. "You don't know what it would be like if they decided to tell."

I can't think about what happened at my old school. I don't want to think about the news spreading on Facebook, moms complaining about their daughters sharing bathrooms and cafeterias with me. When I think back, what I remember most is how completely unprepared I was for everyone to turn on me. I feel unprepared *now*, at a different school two hours away.

"We should tell someone," Lydia says, glancing between us. "Maybe a teacher. They can help, right?"

I grimace.

"Look." Claudia claps her hands together. "I don't give a shit who this person is. They could be the president for all I care, all right? They don't get to control your decisions. And if you don't wanna tell a teacher, I think you should just ignore them."

"I can't just ignore them," I say. "Not if they're following me around."

"So why don't you *tell the principal*?" Lydia asks. "This is the sort of stuff she's there for."

"No," I sigh, running a hand over my face. "If I tell the principal, I'll have to tell her that I'm positive and then tell the entire backstory. For all I know, the principal could be freaked out about HIV, too. I'm not taking that chance unless I absolutely have to."

Lydia shakes her head.

"If you don't want to tell any adults, I'm not sure what to do." She chews at her thumb. "I wish I did."

"I can track the kid down and kill them, if you want," Claudia offers. "It wouldn't be a problem."

"No, you can't kill anyone." I lean against my chair, exhausted by the entire situation. "I'm just worried about everyone finding out, especially Miles. I know I'll have to tell him. I'm just afraid."

"Of what?" Lydia asks, cocking her head. "That he won't want to hang out with you?"

"Yeah, that." I bite my lip, staring at the table. "*And* that he won't want to have sex with me."

My eyes dart up to see Claudia and Lydia sharing a glance.

"I don't wanna sound like your parents, but sex isn't everything," Claudia says. "I can still have a good time with Emma without having sex. It sounds corny, but sex doesn't always make a relationship."

"I *know*, but I still *want* to. I just don't want him to regret it." My voice sounds so small, smaller than I've heard it in a while. "We kiss and he doesn't think anything of it, because he doesn't know. I'm afraid he won't even want to touch me when he finds out. Why would he?"

"Don't say that," Claudia snaps. I glance up to see that her eyes are dark. "Never, ever say that, okay?"

"It's *true*."

"It's *not*," she fires back. Lydia stares between the two of us with wide eyes. "There are—damn, Simone, you're not the only one with HIV. There are so many people who have it. You guys are people, like everyone else."

"I know that." My voice rises. Claudia talks like *she* is the positive one, but I'm the one living with HIV. I'm the one who takes a hit every time someone makes a stupid comment without thinking about it. "It's just different, Claudia. Everyone is shallow, and I don't think anyone would want to be around me if they knew."

"We know and we're still here," Lydia says, squeezing my shoulder. "I'm so glad that you told us."

Tears well up, and I blink to keep them from rolling over.

"Yeah." I wipe at my eyes. "God, I hate this. I wish I were ace."

"Girl, it has its own problems." Claudia kisses her teeth. "You don't know *how* many talks Emma and I have about it. I feel like we're talking about it every single week. *No, dear, I don't like when you go down on me, even though I'm sure you're really good at it.*"

A snicker escapes my lips. "*Dude*."

"It's *true*."

Part of me wants to laugh, but I'm still thinking about what she said before. I'm not the only one with HIV. There are tons of kids at St. Mary's Hospital who go to get checkups each month, like me. We can't all be lonely, unwanted members of society. I wouldn't even *want* to be with someone who thinks badly of me because of the virus.

"I mean, I get why someone would be more, I don't know, *cautious*," Claudia says, lowering her voice. "But if you tell Miles and he's a jerk about it, he just doesn't deserve you."

"I know." I glance down at the hand holding Lydia's. "I just really like him. I wish I didn't have to do this and worry about how he'd react. It freaks me out."

"It's not fair," Lydia says, pulling me closer. "I'm sorry."

This time, I can't control the tears. I rest my head on Lydia's shoulder. Claudia scoots closer so she can rest a hand on my back. Even though I'm crying, wiping at my face so the waitress doesn't notice me, I don't regret telling them. I don't regret the weird comments or the awkward silence. They are officially a million times better than Sarah. I've thought about it before, but today makes it a fucking fact.

CHAPTER 9

My new vibrator is small but mighty.

I picked the bullet because I figured it would be simple—shaped like a small baseball bat, silicone, no fancy features—but I was mistaken. There are *twenty* different settings. I'm not even sure where to start. There's an instruction manual, but after looking at words like *nonporous* and *multispeed* and *vibration patterns*, I just want to test it out myself.

I flip it on, watching the shaking intensify with each level. There aren't any fireworks when I press my finger against it. The good news is that it doesn't make much noise. At least I know my parents won't hear it and walk in on me.

Okay. I can do this. I have the time and the privacy and the equipment. It'll be fun. Probably. I just need to be done before Claudia and Lydia come over, in about an hour. I take a deep breath, plopping on my bed before I switch it back to the lowest setting.

"*Whoa*," I say into the empty room. My voice is breathy like a porn star's and I'm sure my eyes are bulging like a cartoon character's.

It's not like using my hand, that's for sure. It feels like I'm finished five minutes after I start, groaning into my pillow.

"Fuck," I say, the word muffled. "Thank God for the Pleasure Chest."

I'm still walking on air after I shower and make my way downstairs. Claudia and Lydia have been coming over for dinner for, like, the past two months. Dad does most of the cooking, which is funny, considering he's usually on call or working late hours. Today, he's making weird tiny little chickens that look so cute and utterly dead.

"They're rosemary-crusted," he says when I mention this. "So they're going to taste delicious."

"Oooh," I say, peering over his shoulder. "Look at you."

The bell rings, but Pops gets to it before I can. It's been only a few hours since we met up, but my friends are totally put together: Claudia's holding a bouquet of flowers. Lydia is hiding behind them. My parents are so glad about me having friends that they don't need to bring anything. They do it anyway. I'm an only child, and there's still competition to be the favorite.

Actually, that's not fair to say. My half-brother still lives in New York with the rest of our extended family, while we moved out here when I was five or six. I'm not supposed to refer to him as my half-brother, but that's exactly what he is. He barely speaks to me *or* Dad during the school year and lately, when we visit him over the summers, he just seems bored.

"Hope we aren't late," Lydia says, glaring at Claudia. "*Someone* doesn't know how to drive."

"Lydia's just a hater." The corners of Claudia's mouth turn up. "Anyway, we brought flowers."

"They're from my mom," Lydia says, stepping inside. "She wanted to thank you for having me over all the time."

"That's so sweet." Pops smiles down at the bouquet. "You'll have to thank her for me."

I lean against Claudia. Things feel more normal than they did earlier.

"Hey," she says, nudging me. "You never told us if something special happened at rehearsal today or not."

A smile blooms on my lips before I can stop it.

"Simone can tell all of us at the table," Dad says. "I didn't make Cornish hens for them to go to waste. Hi, girls."

They wave. I huff, hiding my face in Claudia's shoulder. I'm definitely not talking about Miles in front of my parents. It's like Dad picked up on it before Claudia even asked. I swear, my parents must have boy radar or something.

Claudia nudges me again as we move toward the table.

"Your parents are great," she says, voice lowered. "You don't need to complain."

I hold back a groan. It isn't fair when she does this.

"I'm not *complaining*," I say. "I never said anything."

She shrugs. "It could be so much worse. You could live at my house."

Claudia's parents are super controlling, and they've been especially harsh since she came out as lesbian and ace. Her father had her sent to a mental hospital once—I shit you not. I'm glad I don't get invited over there, because I'd punch the guy.

Once we sit down, Pops turns to me. "What happened at rehearsal today, Simone?"

I try to think of a way out of the question. Anything that happened at rehearsal apart from Miles: the scenes we rehearsed, new sets, *anything*, but all I can focus on is the way Miles and I swung our hands back and forth like we were the only ones onstage.

God, I hope I'm not blushing. I stab one of the baby chickens—the hens, whatever they're called—with a fork. I guess I can go with something that'll make them laugh.

"Actually, something funny happened at school on Friday. We were supposed to share in psychology, right? I don't know why I keep doing it, because everyone is so stupid," I say, trying to slide my meal onto a plate. "This kid kept *asking* what I call my parents, since I have two dads. And I kept ignoring him, because I feel like that's a self-explanatory question."

"Mone, it kind of isn't," Dad says, cutting into his food. "I could see where the kid would be confused—"

"I think he was being homophobic," Lydia says. "In her defense."

"Fine." Dad presses his lips together. "I approve."

Claudia snickers.

"*Anyway*," I continue. "I finally go, 'I call my parents Ebony and Ivory.' And he told me I was racist."

Pops snorts, a bit of water sloshing out of his cup. He glances at Dad. "I can't believe *we* didn't think of that."

"You missed out!" Lydia says. "Claudia, you should've been there."

"I guess so," Claudia says, winking at me. "But I'm sure rehearsal today was better."

God, she's such a jerk. I had finally succeeded in thinking

about something other than Miles for the first time in hours. Dad and Pops notice *everything*, so I gulp at my water glass to hide my reaction. I don't need another lecture about remaining abstinent. I've had enough to last a lifetime.

"Oh yeah," Dad says, glancing over. "What happened at rehearsal today?"

"Dr. Garcia, did you know Simone said she wants five kids?" Lydia asks, changing the subject. Thank God for her. "It's ridiculous."

"*Five*?" Dad scoffs. "I've never heard her say that."

"Kids are cute and magical," I protest. "I didn't get the whole sibling experience, so why not make a statement by having a ton?"

"That's not how it works," Claudia says. "Seriously, dude. That's not why people have kids."

I ignore her. "And none of the black babies ever get adopted, so I can just be like an old cat lady, except with babies."

I feel my phone vibrating, but I don't have to check the screen to know who it is. Answering a text from Miles at dinner would be totally a bad decision.

But still. It would be rude to leave him hanging.

"Cute black babies become grumpy black teenagers," Pops points out. "Trust me—we know."

"Fine," I say. "I'll just send them to boarding school after they turn four."

Another vibration makes me squirm. Pops raises a brow. Claudia and Lydia are really the only people I talk to, and they're both here. I can see the gears in his brain turning.

"I completely tune you out every time you bring this up," Claudia says. "Because every time you say you want ten kids—"

"Five."

"I think about that time when we went to see the new *Avengers*—"

"That's not fair," I say. "I was, like, *fifteen*."

"It was literally a *month* ago. I didn't even *know* you when you were fifteen."

"*Oh*, I remember that," Lydia says, her voice a smile. "If you can't handle my little brother blabbering during a movie, I doubt you'll be able to handle five kids running around every single day. What are you gonna do if you want to watch a movie? You can't just scream at them like you did at Matt."

"I was having a rough day," I say, picking at my hen. "And I'd put them outside. I'm sure they can handle that for a few minutes without dying."

"Remind me of that the next time you want something from me," Dad says jovially. "They never told us that locking the door was an option at Dad Camp."

"I think my parents would do it more, if they could," Lydia chimes in. "Only, I'm the perfect child. It's the *other* one they have to worry about."

I pull my phone out, the screen flashing with more messages. Technically, we don't have a rule about phones at dinner. That doesn't stop me from hiding it under the table like I'm at school.

I'm watching Sweeney Todd and I don't get why he's having a shaving competition with this Italian guy. When does he start slicing throats?

I stifle a giggle. Tim Burton's adaptation of the musical wasn't bad, but I'm still bitter that he cut the opening number. I don't know why Miles is watching it, though. It's not exactly the type of movie you watch by yourself on a Saturday night.

"Something you wanna share with the class, pal?" Pops sounds like he's teasing, but I know he's probing.

"I was just thinking about the kid who set off the stink bomb in school," I say, placing my phone in my lap. For the first time, I'm glad that Pops doesn't teach at my school. "Did they suspend them yet?"

"I don't think they figured out who it was," Claudia says, glancing at me out of the corner of her eye. "And I hope they don't. That kid deserves to run wild, pulling something like that off."

I slip a quick text without looking down: *I'll call you in like an hour.*

It can't hurt to talk to him about a movie, right? Besides, it's not like I'm ignoring everyone here because he's the only one who will talk *Sweeney Todd* with me.

"So," I say, taking a deep breath. "What's for dessert?"

CHAPTER 10

I've never rushed out of dinner this fast before, but as soon as Claudia and Lydia are out the door, I'm running upstairs. Then again, I've never had a cute guy blowing up my phone.

"Dude, you *gotta* stop live-texting me." I hold my phone with one hand and slam myself into my room with the other. "Start a blog, join Twitter like everyone else, I don't know. But you can't just spam me like that. My parents are gonna think something is up."

"*Is* something up?"

"I mean," I say. "We kissed and everything."

"We did. Is that . . ." He pauses. "Bad? You kissed back, so I thought—"

"No, it was fine. It was great. It's just . . ." My voice trails off. What am I going to tell him? That it's complicated? It's the truth, but it sounds like a lie. I'm certainly not about to tell him my life story. "Look, there's just a lot that goes into it. Okay?"

"Do you have a boyfriend or something?"

I almost laugh at the idea.

"It's not like that," I say, sitting on my bed. "There's just a lot going on, all right?"

He's quiet for a moment, and I hear shuffling on his end. I force myself not to think about where he might be right now—maybe at his own dining-room table, or in his bedroom. It's so creepy to imagine someone else in their bedroom.

"We'll just talk about the movie, then," he says. "That cool?"

I want to kiss him again—in a platonic way. Wait, that doesn't make sense. Ugh.

"It's not as good as the actual musical," I say, lying against my pillows. "Burton cut a *ton* of songs. It's more like a regular movie than a musical, but that's no fun. There's nothing to sing along to."

"Oh *no*," he says. I picture him smiling. He makes that easy. "I can't believe I'm missing the Simone remix. Why should I keep watching *now*?"

I snort. "The movie is fine—there's lots of blood and dead people, like *Game of Thrones*. Anyways, I *suck* at singing, dude. Be glad you've never heard me."

"I don't believe you. Maybe you haven't found the right song yet."

"I don't think that's how singing works," I say, propping myself up. "Well, actually, I can kind of pull off *Chicago*."

"We'll have to watch it sometime," he says. "I've never seen it."

"I've seen it on Broadway and then watched the movie a million times."

"I figured you'd have it memorized." There's more shuffling. "Hey, hold on. It's on Netflix. You should watch it with me."

"I thought I was supposed to be the big fan." I grab my laptop from my nightstand drawer. "Wait, is this what you've been doing since rehearsal ended?"

"Not exactly," he says. "I watched *Grease*, but I wasn't gonna tell you about that because I hated it."

"*How?*" I lug the laptop onto my lap and fish for my earbuds. "*Grease* is a classic."

"I regret watching it. Everyone looked forty. It was depressing."

"You're so dramatic," I say, logging on to Netflix. "Okay, if we're gonna do this, we have to make a deal. You have to stay on the phone the *entire* time. Got it?"

"Totally," he says. "At the count of three. One, two—"

"Three." I tap play, and I can hear the movie starting on the other end. It's like a disjointed robot. "If you need me to explain anything, just let me know."

"Please," he scoffs. "The student is becoming the master."

"You *wish*."

. . .

When I blink my eyes open, the light that was coming from the windows is long gone. I can't hear anything except the faint sound of the coffee machine from downstairs. My laptop is still on my lap, warm like a blanket. The movie is over, the screen black. An earbud is still in my ear, but I can't find my phone.

I roll over. The clock on my nightstand tells me that it's five in the morning. *Five.* I don't wake up that early on school days. Five means it's Sunday, and I've spoiled a perfectly good morning for sleeping in. *Ugh.*

"Miles?"

He hasn't said anything in a while. At least, that's what I think. I could be dreaming. I *definitely* lost track of time, since I managed to doze off. I fumble around for my phone before holding it to my ear. There's the sound of soft breathing on the other end. My chest tightens at the thought of him sitting up in bed, like me, with a computer on his lap. I press the end call button.

I'll never get back to sleep now, so I pad down the steps, following the dim glow of a lamp. It's hard to tell which one of my parents could be up this early, because as far as I know, they both live for early mornings. It's disgusting.

Pops is the one at the kitchen counter, reading the newspaper and sipping from a cup that reads WHITE TEARS. He smiles as I walk in.

"Hey, Poppa," I say, sliding next to him. "What's up with you?"

"I was having trouble sleeping," he says. "Want a cup?"

I nod. Coffee has never tasted good to me, but Pops knows that, and makes it accordingly. I'll drink anything if it's filled to the brim with cream and sugar. Plus, the smell reminds me of being little, sitting on his lap while he read me picture books in funny voices. I settle myself on a stool next to him while he fixes my coffee. His hands are slow but steady.

"I don't know why I'm up so early," I say, trying to stifle a yawn. "I hate waking up this early on a *normal* day. Does coffee actually help keep you awake?"

"It does once you're hooked," he says, sliding a cup over to me. I bring it to my lips, blowing steam away. He's watching me with smug eyes, like he's waiting for something. "Of course, I'd be tired, too, if I was up all night making strange calls in my bedroom."

I splutter a bit of coffee, scalding my tongue. It's obvious that I was texting during dinner, I know, but I didn't think I was being

93

that loud when we were watching Netflix and chilling in the most literal sense possible. I can't say that I was talking to Lydia or Claudia, because they had *just left* when me and Miles started talking. Pops knows me too well. His expression says it all. I almost resent him for it.

I put my cup down, bracing myself for a lecture. It could take a bunch of different forms—he could start talking about abstinence, or keeping secrets from him, or even talking on the phone too late.

"Uh," I say, staring at my phone on the counter. He glances down at it, raising a brow as he looks back up at me. "Um, yeah. You know . . ."

"Who were you talking to, Simone?"

I watch the steam rising off my coffee.

"Well, it's not like we were talking about anything weird," I say, scratching the back of my head. I never got the chance to twist my hair last night, so now it's a matted mess. "We were just watching *Chicago*. No big deal."

"Why do you need someone on the phone with you while you watch a musical?"

"I don't know." I shrug. "Why did Elphaba end up with Fiyero when Glinda was right there?"

I can't tell if Pops is mad or not. He makes a face, eyes narrowed and lips pressed together. I tap my fingers on the counter, waiting for him to say something, but he's silent. He just takes a long sip of coffee. I wish he'd say *something*. The last time I got in trouble was probably . . . Well, I can't even remember.

"You were up at all hours, talking to a boy?" he asks. I've

never seen him at school with his students, but I imagine he's a lot like this. "I was beginning to think that you weren't interested in boys."

"Um, that's wrong." I frown. "I like boys, Pops."

"I didn't say there was anything *wrong* with it."

"Lydia likes boys, too, you know," I say, bending my fingers back. "I'm not the only one who likes boys. It's a totally normal thing."

My tone is defensive, but I can't help it. I don't know how I'll ever get to the point where I'm comfortable enough to talk about *this*. Sarah used to say that bi girls are just straight girls with a need for attention. I don't want Pops to think the same about me.

"You're right," he says, pausing.

"Pops?" I raise a brow. He never talks about *before* Dad, not really. I know he doesn't talk about his family because they're homophobic. It makes me feel worse about the whole *I might be bi* thing. If Pops goes out with Dad, people know he's queer. If Claudia goes out with Emma, people know she's queer. If you're bi, like Lydia, you can go out with a boyfriend and strangers will assume you're straight. It doesn't seem fair.

"You shouldn't be on the phone that long." Pops puts down his cup, startling me from my thoughts. "It's inappropriate."

"It wasn't a school day," I offer, swirling my spoon around in my coffee. "So at least there's that."

He looks like he's going to say something else, but my buzzing phone interrupts him. I start, like a deer in front of a car, but I don't move to answer it. Miles still doesn't have a contact name in my phone, so it's just a random number on the home screen. But judging by the look on Pops's face, he knows what's up. He stares at me, but I just blink.

The buzzing stops. Then a second later, starts again.

"You should probably answer that," Pops says, sounding . . . Is he *amused*? "It's rude to ignore people."

My cheeks flush. Talking to Miles in front of Pops is probably the worst punishment of all time.

"It's too early for a phone call," I say, giving Pops a smile. "Especially not when I'm spending time with *you*. Everyone else can wait."

"How kind," he says. "But it's almost six. You're up at this time for school. Come on, why don't you put it on speaker? I want to hear about the kid who has you up all night."

"Ew, Pops."

With a sigh, I accept the call and turn on speakerphone.

"Hey," I say, casting a side-glance at my father. "Before you say anything, you need to know that you're on speaker and one of my dads is in the room."

"*One?*"

"I have two," I say. "They're gays who want to repopulate the Earth with more of their kind. I think Pops is pissed that I ended up straight."

I almost expect him to hang up after that. I think anyone else would, since it's my stupid idea of a joke. But Miles just laughs. It's not very loud, I guess because he might be half-asleep. The sun is barely up, so he must be.

"I thought you were exploring?" Pops asks. "Was that a lie?"

"Pops," I hiss. "*Really?*"

I haven't even told my friends about my *exploring*. Miles doesn't need to hear about it, especially not from my father.

"Hi, uh, Mr. Hampton? Or Mr. Garcia?"

"Hampton. Garcia is a doctor," Pops says, using his teacher voice. I shoot him a look. He never talks like that around my friends, and Miles is one of them now. "What's up? Is that what you kids say these days?"

I facepalm.

"You *work* in a *school*," I say, rubbing my forehead. "You *know* how we speak. God, I'm sorry, Miles. He's—a big goof. It's really embarrassing."

"This is what happens when you call someone before the sun is fully up," Pops says, leaning close to me. "*Miilless*."

"Oh G—"

"Gosh?" Pops chides. He's too close to my side. I need my *space*.

"Hey, Miles," I say, sliding away from my father. "Maybe you can just text me?"

"I mean, I already have you now, so it's fine," he says. He doesn't even sound bothered, which is definitely different. *I'm* more bothered by the man, and I live with him. "I just want to know if you're doing anything later."

My stomach drops like I'm at the top of a roller coaster. Pops raises his eyebrows at me, but I try to ignore him. He's worse than Claudia and Lydia *combined*.

"Uh, I don't think so," I say. "But I probably can't hang out. I think I have a family thing to do. Or something."

I stick my lower lip out at Pops. He understands everything; he should be able to understand this. I'm getting too close to

97

Miles—first it was kissing, then watching musicals, and now dates? After dates comes more kissing, which leads to sex. I'm pretty sure that's how it works. I'm not ready for this to shift from something light and fun to something that could possibly make me feel like shit.

"Actually, that *family* thing isn't until much later," Pops says, nudging me. "Much, much later. You two have been talking all night, after all. Go have some fun."

"But—" I rack my brain for another excuse. "Homework. I always do homework on Sundays."

I try the widest puppy eyes ever attempted. *Please help me out here.*

Pops smiles. "You can do it later."

"Okay," Miles says. "So I'm going to take a shower, and then I'll call you back and we can figure out where to go, okay?"

"I guess so."

I glare at Pops as I hang up the phone.

"You're the worst," I say. "I never ask you for *anything*."

"That's the biggest lie I've ever heard in my life," he says, picking up his cup. "But I suppose you've learned your lesson. My work here is done."

I groan. I can't trust him *at all*.

CHAPTER 11

Miles suggested I pick a place to meet, so I chose the park. Everyone is so caught up on Golden Gate Park, but Dolores Park is my favorite. It has all the normal *park* things, like tennis courts and a soccer field. It's big enough that I've never run into anyone from school, but close enough to feel like it's part of my neighborhood.

Sometimes, when we don't have anything to do, the girls and I come to watch dogs run around. The south half of the park is the best, because you can see *everything*—downtown, Mission District, and the East Bay. It's not a bad place to meet the boy I like. Too bad the bus takes forever to come and I end up being fifteen minutes late.

I speed walk through the park entrance, but I don't see him right away. My hands dart up to my hair. When I get nervous like this, I wish I still had braids. I'd unbraid and rebraid them over and over so that my fingers would have something to do. Ever since I did the Big Chop before starting school in September, I can't do much with it. Even though I go to bed with tiny twists, my hair never comes out in the tight, crisp curls I see other women walking around with. Then there's the whole fog issue—it deflates my hair in mere seconds. I should've brought a hat.

"So what's the big deal with the school play?"

I blink. Miles is standing in front of me, wearing a blue-and-white hooded sweatshirt. I was pretty sure people only wore school colors as some sort of joke, but I guess not. He has a vanilla ice-cream cone, but instead of licking it like a normal person, he's sucking it like a Popsicle. The dark pink of his lips is flecked with white. His tongue darts out to wipe it away.

"What do you mean? It's *Rent*. You know that," I say. We sit on a bench, his body is warm next to mine. "So it's about a bunch of people who live in New York and have to deal with AIDS and relationships and stuff, but they sing."

"I know," he says, the corners of his mouth turning up. "I've read the script."

"Okay. So you know the 'big deal.'"

"Not really. I don't understand why Ms. Klein is always freaking out."

I glance up at him. Now that I'm close, I can see the barest hint of a mustache over his lips. Sometimes, when I look in the mirror, I can see the hint of freckles along my cheeks, but Miles doesn't have any of those. His skin is consistent, no blemishes, just smooth darkness.

"Because it's the first time she's directing something and all those parents were freaking out about the show, so she wants to *prove* herself."

"Wait," he says. "What happened with that? People were freaking out?"

100

"It was this whole thing at the beginning of the year," I sigh. "Tons of people in the PTA Facebook group were talking about how they objected to the show's 'portrayal of prostitution' or the characters' drug use or something."

"Seriously?"

"Why are you so surprised?" I say. "The PTA is wild. You know Mike Davidson's mom?"

Miles nods. "She's the president. She does all the fund-raising stuff."

"Right, so she came to rehearsal once and actually lectured Palumbo about it." It's hard to keep the heat out of my voice. "She spent, like, twenty minutes talking about how inappropriate it was and that it wasn't setting the right example for high school kids."

"But we aren't even doing the real version," Miles says. "There are—Jesse was talking about how all the lines were changed."

"Yeah, we're not even getting the full *Rent* experience, and it's still not good enough for Mrs. Davidson," I say, shrugging. "Anyway, I think that's why Ms. Klein wants us to win at the High School Theater Awards. It'll make her look good or something. And it's not like we're doing an easy musical. *Rent* is a modern classic. She's probably nervous about pulling it off."

"You know a ton about musical classics," he says, nudging my shoulder. He taps a finger against my forehead. "Do you have a library of musicals up there?"

"Yep." I smile. "Needed to fill all that space up *somehow*."

He snickers, the finger tracing my cheek. It feels like my skin is about to catch fire.

"When was the first time you watched *Sweeney Todd*?"

"Bro, I didn't watch the *movie*," I say, raising my eyebrows. "I saw the musical on Broadway."

"Of course." He laughs. "I forgot who I was talking to. You probably saw the original cast and everything."

"I'm not *that* bad," I say, leaning against the bench. "My pops took me when I was ten or eleven. I think my dad was kind of nervous about all the violence, but it wasn't that scary. I mean, the murderer has to stop every few minutes to break into song."

"Wait, wait," Miles says, moving his ice cream away from his mouth. "Which one wanted to talk to me earlier?"

"Oh, my pops. Dude, he's so *messy*," I say, heart fluttering as he laughs. "He doesn't like to punish me, I guess, so he does these weird life lessons. I think it's because he's an English teacher. He always wants to find teachable moments."

"Your parents don't punish you? Are you even *black*?"

I shove him, and he moves his ice cream cone to the other hand.

"Punishments aren't part of black culture," I say. "Some things are, like getting your hair done, maybe, but not punishments."

"Whatever you say. At least my parents don't care if I talk on the phone."

"That's because you fell asleep," I say, a teasing lilt to my voice. "It doesn't count as talking when you're out cold."

"You fell asleep, too!"

"Not first," I say, even though I can't remember. "That was totally you. I bet you don't even have a curfew, because your parents know you'll be in bed by seven-thirty."

"Oh, shut up." He tosses an arm around my shoulder. "When

102

I still had lacrosse practice, I didn't go to bed until eleven a lot of nights."

"Eleven?" I gasp dramatically. "How did you function?"

He tries to frown, but the corners of his mouth keep turning up.

"What made you pick lacrosse, anyway? It's so *violent*." I shudder. "Might as well choose football."

"Nope. *No*. Football and lacrosse are completely different." He shakes his head. "That's insulting."

"What's the difference?" To me, all sports that don't involve Serena Williams are the same. "They both involve guys running around a field, throwing a ball, and shoving each other."

"Lacrosse is actually *fun*," he says, as if it's the simplest thing in the world. "And my best friends are on the team. We've been doing it since third grade, you know? It feels like the only thing I'm good at."

My eyes roam over his face. He said I look different when I talk about musicals, and I'm trying to figure out if it's the same with him and lacrosse. Do his eyes light up? Can I actually *see* his love of the game? But then I realize that Miles always looks excited like that. His mouth turns up and he moves his body forward and grabs hold of your attention.

And sure, maybe I don't get the love of lacrosse, but I'd still listen to Miles talk about anything. He could read from my physics textbook and I'm sure it'd be interesting. I guess the difference between the two of us is that he seems like he's into *everything* and I don't care unless there's singing.

"I suck at sports," I finally say, running a hand through my hair. My fingers snag, so I yank them out, trying to hide my wince. "I think I'd get hit in the face every time I got on the field."

He laughs, licking his ice cream. It's dribbling onto his hand now.

"Everyone gets hit at some point. It's part of the fun, Simone."

I love the way he says my name. It's like he's never heard anything like it before. God, if he's never heard Nina Simone, I don't know how this is going to continue.

"I'd rather stick to my musicals, thanks."

"How many classics *are* there?"

I lean back. A woman with blue weights in her hands runs past. It occurs to me that this could be considered a date. It's surreal that I'm on an actual date with Miles. It's not a super-dramatic, grown-up one, with candles and flowers and fancy dinners. But we're together at a place other than school. A breath hitches in my chest. I've spent a lot of time with Miles since the note, at school and now outside of it. Could the note be an empty threat? As much as I hope it is, I have no way of telling.

The easiest thing would be to leave. I could tell him that I don't feel well, maybe ignore his calls until school on Monday. But I *like* Miles. I like watching him smile and eat ice cream like a weirdo. It feels right. If I don't have to give him up, I'm not going to.

"Well, *Hamilton* is probably going to be a classic, but I think the rule is that you have to wait a few years," I say, folding my hands together. "There's *The Phantom of the Opera*, which is the first musical everyone sees on Broadway. Oh God, *West Side Story*, definitely. It came out in 1957 and really had a big influence on the way musicals were choreographed and staged and *everything*. And definitely *Les Mis*. They revive it so much that everyone can see it, really, but it's completely epic. And *Guys and Dolls*! It's pretty funny. Oh, and *A Chorus Line*. It's about a bunch of dancers getting ready for an audition, and it won like a *ton* of Tony Awards before *Hamilton* did. It was revolutionary."

He's staring at me, eyebrows raised.

"What?" I bite my lip. "You don't have anything to say?"

He gives himself some time to be obnoxious with the ice-cream cone again. He knows what he's doing—I can see the smile in his eyes. It makes me think about all the other things he could be doing with his mouth.

"Well," he finally says, "I'm trying to figure out how many of those are Webber productions."

"Oh my *God*, Miles."

He snickers, and I can't help but laugh with him. It's starting to feel like summer, with the sun hitting my face as I talk to this guy about *musicals*. Even my parents would've cut me off by now. I never thought I'd be able to do something like this with a boy like Miles.

The ice cream makes it worse. It's hard to ignore him licking ice cream off his hand.

"You need a napkin?"

"I'm fine."

"Isn't it a little early for ice cream?"

"It's never too early for fun."

I don't know if I'm uncomfortable or . . . Well, it would be pretty inappropriate to be horny in the middle of a park. But this is most definitely something I'll think about in my room.

Miles purses his lips, like he's considering something. He holds the hand with the ice cream all the way out to the side, far away from me. I open my mouth, but I don't get to say anything, because he kisses me.

His lips taste like vanilla and they're soft, *so* soft. If I thought we just got lucky on the first few kisses, I was wrong. I grip his hand in mine but forget the stupid cone. It crushes in my fist, and sticky ice cream squelches between my fingers. I pull back, staring down in disgust. He doesn't have any napkins, because of *course* not.

"Well," he says, staring at my hand. "Maybe it *is* too early for ice cream."

I resist the urge to snort.

"God, Miles," I say, reaching for my jacket. "Everyone knows how to eat an ice-cream cone *normally*. You're basically an adult."

I start to wipe off my hands with my jacket. He reaches into his pocket, pulling out napkins. My eyes narrow.

"You had those the *whole* time?"

He doesn't answer, just grabs my hand. His laughter is loud as he gently wipes off the ice cream.

"I wouldn't have to do that if you weren't oblivious," he says. He won't look at me. "I've been totally fucking obvious."

I swallow. "What are you talking about?"

"I started it both times. It's only fair that you lead this time."

"Well, I did *try* yesterday at rehearsal." I put my hand on the back of his neck, and he goes a little stiff. "It didn't exactly work out. You should've said something."

"You like when I do things with my mouth." It isn't a question. The smile on his face is too cheeky. "Don't lie. I watch you. You *like* it."

My cheeks flush. "I don't know what you mean."

"Okay," he scoffs. "Next time I eat ice cream—"

"You're *horrible*," I say. "Completely horrible."

Then I kiss him so he can't argue.

CHAPTER 12

I make the mistake of grabbing yesterday's mail from the mail-box on my way inside. An envelope has my first and last name on it in bright red ink, but no address or return address. My stomach wobbles as I rip it open.

Miles won't want to hang out with you if he finds out the truth. And he will find out.

How the fuck did the note-leaver figure out where I live? I stare down at the envelope like it'll reveal the secret. Fuck, fuck, fuck. This is a million times worse than finding the first letter in my locker. Whoever wrote this doesn't just know where I live—they were *here*. A shiver runs down my back.

"How was it, baby?" I glance up to see Pops and Dad standing in the doorway. "Did you have fun?"

My mouth opens, but nothing comes out.

"What's wrong?" Dad frowns. "Did he hurt you?"

I shake my head, not trusting myself to speak, before sliding past them. Of all times, the note had to come *now*? When my parents aren't going to leave me alone? I don't even know how to act like everything is normal. Part of me wants to tell them, so they can make everything better like they used to when I was little, but I push it down. They'd never let me stay at this school if they found out. I'd rather deal with *this* than switch schools again. Not junior year. Not when I'm directing the musical, not when I just met Claudia and Lydia at the beginning of the school year. Not now.

"Come on, baby," Pops says, following me into the kitchen. "You can tell us if you didn't have a good time. Sometimes that happens."

"No," I say, shaking my head. "It was a lot of fun, actually."

I look up to see them sharing a glance. Dad still has his lab coat on, which means that he is using his break to grill me about the date. *Ugh*.

"What?" I finally ask. Their silence isn't doing anything to help the knot in my stomach. "Is something going on?"

"You have something on your neck," Dad says, brushing his own neck as an example. "I don't think you'll be able to wipe it off."

My hand snaps to my neck, but it's too late. *Fuck*. I think there was maybe a moment where Miles was kissing around my neck, but only for a second. I touch the mark, but it doesn't hurt.

"Oh," I say, my cheeks burning. "Yeah. *About* that . . ."

Neither of them says anything. I swallow, turning to the pantry and raiding the box of Oreos. The fact that neither one of them is talking is worse than a lecture. I normally don't *mind* sharing stuff, but this is a completely different playing field. I don't know how to talk about boys without freaking them out. Hell, *I'm* freaking out. If they noticed, I'm sure the note-leaver will notice, too, if they're watching me so closely. And who's to say that creep wasn't at the park today? It's like I'm not free to do anything I want, anything that would make me feel good. I suck in a deep breath. My hands are shaking.

"So, is it official?" Dad folds his arms. "Are you seeing this boy now?"

"I don't know if we're *seeing* each other, exactly," I say, which is the truth. I turn to face them, but neither one appears amused. "But I like to kiss him. And we talk about musicals. We watched one together on Netflix."

Another shared glance. Dad clears his throat.

"Are you actually *watching* the shows, or—"

"We watch stuff, Dad," I say, trying not to roll my eyes. "It's not like he's ever been over here, so we can't really do anything else *but* watch."

Pops makes a face. "Well . . ."

"Ew. Oh my gosh, no, I can't do this," I say, covering my ears. "If you're going to be creepy about sex, I can't listen to this. I've been scarred too many times over."

"Don't be so dramatic." Pops steps forward, moving my hands. "If you're going to start dating, we need to be open about it, like we are with everything else. Sex is a big decision, Simone. Especially because . . ."

"Because I'm positive."

"Well." Pops glances at Dad. "Yeah, actually. That complicates things."

I know what comes next—*When are you going to tell him?* And that's the hardest question. I'm going to have to do it eventually, if we keep *hanging out*, especially if the note-leaver already knows. I just wish I didn't have to worry about it. I wish I could just think about ice cream and backstage crew and the way Miles looks when he smiles. It's not fair.

"All right," Dad says, breaking the silence. I can tell he's trying to hold back on a lecture. "We aren't saying you can't see this boy, Simone. You just have to be mindful. Maybe have a conversation with him about remaining abstinent. It's important that you communicate about this."

"I know," I say, drumming my fingers against the table. "But it doesn't really matter. I don't—I haven't told him yet. We haven't—he doesn't need to know right now. And once I tell him, I doubt he'll stick around for a conversation about *abstinence*."

"Well, things can't move forward if you don't tell him," Pops says. "Did something happen?"

"Nothing happened," I say, sighing. "I'm just saying that nothing is *going* to happen if I tell him—which I have to. Basically, there's no reason for either of you to worry, because we're not going to get close enough for that to happen. The only reason we got this far is because he doesn't know."

I stare down at the table, surprised to find myself blinking back tears. HIV is usually at the back of my mind. Taking my pill each morning is automatic, and so are the doctor's appointments. Before I started thinking about boys and sex and other stupid things, the only time I *really* thought about it was at Group.

"*Cariño*," Dad says, shocked. "You're smart and funny and dedicated to everything you do. You're an amazing friend and daughter. Anyone would be lucky to date you. Your blood doesn't change that."

"I know." I blink a little bit faster. I'm *not* going to cry. "But other people don't know that."

"So you find the smart people who do," Pops says. "I'm sure Claudia and Lydia do."

I glance up. Pops's face is soft. I don't know how he figured out I'd told them. Technically, I broke one of our big rules by telling. The last time I broke it, I had to move to a different school. Maybe that's why they haven't chewed me out: they figure I've learned my lesson.

"You know," Pops starts. "I was nervous about adopting an HIV-positive baby."

"Pops—"

"I'm *serious.* I was worried that I wouldn't be able to hold you or kiss you. Not because I thought *I'd* get sick. I thought I would have to watch you suffer all alone."

It feels like there's something stuck in my throat. I've heard this story before, millions of times. It's comforting, like a song you can recognize just from the opening notes.

"I think there's something symbolic about the fact that you were positive, being adopted by us," Pops says, his voice quiet. "We lost so many people we loved from AIDS. I know I keep telling you, but the first person I came out to—my best friend—I watched him die. And I didn't think I could watch my child go through that."

"Fear is powerful," Dad says, nodding his head. "And I think that's the reason why so many people are ignorant. They're worried about something horrible happening."

"But that doesn't mean they should *project* that onto me,"

111

I say, shutting my eyes. It's hard not to think about the stupid notes. I don't even *know* who wrote them, but whoever it is thinks they know me. "I'm not—I'm not trying to kill anyone. And it's not my *fault*. I'm not any different, you know?"

Pops squeezes my shoulder. "Of course we know."

"We wanted you before we knew you, but after I found out how strong you were, I wanted you even more," Dad says. "You were such a fierce little thing. And you've always been resilient. Every time we take you into that hospital, we see kids like you living their lives and thriving. We knew you could have a life."

"But—"

"I know why you're upset, Mone," Pops says. "But you can't control ignorant people. There are so many factors at play. Some people don't understand, and some are just plain hateful. Some people hate HIV because of who they picture having the virus. People like us."

"I wish they didn't exist."

"We can't live by them," Dad says, his voice firm. "We continue living our lives and fighting the fight. You can't just let people control you with their hate. You keep living, Simone."

I hold both of their hands in mine. With my parents, I don't have to worry about disclosure or people being afraid of me or getting angry. Here, I'm just part of our family, and there's nothing but love.

CHAPTER 13

Look, I don't *hate* going to St. Mary's every three months. I've been going to Dr. Khan for my checkups ever since I was little, and she's basically my third parent.

I like spending time with my parents, and the hospital isn't a bad place to be and it gets me out of morning classes for the day. But today, I'd rather jump out of the car than listen to Dad sing along—horribly—to Bowie's "Changes". Part of it is because it's a Monday, and I *hate* Mondays. But there's another part, too: I want to talk to Dr. Khan about sex, no matter how awkward it is.

As if to twist the knife, Dad hits a particularly high note. I wince.

"Pops, if I were you, I'd leave Daddy," I say, a hand pressed against my chin. "He can hardly carry a tune. You need someone with *flare*."

Pops glances up at me in the rearview mirror and grins.

"Naw, I'd never leave your daddy," Pops says, casting a playful glance in Dad's direction. "Not for anyone. Well, maybe Idris Elba, if he showed up."

Dad gives him a shocked look. I snicker into my hand.

"What happened to 'till death do us part'?" he asks. "Idris can't promise you that, not with all the people waiting on *his* doorstep. He can't give you—"

"If this is turning into some weird sex talk, *please* leave me out of it," I say, twirling an earbud around my finger. "It's not necessary for me to hear anything more than I already do."

Dad's face reddens a little bit, but Pops just waves a hand.

"Don't be so dramatic," he says, scoffing. "It's perfectly normal for your parents to love each other."

I roll my eyes as he pulls into the hospital's gigantic parking lot.

"Come on, you two," Dad says, sliding out of the front seat. "Let's grace the lovely Dr. Khan with our presence."

We walk into the hospital like we own the place—and honestly, we sort of do.

The Infectious Disease Clinic (ID for short) is on the main floor, behind a gray door plastered with smiley-face stickers. It makes *me* smile; it's like looking at the posters I used to keep on the walls of my bedroom.

"Simone!" Auntie Jackie calls from the front desk. "It's barely been a month, and you already look like you grown. Stop getting so big!"

Auntie Jackie is loud and small and perfect. When I was little, she'd give me candy like M&M's or Mike and Ikes to help me practice taking my meds, and she told Pops that I should leave my hair in braids when I went to school. She sends me cards on my birthdays, came to my eighth-grade graduation, and she's always the nurse to take my blood. I started calling her my aunt when I was six.

"Simone's still a baby," Pops says, giving her a quick hug. "Even if she *does* think that she's too grown for our house. Don't go giving her any ideas."

"How have you boys been?" Auntie Jackie sneaks a hand around Dad's neck as she leads us toward the examination rooms. "Doing good?"

"They've been talking about *college*," I say, stretching the word out. We pass Nurse Patty in another kid's room, and wave at her. "I don't know why they would ever want to get rid of me, since I'm obviously the best."

Pops just scoffs, while Dad rubs my shoulder.

"Education is a blessing, Miss Simone," Auntie Jackie says, casting a glance at me. "I'm sure that a little time on your own would toughen you up."

"What's *that* supposed to mean?"

"I always say exactly what I mean."

We reach the examination room and I hop on the table, swinging my legs like I'm five again. The walls are decorated with stickers of superheroes and Barbie dolls. I'm probably too old to be coming to the pediatric section, but whatever. I wouldn't want to go anywhere else.

"All right, you know the drill," Auntie Jackie says. She ties the tight blue elastic around my arm while Dad and Pops get comfortable. "College ain't so bad, baby. I wish I had gone earlier."

"I've heard that a few times." I stare down at my arm as she sticks the needle in. She has a bunch of little vials that she switches out seamlessly. "But that doesn't mean I'm *excited* about it. It doesn't mean my parents should be so eager to get rid of me."

"Just because you said that, we're going to throw a party the

115

day you leave," Dad says, fiddling with his glasses. His other hand rests in Pops's. God, they're so corny. "Then we'll change the locks."

"I don't know how you watch her do that," Pops says. My eyes, which were focused on the needle and the vial, snap over to him. He's staring down at his shoes.

"What?" I ask. "The blood? Are you afraid I'm going to drink it or something?"

Auntie Jackie snickers. "Don't disrespect your father."

"It's not something we need to watch," Pops says, rubbing a hand over his face. "Blood is just . . ."

"You have blood, too," Dad says, nudging his shoulder. "Do you scare yourself?"

"Man, I can't trust none of y'all," Pops snaps. "You're not too old to be smacked, Simone."

I roll my eyes. He's been saying that since I was five, but he's never actually done it. I think it's just something he heard growing up.

"She'll be an adult soon enough," Auntie Jackie says. She gently pulls the needle out of my arm, taping some gauze down. "How's your new school? I don't have to show up and kick someone's behind, do I?"

"You asked last time," I remind her, rolling down my sleeves. "It hasn't changed much. Um, there are lots of rich kids. I don't know. It's school, Auntie Jackie."

"I think she's enjoying it," Dad says, giving me one of his knowing smiles. "She's the director of the school play, and her teachers rave about her."

"I don't expect anything less," Auntie Jackie says with a wide smile. "I'll see you on opening night, all right? I'd better hear about those tickets."

I give her a small smile. I want to tell her about Miles—about how he watched *Sweeney Todd* just because I talked about it so much, about how he looks at me, how he makes me feel like I'm floating after he kisses me.

Maybe Auntie Jackie would understand what it's like to want to have it both ways: to disclose, but also to forget about HIV when I'm with him.

Auntie Jackie was one of the first people who found out what happened at my old school. She kept saying everything I've always heard when I come here: "There's no reason to be ashamed, but you still have to keep it a secret." I don't know if I can keep doing both.

Dr. Khan strolls in just as Auntie Jackie leaves. The door's open for just a few moments, but I hear the sound of a baby wailing.

Dr. Khan has a different hijab on every time I see her. I'm sure they're meant to impress the little kids, but I still think they're cool. Today, it's red with elephants running down the sides. Her earrings have the same pattern, even though they're shaped like giraffes.

"Look who's here!" She flashes a bright smile to everyone in the room, a clipboard tucked under her armpit. "How are you doing, Simone? What's up?"

She settles herself down on the rolling doctor's chair, which I used to zoom around on when I was ten and got pneumonia. It was super fun, until Pops found me and started freaking out.

"Just school," I say, shrugging. "Trying to survive when I'm there, and do nothing when I'm not."

"She's not doing *nothing*," Pops corrects me.

"I'm not helping orphans with AIDS in India or anything cool like that," I say, glancing at her.

She scrunches up her mouth. "Not everyone has to join the Peace Corps," she says, tapping her pen against the clipboard. "There are plenty of ways to make a difference."

I shrug again.

"Have you been taking your medication?"

"Yup." I pop the *p*. "I'd get in trouble if I didn't."

She might be thinking about the time I did exactly that. Judging by the look on his face, Pops definitely is. In my defense, I only stopped taking my meds because the liquid stuff was so nasty and I couldn't swallow pills yet. The doctors said I was only getting half of the amount of medication I needed by the time I got pneumonia. Such a little rebel.

"Okay, so your CD4 count is at almost 1,000," she says, glancing over at my parents. "We remember that the CD4 is a measure of the immune system's health, yes?"

"That's really good," I say, actually surprising myself.

"It is," she says. "That's totally normal even for someone without HIV, so I'm thrilled with that number. And your viral load is undetectable."

It's the first time it's been undetectable on this combination of drugs. Pops claps his hands together like I've scored a goal. Dr. Khan smiles.

"But it's important that you keep taking your medication. Your count will go down if you don't."

"I *know.*"

"I know this all seems simple to you, but I've lost patients because they stopped taking their medication," Dr. Khan says, fixing me with a hard stare. "There are so many reasons why— denial, depression, sometimes plain rebellion. If you're able to keep those things in check, you'll have a normal life expectancy. Your life doesn't have to be any different from that of someone with a chronic disease like asthma or diabetes."

Maybe I don't mind this part so much. I like to be reminded that I'm not so different. Everyone talks about HIV like it's the plague, but I'm pretty sure that measles outbreak at Disneyland was worse than anything I've experienced.

But I'm undetectable now. That means I have to ask—even if it'll make things extremely awkward. I shift on the table, trying to get comfortable.

"So," I say, swallowing. "Um, I have an undetectable viral load, which means, hypothetically, I could have sex without transmitting HIV. Right?"

I can feel my parents staring a hole through my back. I bite my lip.

"Right, although we recommend waiting six months," Dr. Khan says. "Speaking of which, did you see Dr. Walker, like I recommended? How did you feel? Did she answer all your questions?"

"Sort of," I say. "She mentioned that there's, like, this medication negative people can take when they're exposed to HIV."

"We call it PrEP," Dr. Khan says, voice gentle. "It's a pill the HIV-negative partner would take every day, that lowers the chances of them contracting the virus."

It doesn't feel fair to ask Miles to start taking pills before we have sex. Lydia started taking birth control because she's dating Ian, but it doesn't seem like the same thing. Ian never *asked* her to do it. And even if she hadn't, they could probably go on and have sex. What would Miles be comfortable with? I have no idea.

"That sounds cool," I say, licking my lips. "But what if someone doesn't want to take medication, like, a month before having sex? What if it's more spontaneous than that?"

"That won't be happening," Pops says. Dad makes a noise of agreement.

I sigh. It would probably be better if they weren't here, but we've always done this together. It's just grown to be more painful.

"I understand your concern, Mr. Hampton, Dr. Garcia," Dr. Khan says, ever the diplomat. "But, with all due respect, Simone's questions are natural. And it'll be quite beneficial to both her and her future partners if she's prepared before entering a situation where sex could be involved."

"And that doesn't need to happen at her age," Pops says. I turn and stare down at his shoes. He's wearing a pair of Jordans that look like they're from the eighties. I would've stolen them this morning, if I had known where they were, and shoved newspapers in them so they'd fit me. It's not fair that he has a cooler wardrobe than me. "She's *way* too young."

"But *hypothetically*," I butt in, "what if we didn't have the PrEP stuff?"

"Well, first of all, it's less likely for a cis woman to transmit

120

HIV to a cis man." Dr. Khan turns back to me. "But even then, there was a study where researchers found no evidence that partners without HIV became infected after having condom-less sex with an HIV-positive partner when their viral load was undetectable. And this was over the course of sixteen months with 900 couples—a total of 60,000 sexual acts."

My chest feels a little lighter. It was just one study, okay, but if these couples had sex 60,000 times without anything happening to *any* of them, that has to mean something. If Dr. Khan was confident enough to say it out loud, it means that she believes it.

"There's still a small risk," Dad says, like he's reading my thoughts. "You have to keep that in mind when you're about to have sex with someone."

"But there's always a risk if you're having sex with someone," I fire back. He raises a brow, and I almost regret snapping at him. *Almost.* "I could get herpes or crabs or the clap or something, even if I trust the other person."

"And, quite honestly, there shouldn't be a problem if your viral load is undetectable," Dr. Khan adds. "Which it is."

I feel like there's some sort of unspoken girl code going on here, just like when she convinced my dad to take me to a gynecologist.

"But you should still disclose," Dad says. "And be honest with your partner."

Right. After getting to undetectable status, that's the other part that makes the sex thing so hard. I bite my lip.

"Simone," Dr. Khan says, placing a hand over mine. "You

know I'm always available to talk. You can call whenever you want."

"I know," I say, giving her a small smile. "Thank you."

Even though I didn't want to bring it up, at least I got what I needed—an undetectable viral load—and it wasn't so bad. It looks like Dr. Khan's got my back.

CHAPTER 14

Since Lydia and Claudia refuse to set foot in the cafeteria anymore, due to the Miranda Cross and "slut" incident, we usually eat lunch in the old science building. Ms. Ingall was the last teacher to have a classroom down here, but ever since she went on maternity leave at the beginning of the year, it's been the unofficial meeting place for the GSA.

"I don't know why you're still doing this," I say, pulling my bag over my shoulder. Lydia is beside me, Claudia leading both of us along. "You guys don't even have an advisor anymore. What if you get in trouble?"

Claudia rolls her eyes at me over her shoulder. The lights are still on in this part of the school, and she pushes her way into an empty classroom. I should probably know where I'm going by now, but compared to Claudia, I'm clueless. She walks around like she owns the place.

"Ms. Ingall was the advisor," Lydia says, leaning against me. "But the sub they got to cover her classes hasn't continued with the Gay-Straight Alliance, like, at all."

"We don't need her, anyway," Claudia says, throwing her bag on a lab table. "The GSA was such a mess. All we did was sit around and stare at each other."

"At least Ms. Ingall tried," Lydia argues. "Her sub doesn't even care."

There aren't any chairs, but we settle down on the lab tables around the room. Slowly, kids begin to trail in, and it gets louder. One kid sits next to Claudia, bumping shoulders, while another gives Lydia a hug.

Of course Claudia and Lydia have other friends, but it always makes me feel like an outsider when I come to GSA. My parents might be queer, but I'm not. Or at least I'm not sure.

Anyway, I think they'd laugh if I called myself queer after my assortment of celebrity crushes and the *one* real-life crush on a girl. But it's not all about me. I like that Claudia has a place where she's not different. I like that she and Lydia have friends they can talk to about things I don't understand. It's just that I wish I did, too. I wish I felt queer or straight and not like I'm floating somewhere far away from both.

"Hey, I didn't know you came to GSA."

I glance up to see Jesse standing in front of me.

"Sometimes," I say. It's weird to see my world—Drama Club—intersecting with Claudia and Lydia's domain. "I can't believe I've never seen you around, though."

"Yeah, I'm here pretty often," he says, gesturing toward a group of kids behind him. "I need *someone* to complain about boys with."

I snort. "I'm sure you could do that at rehearsal."

"True," he says. "But it definitely wouldn't be as fun as doing it here."

"We have tons of fun here," Claudia says, appearing beside

me. "Jesse has been telling us all the ways you embarrass yourself in front of your boy toy."

"Ugh," I groan, tossing my head back. "*No*. Jesse, I thought I could trust you!"

"I'm sorry!" he says, holding up his hands. "I promise it's nothing bad."

"All of it's bad," Claudia deadpans. "Come on, Simone. We tease Lydia about Ian all the time."

"Yeah," I say. "But Miles isn't Ian. He's actually attractive."

"Okay." Claudia smirks.

I try to glare at her, but I can't take myself seriously. It feels a little like a rite of passage to be made fun of for having a crush. Maybe it doesn't hurt because it's coming from one of my best friends—and because Miles likes me back.

"I'm shocked and appalled, Jesse," I say, turning to him. "I thought we were a team. A Drama Club *team*."

"We are," he says, placing a hand on my shoulder. "Sadly, my loyalty is to the *gay* part of the Gay-Straight Alliance."

Claudia laughs along with him, but now I can't bring myself to muster up more than a weak chuckle. Which part do I feel loyal to?

"Hey," Lydia says, bumping my shoulder as she passes by. "Do you want to share my sandwich with me? My mom made brownies and I saved you some."

I can't tell if she knows how I feel or not. Lydia has this gift for reading people, which is one of the reasons why the club is so popular. Claudia may not mean to be harsh, but sometimes she just is. Lydia always balances her out.

"Of course I'm going to eat your brownies," I say. "Do you even have to ask?"

CHAPTER 15

Tuesday morning sucks. I wake up late, so I miss my ride with Claudia and Lydia. My pants rip just as I'm walking out the door, and I have to go back inside to change. When I finally get to school, I walk into the wrong classroom for homeroom. And during AP US History, Mr. Thompson gives us a pop quiz on the Marshall Court, of all things.

It doesn't help that I feel Miles's gaze on me during class. I'm not sure how to act after this weekend. Do I wave? Kiss him in the hall? The worst part is that I can barely focus on anything when I know he's looking at me. As soon as the bell rings, I dart out of the classroom, but his footsteps are heavy behind me.

"Hey, Simone." He's next to me, fingers brushing against mine. My hand tingles like it's fallen asleep. "What's up?"

My eyes are glued to our fingers, resting against each other. I can't believe he's acting like this isn't a big deal. All this time, I've been trying not to imagine too much about him. I used to think tons of people were pretty in middle school—celebrities in magazines, the older girls. I never thought about anything happening. High school has made it so much worse because things *happen* here. People kiss in the hallways and hold hands. People are dating, having sex, at least *pretending* to love each other. I never thought I'd have that, at least not until I graduated.

But here I am, standing in the hall with Miles, who holds his hand out like an invitation. It's one thing to hold hands, but Miles doesn't have an air of cool indifference when he does it. He breaks all the unspoken rules, the ones everyone is supposed to know about. Maybe he just doesn't care. I wish I didn't. I want to enjoy this, to grab his hand like it's no big deal, but the person who wrote the notes could be anywhere. I glance up, around us, before grabbing his hand as discreetly as I can. He smiles at me. Hopefully, the note's writer isn't around. I focus on untwisting the nervous knots in my stomach.

"So there's a lacrosse game today," he says, swallowing. I tug him behind me as I dodge kids chilling by lockers and another trying to skateboard down the middle of the hall. "It's home, at four. And rehearsal ends early today."

"Yes," I say, raising a brow. Lacrosse is a welcome distraction from everything I'm stressing about. "It does."

Usually, I try to hang out with Claudia and Lydia after rehearsal. It's not a set appointment every day, but it's been three days since we went to the sex shop, and we haven't been talking much since then. I know it's because of me. Neither of them has said anything, but that doesn't stop the ball of guilt forming in the pit of my stomach. Lydia and Claudia both date and still figure out ways to hang out. Miles and I aren't even dating, not really, and I already feel like I'm slipping away from them.

I glance down at our hands.

"So I wanted to go watch my guys play. And it would be cool if you came with me."

"Oh." I blink. "I mean, I might stay after rehearsal a little bit, so I can talk to Palumbo. We're getting closer to opening night."

It's already November, and the musical opens at the start of December. I can't believe how quickly time is flying by. The thought makes me nauseous. I feel like time goes even faster when you're *in charge* of stuff.

"That's cool." He nudges my shoulder. "As long as you get there in time to see us win, I'm good."

"You're so cocky," I say, shaking my head. "What if the Spartans lose?"

"We always win."

I roll my eyes, shoving him lightly, but there's no weight behind it.

"Where's your faith?" He wraps an arm around my shoulder. "I thought you believed in me."

As we walk down the hall, my cheeks are flaming. If Claudia were here, she'd undoubtedly make fun of us. The thought makes my heart pang. After the game today, I'll call her, and try to talk about anything *but* Miles. I don't want to be *that* girl.

And if the note-leaver were here . . . I swallow the thought down, but it just makes my stomach hurt.

"Well, *you* aren't going to be on the field," I remind him. "And I still don't understand the game. So I'll go watch, but they could suck and I wouldn't even know."

"Come on, that's not fair." He leans down so his voice is close to my ear. "I don't understand musicals, but I still know you're good."

"That's different," I say, trying to hide my smile. "It's not just me. Mr. Palumbo does a lot of work to make sure everything looks good."

"And the Spartans have a coach." He smirks at me. "I know everything I do looks completely effortless, but—"

"Oh, please." I bump his side. "A musical is totally different from lacrosse. *Music* is different. You could watch an Italian musical and still understand it because music is so universal. It transcends languages."

"Lacrosse doesn't have a language," he says. We're quickly approaching my physics class, but if he notices, he doesn't show it. "I think that means I win by default."

"Whatever." I reluctantly untangle myself from his arms. "I have to go now."

He glances at the classroom, then back at me. "The bell didn't ring yet."

"Miles, I gotta go." I cross my arms, but my entire body tingles, right down to my toes.

He smiles, bending down to kiss me.

I've thought about kissing him again more times than I can count. It's like all the time I've spent with him is separated into *before* that first kiss at rehearsal, and after. *Before*, I thought about kissing him sparingly, like my thoughts needed to be hidden away. I'd think about it late at night, right before I was about to slip off to sleep.

But this is real. I get to kiss Miles in the hallway and in the prop closet during rehearsal, and see him after school. I know it's true, but the awe is still there, in my fingers, in my cheeks, in my lips. Girls like me *can* have this.

I suck in a breath as his fingertips slip under my shirt. They press against the skin near my jeans. My hands jerk to his wrists as I pull away. Miles stares back at me, but I can't read his expression. My head rests against the wall.

"That," I say, voice quiet, "isn't something you do in school."

"Right." He swallows, eyes fixed to a spot on my neck. My hands are trembling, and he can probably feel it. "You're right. Sorry."

If we were literally anywhere else right now, I'd probably take off my pants. I'm not even kidding. But there's no way I'm letting Miles feel me up in a hallway.

"Hey." I swipe a thumb under his chin. His eyes snap up, and I freeze until a smile appears on his lips. "It doesn't mean *never*. Just not here, where everyone can see. You know what I mean?"

"Right," he repeats. His hand wraps around mine, pulling it away from his chin. "Wouldn't want you to get embarrassed."

"Oh, *please*," I scoff, snatching my hand away. "In your dreams."

Instead of saying anything, he just stands there with that stupid smile on his face. I probably look the same way. It's like we're sharing a secret.

I should say something else, tell him goodbye, but then I notice someone standing behind him. Most people are either rushing to their classes or chilling by the lockers, but Eric and Jesse are just standing here.

"Uh, hi," I say. "I didn't see you guys there."

Miles turns around like we weren't just making out in a hallway. Eric rolls his eyes, flouncing off. I glare after him.

"What's his problem?"

"Ignore him," Jesse advises. "You know he can be a little dramatic."

"A *little*?"

"It's probably no big deal," Miles says, squeezing my hand. "I didn't know you two had lunch this period, Jesse. You're lucky. We were just stuck in APUSH."

"Oh, I don't know if Eric does. I just ran into him on the way to my locker," Jesse says, waving a worn copy of *Hamlet* in our direction. "You know how Bernstein gets when you're *unprepared*."

"Oh yeah," I say. "He makes you sit in the front of the class. It's like a punishment thing."

"He does that?" Miles wrinkles his nose. "I thought it was a rumor."

"It's definitely not," Jesse says, wiggling his eyebrows. "But don't let me interrupt. Pretend I wasn't even here."

He disappears down the hall with a wink.

"Oh God," I say, rubbing my forehead. "He's so embarrassing."

"How?" Miles glances at me. "He was nice."

"But now he's gonna tease me about it forever," I say. "And that's *after* he tells my friends at the next GSA meeting. I bet ten bucks they'll follow me around making kissing noises next time I see them."

"Come on." He snorts. "That's how friends are."

Is Jesse my friend? I didn't think of him that way before, but the more I think about it, about the teasing, the more the word feels right. I smile to myself. Then the bell rings, snapping me out of my thoughts.

"There's the bell," Miles says, tilting his head toward the

classroom door. "You might wanna get in there now, since I'm pretty sure you're late."

"You suck," I call behind him. "Your name twin Miles Davis would be ashamed of your antics, young man."

"Thanks," he calls back. "I'm sure Nina Simone is proud of your delinquent activity. I bet *she* never skipped class to kiss a hot guy."

"*Miles*."

"It's okay," he says, sticking his head around a corner. "If I had been around, I'm sure I could've made her late, too."

He knows Miles Davis *and* Nina Simone. I'm not sure if I should kiss him again, or punch him for making me late.

CHAPTER 16

Normally, it's easy to throw myself into rehearsal. The show has so many moving parts that there's always something new catching my attention. But today, I can't focus. Maybe it's because Ms. Klein is following me everywhere I move—to the pit orchestra, backstage—like she's making sure I don't screw up.

Eventually, I migrate toward the front of the auditorium, folding my arms over my chest to make myself seem more official. Looking out at the cast fills me with dread. First, there's the way everyone groans once I pull out my notebook. And there's the fact that we're losing time, not gaining it. The more notes I add, the more we have to work on, only we'll have less time to do it.

"Okay, just a few notes," I call out. "Rocco, try not to upstage Wyatt. *Share* the stage. *Share* the wealth. You know what I mean?"

Rocco grins, sheepish, while Wyatt, who plays Roger, sticks his tongue out at him.

"Mia, make sure you *look* at the audience," I say. Mia, playing the role of Maureen, is a sophomore who only speaks when she's onstage. "Don't be shy about it, okay? People want to see you."

She blinks at me. I guess that means she heard me.

"Laila," I say, glancing over at her. "Looking good."

She winks.

"Eric," I say, switching gears. "You're not enunciating your lines properly. At this point, you should just drop the New York accent. It's not working."

His face scrunches up like he just smelled something bad.

"You never have anything bad to say to Laila," he says, folding his arms. "It's always me you have a problem with. Have you guys ever noticed that?"

He looks back toward the other cast members. Rocco slinks out of sight. Wyatt's eyebrows furrow. Mia has already disappeared.

"That's not true," I say. "And I don't have a problem with *you*. Your performance needs some work, but that's why we're rehearsing."

"See, this is what I'm talking about," Eric says. "I've starred in five school productions. How many have you directed, exactly?"

My face is heating up. I hate the fact that his words have an impact on me at all. Everyone knows this is my first time directing a school musical.

"Come on, Eric," Laila says. Her face is red. "She gives me notes all the time."

"Like what?" he asks. "'Smile wider'?"

"That's enough," I say, forcing my voice to resemble something like steel. "We're not going to waste time on this. You guys run lines on your own for a few minutes and then I'll watch again."

They slowly cluster together, Rocco and Laila tossing glances over at me. Eric is the last to move. He stares at me like we're in some sort of battle. I take a step away from them, plopping myself down in a seat. My face is still hot and my breaths are coming out fast. I hate this.

I try not to have favorites, but Laila *is* the nicest, and she hasn't needed as much feedback as the rest of the cast. It's not my fault that she happens to be a quick study. And, God, I wish Eric would just talk to me after rehearsal or something. Calling me out in front of everyone implies that I have no idea what I'm doing.

"Something on your mind?"

I jump, turning to see Jesse. He has his headphones slung around his shoulders like usual, and a clipboard at his side. He's already crossed out half of his list of notes. Show-off. With the amount of notes I take, it feels like I'll never get rid of them before the show in December.

"Just thinking about everything we have to do," I say, squeezing my arms around my stomach. "We have to finish costumes, get everyone off book, make sure the choreography looks great. . . . It feels like everything is going by so fast. It'll be December before you know it."

"It's always like this," Jesse says, glancing at the stage. Ms. Klein is speaking rapidly to Laila and Eric, who stare at her with rapt attention. At least they don't get pissed when *she* gives them notes. "It'll be even faster next year. You'll see."

"I guess so." I run a hand through my hair, letting out a sigh. "Do you think Lin-Manuel Miranda felt like this before *Hamilton* debuted on Broadway?"

Jesse raises a brow, but if he thinks I'm full of myself, he doesn't say so. "I think it goes by fast for everyone. Even Lin-Manuel Miranda. He did a show every night, right? By the time he got to his last night, I'm sure it felt like he had barely been there before he was passing the role to the next guy."

"Yeah, Javier Muñoz," I say, glancing at him. "He's really good."

Jesse shrugs. "He's okay, I guess."

I raise a brow. Maybe I'm the tiniest bit more protective of Javier Muñoz because he's positive. But *still*. How can Jesse say he's just *okay*?

"You probably haven't seen him perform," I say. "Because if you had, you wouldn't call him *okay*."

"Hey, different strokes, right?" He holds his hands up like I'm attacking him. "I just like the original. That's all. It's not like I hate the other guy."

"Javier Muñoz," I repeat.

"Right," Jesse says, but he's already looking back down at his clipboard. "Him."

I sigh, turning back to the stage. It looks like Ms. Klein trapped some crew members, who are struggling to lift a fake pay phone while she talks to them. Since she seems to be handling things, I can go look for Mr. Palumbo and talk to him about my notes. He always knows how to say things without making people hate him. I could probably learn from that.

Members of the cast usually cool down by stage left, near the door leading to the choir room. Sometimes Mr. Palumbo disappears back there to give pep talks or just mess around with the other kids. I poke my head in, frowning when I don't see him.

"Did you see them?" Claire's voice is low, almost a whisper. Eric and some of the other cast members crowd around her. "I swear to God, they were practically doing it in the middle of the hall. His tongue was down her throat and everything."

Shit. That little punk. What happened to feminism and solidarity?

"Are you sure it was her?"

"Positive," Eric butts in. "But maybe he'll keep her mind off all her *notes.*"

I know I've probably gone overboard, but that doesn't give him the right to be such a jerk behind my back. Besides, what does *Claire* have to complain about? I can't remember the last time I had any notes for her.

I don't know if I should scream at them or just hold it all in. On the one hand, screaming at them will only undermine my authority as director. On the other hand, they're gossiping when we're supposed to be rehearsing. That's something I can call them both out on.

I take a step forward.

"Simone! I've been looking for you."

At the sound of Mr. Palumbo's voice, I freeze. If I yell at Eric and Claire in front of him, he'll probably regret making me director. But if he hears what they're talking about, I'll be embarrassed for the rest of the school year. I don't feel like talking to Palumbo about my notes anymore, but it's the best choice. With a sigh, I turn to face him.

"Hey, Mr. Palumbo," I say. "What's up?"

"We just need to have a little chat," he says, gesturing for me to walk away from the group. "I don't want you to get upset. You've been doing a fantastic job."

Oh no. This definitely *sounds* like he's going to say something upsetting.

"Thanks," I say, biting my lip. "Did something happen?"

"I think your notes are excellent," he says. "You really have a gift for finding weak spots in each performance without being too harsh. But . . ."

Dread rests low in my stomach.

"But?"

"Some students feel you play favorites," he says, apology written in his forehead lines. "Don't get me wrong—it's totally understandable. We all have favorites. But, in the future, maybe you can try to—"

"*Favorites*?" I repeat. "I'm—Mr. Palumbo, I don't have any favorites. I treat everyone the same. You've seen me."

"Well," he says, cocking his head to the side, "I just saw you give some notes to Eric. They were perfectly valid, but I'm sure it was hard for him to hear them in front of other students. You should pay more attention to how you deliver your notes. Try not to single anyone out too often."

Eric is *not* this delicate. He probably has been complaining to Mr. Palumbo to make me look bad.

"I don't single Eric out too often," I say. "He's just mad I say anything to him at all, so now he's acting like an asshole."

"*Simone*."

I glance up. Big mistake. Mr. Palumbo is frowning at me in a way that makes his entire face droop toward the ground. I've never seen him look this disappointed before, not in anyone. If I thought Eric made me look bad, I was wrong. I made *myself* look bad.

"I'm sorry," I say. I'm not sorry that Eric is a prick. I'm sorry that I disappointed Mr. Palumbo. "I didn't mean that."

Mr. Palumbo rubs the middle of his forehead. Heaves a big sigh. It's like I've aged him ten years.

"Look," he says. "I think you need some time to cool down."

"But—"

"It's not a suggestion, Simone," he says, holding up his hand. "Go for a drink of water, or a walk around the school. Just get some air. Okay?"

From the corner of my eye I glimpse Eric leaning against the wall, with his arm around Claire. He catches my gaze, holding it for a long second. If Mr. Palumbo weren't looking, I'd flip him the bird. As if he can read my mind, Eric smirks. If I don't leave now, I think I might punch him.

"Okay," I say, turning to Mr. Palumbo. "But I'll be back."

• • •

I'm halfway down the hallway before I realize I have no idea where I'm going. All I know is that I don't want to come back until Mr. Palumbo has forgotten the whole thing. Maybe I'll hide out in the halls for a week.

Taking a walk *is* sort of relaxing, but I need something else to do. My geometry textbook is still in my locker. Maybe I can get some homework done instead of wasting time.

I head to my locker, another hallway over, and fumble it open. In the silence of the empty hall, this feels like a crime scene. I scan for another note. The welcome packet is the first thing I see.

Shit. And right under it is a folded piece of notebook paper with my name on it. I've been checking my locker every day, and haven't noticed anything new. Someone must've put it in today. I scan the hastily scrawled words.

> *Whatever you're doing is not what I call staying away from Miles. Ticktock, Simone.*

I glance toward the auditorium door. It *has* to be Eric.

CHAPTER 17

I crumpled up the note and shoved it to the bottom of my backpack hours ago, but the words are still burned into my mind. Dad and Pops aren't home, which means I have the house to myself. I shouldn't be home, either. I'm supposed to be at the game with Miles.

I barely made it to the end of rehearsal, and at that point I just needed to get away. Maybe I should feel bad about ditching, but all I can think about is this stupid note. I've been trying to think of suspects, and I come back to Eric every time. He's had a problem with me ever since we started rehearsals, he gossips about me, *and* he complained about me to Palumbo. Then, I guess, there is Claire, who joins him in gossip sometimes. There's just no reason for her to hate me. Yeah, she's all the way in the back of the chorus, but that's not *my fault*.

I haven't been at my school for a full year, and Eric's the only person who has made their hate for me completely clear. But why is he doing this? It doesn't make sense.

The scariest part is that I haven't even noticed him sneaking around. Besides Lydia and Claudia, no one knows where my locker is. He'd have to follow me to figure out where it was, but I don't even use it that often. The bigger question is how he figured out that I'm positive. He would've had to see me at St. Mary's Hospital or read my medical records. But how could he get that kind of access? Why would he actually *care* enough to go through that much trouble?

I drift into my room and throw myself on my bed. The first time my phone rings, playing "Seasons of Love", I ignore it. It's probably Miles. I texted him after rehearsal, but he still might be looking for me. I can't tell him about the note, not when he doesn't even know that I'm positive. I grab a pillow and hold it over my head. "Seasons of Love" stops, and then starts right back up again.

God. Can't anyone leave me alone when I want to wallow? I roll over, yanking the phone out of my pocket. My shoulders relax at the sight of Lydia and Claudia's names. They'll know what to do. Even if they don't, talking to them will make me feel better. It always does.

They're already talking to each other when I pick up.

"It's not a big deal, Lydia," Claudia says. "I did it just so I would *know*."

"Wait," I say, sitting up. "Did what?"

"I'm just surprised," Lydia says on the other line. "*Wow*."

"Some ace people do have sex," Claudia says, her voice almost irritated on the other line. "Just not *me*. I'm never doing it again. *Ugh*."

"*What*? You actually *did* it?" I shriek into the phone. "I thought you'd be an eternal virgin. I thought you'd just chill. I don't know. This is so *weird*."

"I wasn't even a virgin before," Claudia says. I can practically

142

hear her roll her eyes. "But I guess it was official this time? Since we were using fingers and—"

"Okay," I say. "Maybe that's why you didn't like it?"

"Yeah," Lydia says, voice peaking up on her end. "I hated my first time, but sex was fine after that. Once I found a different partner."

"Nope, never doing it again," Claudia says, way too fast. I stifle a laugh. I know I should tell them about the new note, but it's so much easier to pretend that things are normal. "I told her I wanted to do it just to see how it would feel, and that's what happened. Now I don't need to worry about it ever again."

"What if she wants to do it again, though?" I ask, playing with a strand of my hair. "Are you guys going to get into fights about it?"

"If she wants to fight about it, she can, but I'm not going to," Claudia says. She always sounds so sure about everything. I love that about her. "I can't be with someone who wants stuff that I can't give, you know?"

"But it would suck if it doesn't work out," I say. "Because you love her and everything."

"I do love her." Claudia's voice takes on an uncharacteristically dreamy quality. "I love her hair and her eyes and the way she laughs. I love the way she knows everything." She pauses. "And her boobs. I love those, too. Maybe I'll kiss them and that'll be the sexual part of our relationship."

"Oh my God," Lydia says. "My mom could show up at any minute and see the look on my face. We don't need a play-by-play."

This time, I laugh. Lydia acts like her mom is going to drop dead if our conversations pass the PG-13 mark, but I have a feeling Lydia would be far more traumatized than Mrs. Wu.

"She won't even know what we're talking about if you don't say anything," I say, resting a hand under my chin. "Just try to stay smooth."

As Lydia launches into a monologue about her family dog chewing her DivaCup, I switch to speaker mode. I have my Drama notebook on my bed, and pull it toward me. Every time we have a rehearsal, I try to come home and brainstorm solutions. This time, though, it's taking all my brainpower to ignore the stupid note at the bottom of my backpack.

"I think we need to have another sleepover," Claudia is saying. "I'm tired of living with my family. Lydia's place is my favorite. No offense to you, Simone."

"What's wrong with my house?"

"Your dads are always lurking somewhere," she says. "They want to talk and interact, and sometimes I just want to have girl time."

I can't blame her. When my parents get home, I'll have to stay in my room if I want to avoid an interrogation. I hate that they can always tell when something is wrong. I hate Eric for putting me in this situation.

"You're such a freak, Claude," Lydia says. "They aren't even that bad. My parents would give you the twenty-questions treatment if they weren't so busy with Matt. I swear, you'd think he could handle himself."

"He's *six*," Claudia says. "Have a heart."

That's it. Ignoring it isn't helping. I need them to fix this.

"Guys," I say, voice cracking. "There was another note in my locker. I think Eric left it."

"What the *fuck?*"

"Oh my God. The asshole from Drama?"

Both of their voices screech through the phone at once. It's on speaker, but I still have to push it away. The knots in my stomach unravel a little bit now that it's out in the open.

"Did you tell your parents?" Lydia asks. "If you know who did it, then maybe you should tell."

"No way. They'll flip the fuck out. I'm not telling them *anything.*"

"Who does this kid think he is?" Claudia snaps. "I'm telling you, some people think they can get away with the worst shit. If he hacked into your school records or something—"

"I seriously don't know. Maybe he saw me at the hospital?" I say. I don't think I'm going to cry, but I'm *pissed.* "I don't think he could find it in my school records. He'd have to find my medical records."

"But *why?*" Lydia asks. "Who has the time for that?"

"Maybe he's trying to play a stupid prank?" Claudia suggests. "Boys get crazy when it comes to that shit."

"It just doesn't add up," I say, running a hand through my hair. "I know he doesn't like me because I always have notes for him, but I don't know. I can't . . . I don't know how he can hate me enough to do something like this."

Sure, I'm definitely a pain in his ass, but why would Eric care so much about my relationship with Miles? He did seem, I don't know, *repulsed* when he talked about us kissing earlier. I guess if he somehow found out I was positive, this could be his twisted idea of *protecting* Miles.

"I'll kick his ass," Claudia says. "Just give me his last name."

"You can't kill him, Claudia. I already told you that," I say, pressing a hand against my forehead. "Just give me a second. I need to figure this out."

"Figure *what* out?" she asks. "We know he's a creep and you aren't going to tell your parents. I'll just wait outside the auditorium and beat him up."

"I guess I could help," Lydia says. "But I'm not good at fights. I'd be the first one to get hit."

I open my mouth to say something else, but my phone flashes with a new text. It's an unknown number. My eyes widen and my spine goes straight. I'm barely even breathing.

Hey, Simone. This is Jesse from the crew. Just wanted to check in about sets! I know you wanted to change the cue for the apartment set. When in the scene should it come out?

For a second, I wonder why he has my number. Then I remember the directory we made at the beginning of rehearsals and let out a sigh. This stupid note is making me paranoid as hell.

"Simone?"

"I don't know, guys," I say. "I don't know. I think I'll ask him about it."

"He's not going to admit it," Lydia says.

"Well, what *am* I going to do?" I snap. "I'm not going to let you guys get suspended for beating a guy up, and I don't want my parents to flip out, either."

Not only would Pops and Dad tear the principal apart, but they'd also want me to transfer again. If I can stop this without telling them, I will.

"You could tell Principal Decker," Lydia offers. "Or literally any other adult."

"And they'll tell my parents, which brings us back to the drawing board." I groan, dropping my head between my legs. "I just . . . I don't want everyone to find out. I don't want Miles to hear this from a random person I don't even know."

There's silence on the other lines. My chest feels heavy, but I'm not going to cry. I'm not.

"So don't let him take your chance away," Claudia finally says. "Tell Miles before Eric can."

CHAPTER 18

Wednesday is the first time I'm actually looking forward to feedback from Group. Pops is right: the kids here understand things that no one else does. If I'm going to tell Miles that I'm positive, Group is the best place to go for advice.

"So, I like a boy," I say, trying to focus on a spot at the back of the room. It feels like everyone's eyes are on me. "But he doesn't have HIV—at least, I don't think so—and I'm not sure how to talk to him about . . . well, any of this. It's freaking me out."

Julie sits in the center of the circle, nodding like I'm an episode of a soap opera. Maybe she's surprised that I know how to speak.

"Does anyone have any advice for Simone?" she asks, turning to the rest of the group. "It's very important that couples talk about differences in HIV status, and I'm glad she brought it up. Even if some of you aren't worried about it now, it's something you'll all eventually deal with."

I chew at my lip. My hands are still shaking—have been shaking ever since yesterday. I've been ignoring Miles since I skipped the game, even though I saw him in the hallway and in History class. We definitely aren't kissing against lockers right now. All because of this stupid note.

Maybe it's not fair to ignore him, but I'm still trying to figure shit out. If I get used to acting like his girlfriend and then I tell him I have HIV, it'll be even worse if he reacts badly.

"Act the way you want him to react," Brie says, startling me. Her bangs are pushed back, which is weird enough, because her hair is always in her face. She meets my eyes and doesn't look away. "If you aren't comfortable talking about it, he's going to be weird about it. If you're chill, he'll be, too."

"Yeah, don't even make a big deal out of it," says Jack, nodding his head. The two of them share a *look*. If I weren't so worried about Miles, I'd spend more time analyzing it. "Don't apologize, because it isn't anything to be sorry about, and it's not your fault. Just text him."

"You can't just text him something like that," Ralph snaps. Normally, I'd ignore him out of principle, but he has a point. I *hate* that he has a point. "That's—that's a lot to take in. We live with it every day, but it's a big deal to people who don't."

"So tell him over a candlelight dinner, whatever," Brie says, rolling her eyes. It makes me want to hug her. "The point is that if he's the type of person who would reject you because you're positive, there's nothing you can do to change that."

"Yeah, it's not like waiting longer is going to change anything," Jack agrees. "Tricking him into staying with you isn't going to do anything."

"I'm not trying to trick him into anything," I say, but my voice sounds weak, even to my own ears. "I'm just nervous talking about it. That's why I've been putting it off."

"That's valid," Julie says, her soothing voice breaking the tension. "That's completely valid. But no matter how you decide to tell this person, it's important that you're honest. Honesty is the most important part of a relationship, and you don't want to start something with lies."

I lean back in my seat, ignoring her as she moves on to the next subject. Waiting to tell Miles doesn't count as lying. At least, it shouldn't.

I take the train home alone, letting myself into our empty house. Pops has to stay after school to supervise detention, which means I'll be alone for another hour, at least. Before I realize it, I'm gravitating toward my parents' room. There are prints of paintings on the wall: a Frida Kahlo on one wall and a Basquiat painting on another. It looks like a bunch of scribbles to me, but Pops gets pissed whenever I tell him that.

I toss myself back on the bed. I haven't slept with them since I was really little, around six or seven. But just being in here makes me feel connected to them. There's even a tiny bit of me that feels connected to my bio mom. This is where my parents keep the adoption records: legal papers, letters, and even some photo albums. They're all I have of her. It's never bothered me before. I don't know if it's bothering me now, exactly. I just wish I could talk to her about this.

How did she feel when she found out she was positive? When she found out she was pregnant with me? I've never wondered until now. Did her boyfriend ignore her? Did her family leave her? Her friends? I'd like to imagine that she was surrounded by people who loved her; people who helped pull her out of a bad place. But I really don't *know*.

Most of the time, I hate thinking about her. I hate the idea that I'm not just the daughter of my two fathers. Maybe that makes me horrible. I just hate the fact that I don't *feel* anything for this person who created me, who probably wanted to get rid of me.

I bite my lip. People are supposed to be connected to their biological mothers, to *feel* something. There are stories about people tracking these women across countries, of them hugging and loving each other even if they don't speak the same language.

There are two things that connect me to this woman: she had me, and she passed HIV down to me. I've never wanted to talk to her before, but for the first time, I wish she were here. This is the one thing she'd understand better than my parents do. Maybe she'd know what to do. Maybe, if she were here, I wouldn't feel so alone.

I pull my legs close to my chest and start to cry.

CHAPTER 19

It takes me all of Thursday, but I finally manage to text Miles after rehearsal. That's how we end up in Dolores Park again, sitting on a bench and staring at each other. It's almost like the first time we came here together, but this time neither one of us is talking.

I normally don't mind silence, but I hate it right now. Maybe because I know it's my fault. *I'm* the one who hasn't been talking to him lately. I'm the one who's been ignoring him in the hallways. I'm the one who's about to share something unexpected. God, I feel sick.

At least we're in the park. There's so much noise, between the dogs and the little kids and the strangers wrapped up in their own lives, that even awkward silences aren't completely quiet. It's not foggy, for once, so I should be enjoying the evening. I would be on any other day.

"Are you okay?" Miles asks. He isn't sitting as close as he was last time. If he wanted to touch my shoulder, he'd have to lean over. "Because you look like you're going to be sick."

I swallow, fiddling with the note cards in my hands. I haven't used these since we had to give presentations on our science projects all the way back in middle school. They're numbered and everything, in case I forget where I'm going. It's important that I don't forget.

"Okay," I say, putting my note cards on my lap in front of me. It feels weird to do this in a park, but at least no one here really knows me. This is one of my safe places. "I want to tell you some stuff."

"Okay."

"So, um, I'm adopted. But I feel like you could've guessed that already."

"Yeah." The corner of his mouth turns up. "Kinda."

"My biological mom had HIV," I say, hurrying to get the words out so there isn't an awkward silence. "And I guess she didn't know or there wasn't medication for her or, if there was, she just couldn't get it. I don't know."

I switch to the next note card, not allowing myself to make eye contact with him. My hands are shaking. No matter how much I tell myself that I shouldn't be scared, that this is all on him and how he decides to react, it's still scary. I don't want Miles to think HIV makes me dirty.

"When I was born, I was really sick. They tested me, and I have HIV, too. It's not like I just found out—I've always known, since I was little. I've been on medication forever, and now I'm healthy and everything."

I allow myself to look up, just briefly. He swallows slowly, his Adam's apple bobbing. He's looking right at me, no way to pretend that he isn't. I look away.

"I'm sorry I didn't tell you sooner and I'm sorry for ignoring you and I get it if you don't want to talk to me again," I say, my throat dry. "I was just really scared, because it's always weird when I tell someone, so I *really* don't tell anyone. Like, anyone. But I want you to know, because I really like you, so . . ."

I lick my lips. He hasn't interrupted me once this entire time, like I was expecting. I glance back up, and he's still staring.

I wait. I can hear the sound of squirrels throwing nuts to the ground, strollers moving past. The sun is setting, slowly, like it's lingering to watch *this* mess. Now that I've told him, we won't be able to act the way we did before, just having fun. I immediately wish I could take it back.

"Um," he says. "Can I hug you?"

My brows shoot up. "You want to touch me?"

"Yeah," he says, scrunching his brows together. "Why wouldn't I?"

"A lot of people would be very concerned about now," I say, eyeing him warily. "Do you . . . I don't know, have any questions? You aren't reacting. It makes me feel weird."

"I mean, I'm thinking," he says, biting his lip. "How does everyone else normally react?"

"Um, I don't know. They ask a lot of questions," I say. Lydia and Claudia sort of did. Sarah asked even more, but I can't think about that right now. "I'm not sure how everyone reacts. It's not like I go around telling people all the time. That would . . . I don't think that would be a good idea."

He nods, staring at his hands. I wish I could tell what he's thinking.

"You're not going to tell anyone." It comes out more like a statement than a question. "Right?"

"No." He shakes his head, glancing up. "Of course not."

"Good." I breathe out, my chest a little lighter. "Okay."

"So it's not going to be AIDS anytime soon?" he asks. There's an uneasy look on his face. "That sounds stupid, but, like, are you okay? For good?"

"Yeah," I say, voice soft. "I'm fine."

"So you're not going to die?"

"When I'm eighty, maybe," I say, shrugging. "Eventually. But not now."

"Are you mad at your mom?"

The question makes me pause. Honestly, I don't usually think of her as my mother. Maybe, if she were still alive, she'd be like another aunt. She could answer questions about dating with HIV and how to disclose and when to keep it under wraps. But that feels too raw, too personal, to say out loud.

"I don't think I can be mad at her," I say, choosing my words carefully. "I have been, before, because she probably could've stopped me from getting the virus. But she was really young— I know that—and she had to deal with being sick and pregnant. I think she was probably alone, too. That must've been hard."

I glance at Miles out of the corner of my eye. He's nodding really big. I'm not sure what to make of it at all, honestly.

"Can I ask more?"

I nod, almost too quickly. My hands fumble to put the note cards back in my pocket. I don't need them anymore.

"Do you take a lot of pills?"

"Just one a day."

"Right," he says, putting his hands in his lap. "That's good, right?"

I nod. I almost want to smile. He seems just as nervous as me.

"And . . . I'm not going to get it by hanging out with you?"

The harder question. I wish I had Dr. Khan here to answer all the questions calmly and professionally, but Miles will have to settle for my awkward answers. Strangely, I don't feel so awkward anymore. Thinking about my parents makes me feel better. If they chose me, *wanted* me, other people will, too.

Miles bites his lip. "Was that a stupid question?"

"No, it's . . . normal," I say. "Transmitting HIV by touching is basically impossible, and you can inactivate it with soap if blood spills or anything. The only way you can transmit it is through bodily fluids, like blood or breast milk. . . ."

"Or, like, sperm."

Now I'm flustered again.

"Well, like, semen," I say. "Or cum. I don't know—like, whatever comes out."

He snickers.

"What?" I say, leaning away from him. "It's true."

"You sound so much like a doctor—you have this whole time," he says, shaking his head. "And then you just say *cum*. Completely changed the tone."

"Well, that's what it *is*."

"Yeah," he says, shrugging. "But it's—you know."

I don't know, but I don't think I want to find out. There's too much going on for me to hear *him* talk about sex. It's funny, the way I do it with Claudia and Lydia without it being a big deal. To hear him just say the word makes my skin flush. I hate being embarrassed about this.

"Anyway," I say. "It can't be transmitted if your viral load— like, the amount of virus they can find in your blood—is unde- tectable."

"Is yours?"

"Yeah." It comes out as a squeak. "It is. I found out on Mon- day. But my gynecologist says I should wait until it's been this way for six months."

I don't let myself look at his face. There's more silence now, even though birds are making their nighttime noises, and I can hear trains rushing past. It's probably time for me to get home. I just wish things were more . . . I don't know. Resolved. At least I did it. Now no one else can take that away.

Miles kisses my cheek, and I jump a little bit.

"That's not sex," he says. "No bodily fluids, right? So, we can still do that."

I don't even know what to say. He's *too* good.

"You're right," I say, giving him a small smile. "And anyway, it can't be contracted through saliva. But you should think about it."

"What do you mean?"

"I don't know," I say, heaving a sigh. "Like, I'm still a virgin."

He blinks at me. "And?"

"It's for a reason," I say, putting force behind my words. "There's only a small chance, but there's still a *chance*, so you should think about it."

He blinks a few more times. I'm glad he hasn't called me a whore or run away or anything, but part of me feels like he isn't taking this seriously.

"We don't *have* to have sex right now," he says, almost like a petulant child. "Not everyone has sex all the time, Simone."

I scoff, "You'll *want* to wait."

"You don't know what I want. Even if I *do* want it, I can wait."

"Well, what if you decide you don't want to wait?"

He shakes his head, sliding away from me. It's a little colder without him near me, so I wrap my sweatshirt around my shoulders.

"Do you seriously think I can't go without sex for six months?"

"I don't *know*," I snap. I shut my eyes, willing myself not to lose it again. "It's just . . . I don't know. I don't want . . . I don't *think* anything bad is going to happen, but in the alternate universe where it does, I don't want you to hate me forever."

"I wouldn't."

"If you got HIV because of me?" My eyes pop open. "Miles, once you got on the meds, you'd probably have side effects like throwing up and getting headaches and rashes. Plus, some people would avoid you like you have the plague—maybe even your own family. Most people don't even know anything about it; they're just scared. I think you'd care, even just a little bit."

He's quiet.

"I'm not saying it's going to happen," I continue, lowering my voice. "I'm pretty sure it won't. But I'm still scared that—"

"I don't think any differently about you."

I glance at him. "What?"

"You're acting like I'm going to stop talking to you or something," he says, shaking his head again. "But I'm not going to. I mean, where else am I gonna find someone who can memorize all the lyrics to the original Broadway production of *The Phantom of the Opera*?"

I sort of want to cry.

"You're so stupid," I say, even though I'm smiling. "I know I'm awesome—"

"You are." He puts his hand on top of mine, and I don't pull away. "You're really awesome."

"Okay, but people would stay away from you, if they found out," I say, forcing myself to look him in the eye. "You know that, right? People would be afraid of you. I mean, we both know what it's like to be black. And people hate black *guys*."

He snorts. "I *know*."

"Well, they hate HIV even more," I say. "Put all of those things together, and they'd try to, like, quarantine us on Mars. In the meantime, they'd make our lives miserable."

"Simone, racism's not going to go away if I stop talking to you," he says. "It's not like we can control prejudice or anything."

"I know." I stare down at our hands. "I just want you to know that things could be bad."

"Are you *trying* to convince me to stop talking to you?"

Yes. No. Maybe a little bit. Maybe it'd be easier to stop things now instead of getting hurt later on.

"I'm just surprised," I say. That I liked him first, and he likes me back. That he's still here, even after I *told* him, and he's holding my hand—not for the first time. "I didn't think this would happen."

"Well, I like you."

I flush. "I figured, but like—"

"I hang around you because you're smart and pretty and *funny*," he says. He doesn't rush his words out the way I do. Like saying this doesn't embarrass him. "If I didn't want to kiss you, I think I'd be jealous of you."

"You're . . . God, Miles, you're so weird," I say, rubbing a hand over my face. "I don't even know what to say."

"You don't have to say anything. You already said a lot."

"Well." I turn toward him. "There are a bunch of things I could say. Like, you're my favorite person. One of my favorite people, anyway."

I think of Claudia and Lydia. Miles is somewhere on the same level as them.

"I could also say I love you, but it would be, like, ironically."

"*What?*"

"Because I tell my best friends that I love them all the time," I say, moving my hands as I speak. "They're my favorite people, you know? So, if you're one of the favorites now, I pretty much love you. But not in the super-dramatic way. I love pizza and brownies and *Aida* and—"

"And Webber."

"*And* Sondheim," I say. "I love a lot of things, and you've been added to the list."

"I'm honored, I think." He laughs. "Where am I on the list— before or after pizza?"

I can't take my eyes off his smile. I didn't realize I could like someone this much. I didn't think I could like them so much and they'd like me *back*.

"I like kissing you better than I actually like *you*," I tease. "So, first Claudia and Lydia; then musicals; then kisses, which come before pizza; and *then* you."

"Okay, I'll try to remember," he says, leaning forward. "But I like *you* better than all of the above. I think I should get a prize."

I don't think there's anything I could give him that would be

160

good enough. He's acting like this isn't a big deal, which is how the reactions *should* be, but they never have been before. It feels like my body is filled with the sun. I don't know how to make him feel the same way, but he deserves it. I want to give him the sun.

"You get a secret." I slide my arms around his neck. "I like you better than everything."

CHAPTER 20

When the sixth-period bell rings on Friday, I head down to the old science wing. As much as I want to see Miles, it's been four days since I last ate lunch with my best friends, and I'm sure I'm not the only one who noticed. Last night, Claudia sent a text in the group chat: *SIMONE! come to lunch tomorrow with the GSA pls and thx*, followed by Lydia's text: *You totally should because we miss you!*

Now I'm here. I push myself into the room, but neither of my friends is here to greet me. There are more kids here than last time. I can't spot Claudia or Lydia right away. Geez, why'd they want me to come to *this* meeting? I thought we'd just be hanging out.

The only person I recognize is Jesse, but even he's distracted, laughing in the corner with a group of friends. I shift my weight between my feet. This is so not what I was expecting.

My phone chirps, snapping me out of my thoughts.

Proposition: I'll buy you pizza if I get to move up a spot on the list.

It takes me a second to realize what Miles is talking about—my list of favorite things, the one I told him about in the park.

You're already at the top, tho

He texts back right away: *A guy's gotta maintain his status, Simone!!!*

I grin before I can stop it. He's so corny and I love it. I also wouldn't mind eating pizza instead of my sandwich.

I glance up. Claudia and Lydia are standing around with some kids, totally engrossed in their discussion. I catch only snippets.

"Yeah, I'm pretty sure non-binary people can identify as lesbians," Claudia says. "But I don't really know, since I'm not non-binary."

"We can probably look it up," Lydia suggests. "Or you can talk to Alex when they get here, maybe? They're non-binary, too."

I doubt they'd notice if I left. Most of these meetings consist of them talking while I sit in the corner and nod, anyway, and it looks like today's meeting will be more of the same. We're better off hanging out after school instead of here.

The door is still open. I pull my bag over my shoulder. If they notice I'm gone, I'll make it up to them. I hold my breath and run out the door before either of them can call after me.

CHAPTER 21

Rehearsal is mostly normal on Saturday, even if I keep glancing at Eric every few minutes. If he knows that I met up with Miles yesterday, he doesn't show it.

"Okay, so, notes," I say, fisting a hand in my hair and trying not to sigh. "Eric, like I said, you're gonna want to drop that accent. Everyone in the ensemble: You're doing great, but some of you are reacting a little *too* much and it's kinda melodramatic. Try to tone it down a little bit, especially if you're in the front. Okay, let's try it again."

Everyone heads back to their spots except for the cast members in the front. Eric rolls his eyes. Claire inches closer to him, whispering something in his ear. His laugh is obnoxiously loud. She glances back at me with raised eyebrows, almost like she's daring me to say something.

What if Claire knows about the notes? What can I say? *I know you left me some creepy notes and I want you to stop?* They'd just deny it. Confronting either one about it would make me look even more like I don't know what I'm doing.

Once rehearsal is over, I toss my bag over my shoulder. Miles gave me his hoodie to wear, like we're in a rom-com from the eighties—not that I'm complaining. It's white and blue, our school colors, and too big for me. I like that it smells like him, that it's warm, the way he is.

I told him to meet me outside, mostly so that Eric and Claire wouldn't see us. I think back to that look Claire gave me, and remember how Sarah texted five different girls about my status right after I told her. Sarah ruined our relationship when she told my secret. But Claire and I barely speak, so she has nothing to lose by terrorizing me.

Miles appears next to me, grabbing my hand.

"Hey," he says, sweat running down his brow. We ran sets today, and it looks like he did the bulk of the heavy lifting. "I guess you're ready to meet the guys?"

Oh yeah. *That*.

Normally, I don't worry about making a good first impression. I figure it just happens or it doesn't. The first time I met Sarah was as normal as possible. She was the upperclassman who took me on a tour of my old school before I started. I didn't expect her to be completely horrible, but hey, it just goes to show.

But these are Miles's friends. I like Miles. I want his friends to like me or, at the very least, tolerate me.

"You look so freaked out," Miles says at my silence, shaking his head. "Don't be. It's not a big deal."

"Maybe not to you," I mumble, shrugging out of his hoodie. He's not the one meeting anyone new. If his teammates hate me, will he look at me differently? It should only take five minutes to meet them; all I have to do is smile and wave. I press my lips together and shove my hands into my pockets.

Outside, there are already players on the field. My eyes are drawn to number twenty-four. There's something graceful about the way he plays, running in between other players and cradling the ball. Then he crashes into another guy and the spell is broken.

I open my mouth to say something else, but shut it as a boy jogs over. He pulls the sweatshirt from Miles, staring at him with a stupid grin.

"*Ooooh*, is this the lucky hoodie? I bet it still smells like her," he teases, glancing over at me. "Is that why you let her borrow it?"

"Shut up," Miles says, shoving him. "The last time I tell you *anything*, I swear to God."

The guy grins at me, and I snort. It's nice to know that guys aren't so different from my friends and me. Miles grabs the hoodie, turning back around.

"Here." He holds the sweatshirt toward me. "It's lucky."

"Because it smells like me?" I bat my eyelashes. "What do I smell like, Miles?"

He rubs the back of his neck, like he's embarrassed. When he steps ahead of me, I hold the fabric up to my nose. His scent is still there—deodorant and sweat and something warm, like wood.

"Hey, guys," Miles says. Luck must be on my side, since the coach isn't here. I'm sure he'd make this even more awkward. "This is Simone."

There are about ten guys, all in their pads and jerseys. Some of them have on helmets, but take them off, I guess to see better. It's weird to think that they're looking at *me*. I barely even glance

166

at them when I see them walk around in the halls, with their jerseys and massive lacrosse sticks taking up all the space.

"Hi." I give a wave. "I'm Simone."

They murmur at the same time, words like "Hi" and "Nice to meet you" blending into each other.

"That's Ryan." Miles points to a white boy at the end of the group, and continues down the line: "Beast, Greg, Kevin, Squid, Tom, Dylan, Will, and Chad."

Tom, a Japanese kid I talk to in math class, is the only person of color. Everyone else is white. I don't know how Tom and Miles deal with it. The rest of the school is pretty diverse, and I'm normally not in a room full of white people by myself, a definite step up from my old school, where I was often the only black girl. Being in mostly white groups makes me twitch. It's like I'm more vulnerable. On the bright side, these are Miles's friends, not mine. He doesn't hang out with Claudia and Lydia, and I won't be hanging out with these guys. I force a smile, forcing myself not to say anything about the kids called Beast and Squid.

"Aw, Austin has a little girlfriend," one of them says. I can't remember his name, mostly because it's hard to keep track. He pulls his helmet back on, matting his hair. "Look at you, making friends in Drama Club. It's so cute."

"Shut up, Greg," another guy says, jogging backward. "It's nice to meet you, Simone."

"I like your hair," a kid with freckles says. "It's pretty."

"Oh." I tuck a strand behind my ear, but it doesn't stay put. "Thanks."

"I've always wanted to date a black girl," he continues. "I'm pretty sure it would be more fun."

"What?" I blink, cocking my head to the side. It's barely been a full minute, and the bullshit is already starting. "What does that mean?"

"Chad, what the fuck?" Miles snaps. He takes a step forward, like he's trying to block me or something.

I push him to the side with my shoulder, but he barely budges.

"What?" Chad says, holding up his hands. "It's not a big deal. I'm just *saying*. Black girls are different. Feistier, you know?"

"No," Miles says, voice short. "I don't."

"I'm not a cultural experience for some random white boy," I say, folding my arms. "And, before you go looking for one, I don't know any black girl who'd want the position."

The rest of the team is silent. I can't tell what it means. Maybe they don't know what to say. Maybe they think the same thing, and don't want to get caught up in a fight. Whatever the reason, it reminds me why I don't like all-white spaces. I always have to be on the defensive, ready for someone to say or do something stupid, no matter how "safe" the space appears to be.

"Look, it's no big deal if you don't get it, Austin," Chad goes on, shrugging. "But I can definitely tell the difference."

"Oh my *God*," I say. "Fuck you."

I turn on my heel. There's no way I'm listening anymore. I know where it's headed: He'll keep acting like what he said isn't a big deal. And since we're surrounded by white people, he'll have a pretty easy time of it.

Miles calls my name, but I don't stop. I'm pissed at him, too. So what if it's not his fault? These are his *teammates*. I'm sure they've made tons of comments about how *fun* black girls are to mess around with. Has Miles called them out before? Or did he just stand there and laugh?

I push back into the school, but Miles's heavy footsteps catch up to me.

"I'm sorry, Simone," he says. I don't turn to face him. "He's an ass."

I lean against the wall, still not facing him. "He probably isn't the only one."

"Hey." He steps in front of me, forcing me to look at him. "What's that supposed to mean?"

"Oh, come on, Miles," I say, leaning away from him. "Don't act like he's the *only* one who has 'always wanted to date a black girl.' They've said stuff like that before, haven't they?"

"How would you know?" he asks. The words come out too fast. I know I've struck a chord. "You don't hang out with them. This is the first time you've met them."

"I just *do*." I try to push past him, but he steps to the side, blocking me with his frame. "It's—Miles, it's not just me. They must say stupid shit to you all the time and you just brush it off. I don't get why you're so in love with lacrosse when it's reserved for white guys."

His eyes darken.

"I like lacrosse," he says. His hands tighten into fists and flex out again. "And last time I checked, I'm black, so it isn't 'reserved for white guys'. And there are, what, *five* black kids at Drama rehearsals? I notice that shit, too, but I never say anything about it because I know you like Drama."

"Don't turn it around on me," I snap. "This isn't my problem."

"What are you talking about?" He shakes his head, bewildered. "You're the only one here with a problem, Simone."

I've gotten stuff like this from white people. They don't understand why I hate when people touch my hair, or they think I'm being dramatic when I say I get followed in a store. But Miles is black, just like me. I don't know how he doesn't get it.

"Forget it," I say, shoving my hands into my pockets. Maybe I'll track down Claudia and Lydia and we can go get food together. "I'll see you later."

"No, nah, come on." He grabs my arm, and I snatch it away. "Talk to me about this. I don't get it."

"You don't *get* it?" My voice rises. "Miles, if one of them saw you outside their house at night, they'd call the cops. You know why?"

"It's not about that," he says. "It doesn't always have to be about that all the time. It's about the game."

"I just . . ." My voice trails off as I sigh. "It would bother me is all I'm saying. Hanging out with them and knowing what I know."

"I don't think about it all the time." His voice is soft. For a second, I feel like a jerk. "You don't believe me, but it's easy to forget about on the field. It's like being at rehearsal. We're all part of the same team. This stuff doesn't matter when we're out there together."

"Miles," I say, lowering my voice. "I wish . . ."

I take a deep breath. How do I say this?

"I don't know," I finally say. "Being black isn't something you should have to forget about."

"No, that's not what I mean," he says, shaking his head. "What I want to forget about—it's not being black. It's the way people

170

look at me. I'm *supposed* to be scary on the field. It's different than people seeing a big black kid walking down the block. You know what I mean?"

I *do* know what he means. Sometimes I wish I didn't have HIV, that I didn't have to worry about disclosing before sex, but I mostly wish I could get rid of other people's reactions. It's not fair for me to be mad because he loves something. Miles isn't the one who walks around saying stupid shit.

I pull at his hand, running my thumb over his knuckles. His fingers slip through mine.

"You're completely different from my parents," he says, almost like an afterthought. "They're—God, they're so intense. Dad didn't want me on the basketball team. I guess that's another reason why I picked lacrosse."

"What?" I raise a brow. "Why?"

"They didn't want me to fulfill the *stereotype*," he says, rolling his eyes. "They're big on that. Not becoming a stereotype. I have to be *better* than that."

"Wow," I say, voice soft. Pops might've been irritated if I joined basketball, but that's because he can't stand sports. I don't think he cares what I do, as long as I'm happy. "That's rough."

He laughs. A hand hovers near a spiral of my hair. I lean forward, letting him play with it. It's starting to grow out again.

"I understand," he says. "Sometimes it's a lot. I don't think racist people care if I play lacrosse or basketball, but Mom and Dad disagree."

"I get it. They want you to be the best. You know? More than a stereotype," I say, staring at our hands. "You already are, though. They don't have to worry."

"Careful," he says. His voice is soft, like he's afraid to speak. "It sounds like you like me again."

"I didn't exactly stop."

He stares at me for an extra beat. I should say something funny, but my mind is suspiciously blank.

"Hold on," Miles says. He startles me by plopping down on the locker-room floor, rolling up his jeans. "I wanna show you something."

"What are you doing?" My eyes dart from his hands to his face, but he doesn't meet my eye. If he wanted to strip down in front of me, I'm sure there would be easier ways to do it. "Miles . . ."

Now I see it: a huge scar, so lightly colored that it looks out of place. The scar isn't in a cool shape, or even fully healed, like the one Harry Potter has on his forehead. It looks like it might collapse into itself if I touch the skin. It looks like it should still hurt. I wince.

"The doctors had to slice through to fix the bone," he says, patting a little above the scar. "I thought it would look better once the cast came off."

"Yeah, well . . . at least you still have your face."

Fuck. Why don't I think about the shit that comes out of my mouth? I glance up in horror.

"Wow." Miles just smiles at me, shaking his head. "What a heartfelt reaction."

"It's not such a big deal." I shrug, moving closer to him. "If it doesn't bother you, it doesn't bother me. Everyone has a scar. You know what I mean?"

"Yeah." He bites his lip. "I just wanted to show you. I don't have HIV or anything, but you should see something I've never shown anyone else. The guys on the team all saw me get hurt— this douche from another team checked me, and his teammates basically trampled me—but they haven't actually seen the scar."

"Oh." That's strangely sweet, even if it sounds painful. "Well, I'm glad you showed it to me. I'm honored."

It's a joke, but he doesn't smile. I realize he needed to hear that.

He's closer to me now, his shoulder bumping against mine. Sometimes, when Miles sits next to me, it feels like his body can block everything out. Like he can stop anything bad from existing just by being here.

We're quiet, leaning against one another, and the gravity of the moment strikes me. This is more than sweet. It's like . . . the way my parents look at each other sometimes, or something out of a love story full of symbolism and heartfelt declarations.

Or maybe I'm just taking this too seriously. I clear my throat.

"But you know that you aren't the only person who knows I'm positive, right?" I say, breaking the silence. "So mine isn't a total secret like yours. You have to stop showing me up!"

"Hey," he says, turning to look at me. "Don't worry about that. I wanted to show you anyway."

It just seems like he's better at this stuff than me—always knowing how to say the right thing. I pull his hand up to my mouth, kissing the knuckles. He watches me with dark eyes. Just because he's better at this doesn't mean I can't try.

"Come on," I say, tugging at his arm. "Let's get out of here."

. . .

Fisherman's Wharf is a tourist area, and if there's one thing I hate more than racist white boys, it's tourist areas. It's always filled to the brim with confused travelers and their cameras, smelling of dead ocean creatures and fried food. Combine that with the fact that it's Saturday and it makes for an hour of irritation. I never would've come here on my own. This is what I get for telling Miles to pick the place.

"Come *on*." He notices my expression and tosses an arm around me. "Don't be like that. I wanted to do something fun. I figured we could go to Ghirardelli Square and get ice cream or something."

It's not the first time he's put an arm around me, but I don't think I'll ever get used to it. But I *like* Miles touching me. I like that he's taller than me, and that I can lean into him. I like this more than I realized I could.

"Simone?" He nudges me. "You wanna stay?"

"Have you ever thought about how weird San Francisco is?" I say, touching the arm that's wrapped around me. "Like, I love it here. But it's expensive for no reason and mostly everyone is poor. Except, like, all the tech bros."

"Both of my parents are in business." Miles shakes his head. "Even then, I don't know how they do it. I won't be able to be like them."

"Why not?" I glance up at him. "You're smart."

If Miles is worried about surviving in *business*, of all things, how would I ever survive as a director? How would I even make it to Broadway, in between trying to eat and finding a place to sleep without going completely broke?

"Smart people don't always have money," he says. "Black

people are smart and we're, like, all poor because—you know why. Even rich black people have less money than rich white people."

I wish there were an option for us to turn off racism. I would never want to stop being black, but if I could control the way that society shapes us, I totally would.

"I know," I say, sighing. "I just—"

"Simone? What are you doing here?"

I glance up and frown. Ralph from Group stands in front of me, surprise in his eyes. *Fuck.* If I had seen him earlier, I would've found a place to hide. The last thing I want is one of his condescending comments while I'm hanging out with Miles.

"Hi, Ralph," I say between clenched teeth. "This is Miles. We—"

"*Miles?* Wow," he says, sticking out a hand. "I've never seen you around before."

There he goes again, interrupting me just like old times.

"Did you two meet at Group?" Ralph asks, pumping Miles's arm. His eyes lock on me. "I think I would've noticed someone new."

I glare at him. We both know that Miles isn't from Group.

"No." Miles glances at me with furrowed brows. I let out a loud sigh. "Uh, Simone and I go to school together."

"*Oh.*" He glances over at me, mouth open. I can practically see his gears turning. "You must be who Simone was talking about last time."

I *hate* this kid. "Look, Ralph—"

"Well, I hope everything works out." His smile is as fake as the Christmas tree we're using in the show. "Nice to see you, Simone. And *great* to meet you, Miles."

He walks away before I can get another word in, the stupid jerk.

"Wait," Miles says, blinking at Ralph's retreating form. "*Who* is he? What just happened?"

"He's only the worst person in the history of the world." I groan, tossing my head back. "We're in the same support group together. It's a long story."

"You talked about me at a support group?"

"Well, yeah." I take a step forward. "It's an HIV support group. I was really nervous about—you know—telling you."

"Oh." It's hard to read his expression. His hands are in his pockets, and he stares up at the seagulls flying around in the air.

My cheeks are hot. Group never seemed embarrassing before, but then again, I've never talked about Group to a boy before. Hell, I barely even talk *in* Group. I almost wish I hadn't said anything—but then I never would've had the nerve to tell Miles. He needed to know everything even though it was nerve-wracking as hell; I'm glad he knows. But that doesn't make me less embarrassed. Ugh, screw Ralph.

"Wait." His hand reaches out, grazing mine. "Simone."

I allow myself to glance up at him. His smile isn't as happy as it usually is. It looks like his mouth wants to frown and he's fighting it.

"You don't have to feel sorry for me," I say. "And I promise I didn't say anything weird. I just wanted advice."

"I don't . . . No, that's not it." He swallows. "It sounds like it took a lot for you to tell me."

"Yeah." I scratch the back of my head. "It did."

"But I'm glad." His index finger traces patterns on the back of my hand. "That you did it, I mean. I'm really, really glad."

Suddenly, it's hard to swallow. I spent so much time worrying about what he would think and how he would react. Never did I let myself even *consider* the possibility of this. I lick my lips, glancing down at our hands. It's only been a little while, but I've gotten used to how they look when they're intertwined. They complement each other.

"Me too," I say, voice thick. "I'm glad you listened."

CHAPTER 22

"You still use your locker?"

"Well, yeah," I say, spinning the combination. "When did I say I'd stop?"

It's only mid-November, but it feels like the rainy season has already started. Kids drip through the hallways, toting raincoats and umbrellas. Lydia manages to wear her raincoat the entire day like it's a fashion statement. Claudia just doesn't care. Currently, she's trying not to make eye contact with me, like she's been doing ever since I ditched them at GSA.

I expected her to ambush me, rant about what a horrible friend I am or something, but she never did. She's just stopped talking. Lydia glances at her every once in a while, like she's trying to encourage Claudia to speak to me, but it doesn't work.

She can't ignore me forever. Right?

"I just don't think it's a good idea since you started getting those notes," Lydia says. "It doesn't feel right. Like you're falling into a trap."

"It's fine," I say, pulling out my jacket. As far as I can see, there isn't any note. I breathe a sigh of relief. "Really. There's nothing there."

My locker isn't what Lydia needs to be worried about, not since that note showed up at my house. But she doesn't know about that. No one does. If I told her, she'd tell the principal on my behalf, and then all the secretaries would know my business. Who knows how fast news spreads in the teachers' lounge?

"Seriously. I can handle it."

At least, that's what I keep telling myself.

"What about Miles?"

My eyes snap to Claudia. She's staring straight at me, for the first time in ages.

"Uh." I tug at my backpack straps. "What about him?"

"Does he know about the notes?"

"No."

"Maybe he should."

"Why?" I ask, narrowing my eyes.

"You're getting them *because* of him," she snaps. Then, lower: "And blowing us off because of him, too."

"What?"

She raises a brow, as if daring me to disagree. I hold back a groan.

It's not Miles's fault I skipped GSA—it was mine. I don't want her to blame him. I want to talk to her about what it's like to officially date Miles, how we stare across the classroom during AP US History, making a game out of trying not to get caught. I want to tell her about trading the lucky sweatshirt back and forth, how I pretend I don't sit around my house with it on, the scent of Miles around me while I watch TV. But I know Claudia doesn't want to hear it.

"I swear to God, you are *so* far gone," she says. We walk down the hallway, with Lydia on the left and me on the right, like always, but the tension between us is far from normal. "Do you ever stop to think about anything else?"

"*You* brought him up," I say, balancing my books in one hand while holding my jacket in the other. "And anyway, you know I think about other things."

"Like what?"

"Like . . . musicals," I say. "And food. I'm always thinking about food."

"Is that why you hang out with him?" Lydia raises a teasing brow. "Because he buys you food?"

I'm startled at her voice. Almost irritated. She and Claudia were friends before I came along. If anyone can get Claudia off my back, it's her. But she doesn't say anything about our weird confrontation, just like she hasn't said anything about GSA. She just grabs a book off the stack I'm carrying.

"I pay for stuff," I protest. "I'm gonna pay for my own stuff today."

"Yeah, sure." Claudia scoffs. "I'm sure you'll have to."

"What do you mean?"

"I'm surprised Miles isn't broke yet," Claudia says, not looking at me. "You go out for lunch so much. I'm sure he's spent a fortune."

"Okay, what's up?" I stop walking. "Are you still pissed about Friday? Just yell at me so we can get over this."

Claudia frowns. "It's not—"

"Um, guys?"

Lydia holds my copy of *Hamlet* open in one hand and a square piece of white paper in the other. *Shit.* My legs stutter, textbooks toppling out of my hands.

Claudia snatches the paper and reads aloud:

Thanksgiving is less than two weeks away. End it.

"Who the fuck is this kid again?"

My stomach rolls. I swallow to keep from throwing up.

"I'm so sorry, Simone," Lydia says, bending down to help. "I thought the notes stopped coming."

That's what I had hoped. I can't bring myself to touch any of the other books. How the hell did the note get in there? It couldn't have been slipped through the vents like the others.

I figured that telling Miles would give the note-leaver less power, but they could still tell everyone else about my secret. In some ways, it could be worse than what happened at my old school. People wouldn't just give *me* a hard time; they'd bother my friends, and Miles, too.

A shiver runs through me. I didn't even notice Eric go anywhere near my locker.

"Why don't you *tell the principal*?" Lydia asks. "This isn't getting any better. I know you don't want to, but I don't think it would be so bad for one person to know, especially if they'll help make this go away."

"No," I sigh, grabbing my books and rising to my feet. "Not unless I absolutely have to."

"Well," Claudia says. "What else can you do?"

"I don't know," I say. "I just don't *know.*"

The two of them share a glance. Lydia and Claudia are the smartest people I know, and even *they* don't know what to do. Telling the principal isn't a bad idea, but I can't bring myself to do it.

"Is something going on?"

At the sound of Miles's voice, I crumple the note in my hand. There's no way in hell he's seeing this.

"Nothing. I just dropped my books," I say, gesturing to the pile with my chin. "You know Claudia and Lydia, right?"

"Yeah," he says, frowning. I'm sure it's obvious something is wrong, but that doesn't mean I have to admit it. "It's cool to see you guys. Do you wanna come out to lunch with us?"

"No, thanks," Claudia says. Somehow, she's able to act like everything is normal. It's a skill of hers. "We have a GSA meeting."

My eyes snap up. She's smiling, but I can't bring myself to return the favor.

"I forgot," I say, voice falling flat. "But you can still come, if Miles doesn't care."

Claudia presses her lips together but says nothing. We both know that I don't actually expect her to come. I can tell by the twitch under her eye, the way that Lydia nervously glances at her. Can they blame me, though? It's not a secret that we haven't been spending as much time together as we used to, but it's not like I'm *ignoring* them. Hell, I'm allowed to have lunch with someone other than Claudia. It's not just about having a boyfriend.

"We could go to my house," Miles offers. His words are hesitant, like he knows he's stepping into a fight. "It's close, and we have sandwich stuff."

"No, it's fine. We have to go to GSA," Lydia says, jabbing Claudia's ribs. "Right, Claude?"

"Sure," she says. Her eyes don't move from my face. I'm not sure when *this* happened, or why it has to happen *right* this second. "You guys go. Have a *great* time."

I roll my eyes, shrugging on my coat.

Lydia frowns. Claudia walks down the hall, not sparing me a second glance.

CHAPTER 23

"Do I get any hints?"

"None," Miles says on the other end of the line. "Just trust me. And meet me at Dolores Park in an hour. But don't bring any chairs!"

"I wasn't planning on bringing chairs."

"Good," he says. "I'll see you then."

I'm a little bit suspicious, mostly because he spent all of yesterday sending me weird texts (*What's your favorite snack? On a scale from one to ten, how do you feel about Hugh Jackman?*) and was grinning at me during Saturday rehearsal this morning. I mean, he usually smiles at me, but this was way different.

"Make sure you text me when you get there," Pops orders. "It's always busy on Saturdays and I don't like all of this secrecy."

"Well," I say, grabbing my bag. "It's just the park."

"Right." He narrows his eyes. "Is that a new slang term?"

"Ugh," I say. "Bye, Pops."

It's not unusual for Dolores Park to be busy, since tons of people hang out here. What's unusual is all the people with picnic baskets and blankets. Did everyone collectively decide to have a gigantic picnic or something? I wouldn't put it past San Francisco.

Miles is waiting near the entrance when I walk up. He has a picnic basket, too. I bite my lip to hide my smile.

"Are we having a collective picnic with everyone in the park?"

"What?" His face scrunches up. "No. I mean, I guess you could think of it that way, but that's really not what it is. Just come on."

I'm not sure how long the surprise is supposed to last. We're only walking for a minute or two before the giant outdoor screen comes into view. People are sprawled out on blankets in front of it, talking and eating.

"Oh, wow," I say, gazing up at the screen. "I didn't know they did this."

"They alternate parks, so it's not always here," Miles says. He hesitates and some people move past us. "Wait, are you actually surprised? I thought the texts would give it away."

"Um, no way." Laughter seeps into my voice. "Come on, how would I get it? *Don't bring a chair*? I had no idea what to think."

"You're not allowed to bring chairs!" he says, gesturing to everyone sitting on the blankets. "I thought that was obviously about the park."

"Oh my God." I snort. "Why would I bring a chair to the park in the first place?"

"I don't know," he says, going quiet. "I just wanted to make sure it'd be good."

My heart sort of melts.

"Well, it will be," I say, voice soft. "As long as they aren't showing something horrible, like *Cats*."

"Is there even a *Cats* movie?"

"God," I say. "I hope not."

We find a spot in the corner and spread out on a blue-and-green blanket. I still can't believe he brought a picnic basket, one that looks like it's from *The Sound of Music*. I want to take a picture of it and send it to Claudia and Lydia, but I can't because of our stupid fight. I'll settle for grinning until my face falls off.

"So we have pre-popped popcorn," Miles says, pulling food out and laying it on the blanket. "Orange soda."

"The best of sodas."

"Absolutely," he says, grinning. "And I tried to make turkey sandwiches, but they might be horrible."

I glance at the aluminum foil–wrapped phallic object and try not to laugh.

"How do you mess up a sandwich?"

"Well." He huffs. "You're just full of questions today, aren't you?"

I want to ask something else—namely, when he started planning this—but then the screen starts to flicker.

"Wait," I say. "What movie is it?"

"*Simone*." Miles puts his hand on his chest. "You want me to *spoil* the surprise?"

"You're not spoiling it," I protest. "We're already here."

"I'm not telling you," he says, shoving some popcorn into his mouth. The screen is still flickering, but the crowd has started to cheer. "If you hate it, I don't want to know until the end."

"I promise I won't hate it," I say. "I couldn't."

He smiles at me then, and I grin back like a little kid.

"Dolores Park!" a voice declares. I glance up to see someone standing in front of the screen. "Welcome to Movie Night! Are you *ready* for the incredible *Les Misérables*?"

The crowd cheers again. I was expecting something more up-lifting and crowd friendly, like *Mamma Mia!* I glance at Miles in surprise.

"I don't know if you're into it," he says, spreading out on the blanket. "But Hugh Jackman is a pretty good Jean Valjean—"

"Wait." I hold up a hand. "You know who Jean Valjean is?"

"I'm not that clueless," he says, a rueful smile on his face. "Google is a thing."

The opening violins begin and everyone starts to quiet down. Everyone except me, anyway.

"But you said Hugh Jackman did a pretty good job." I grin, pointing a finger at his chest. "Did you watch a musical with-out me?"

"I've done it before—"

"Shhh," a woman next to us hisses. "It's starting!"

Miles flashes an apologetic smile, but I ignore her.

"There's a big difference between *Grease* and *Les Mis*, Miles." Little stuff like this reminds me why I was excited to hang out in the first place. "I'm so proud of you. You're moving up in the theater world! Okay, wait. Pop quiz."

He rolls his eyes, but cocks his head to the side, waiting.

I lower my voice to a whisper. "Why did Jean Valjean end up in prison?"

"Because he stole a loaf of bread."

"He stole a loaf of bread!" I clap my hands together. The lady next to us glares, practically seething. "You're right! Okay, another one."

"Simone—"

"What was his number?"

"24601." Miles shakes his head, grabbing his sandwich. "Actually, I'm regretting the whole *Les Mis* thing right about now."

"Oh, come on," I say, lying down next to him. "I didn't even ask about Javert."

This is actually the sweetest thing anyone has ever done for me. Saying "thank you" doesn't feel like enough, but I don't know what else to do. I wish I could just focus on the movie. Miles makes my entire insides feel warm, and it's hard to believe I do the same for him.

"Miles?"

He doesn't glance over.

"Hey," I try again, a little louder. "Miles."

"Hm?" His eyes are glued to the screen. "What's up?"

Oh, come on. Hugh Jackman is great and all, but the vocals in this version are totally weak when compared to any decent stage production. That's what happens when only three members of your cast have musical theater experience. And yet, Miles is completely into it. What a rookie.

Fine. I lean over and kiss his cheek.

His eyebrows rise. "What's that for?"

"Nothing," I say. "Well—for this. It's really nice. I'm—you're—"

More than I expected. Better than I expected. So, so good.

"You're great," I finish. "Thank you."

"It's cool," he says. "I'm glad you like it."

He takes my hand, turning it over. My brown fades into his.

CHAPTER 24

"I just don't get why your *gay* parents would send you to a *Catholic* boarding school. It doesn't make any sense."

"*Brie,*" Julie admonishes, stopping in front of our group. "This is a judgment-free zone, remember?"

"Who said I was judging her?" Brie lifts her shoulder in a lazy shrug. "I just said what we're all thinking."

I snort, tilting my head back. Julie split us up into smaller groups so we could discuss some article she printed out. Obviously, that's not happening. Group is livelier than usual tonight, most likely because Julie bought one of those big-ass bags of candy they sell at Target. There's just something about fun-size candy bars that makes people want to participate.

"It's fine, it's fine," I say, reaching for the big orange bag as it goes around again. Somehow, in between talking about friends and school, the attention ended up on me. "I know it sounds pretty weird. It's just that my dad is Catholic and wanted to 'share the experience' with me or something."

Julie sighs, shaking her head as she walks away.

"You weren't, like, worried about going?" Jack asks, dutifully holding the article in both hands. "That sounds intense."

Brie's folding her article up so that it looks like a bizarre crab with legs coming out of its head. Ralph isn't here today—Thank *God*.

"I mean, they never really saw my parents at Our Lady of Lourdes because it was, like, two hours away," I say, organizing my candy by color. Orange Starbursts go on top of my article, while I rest the actual *good* flavors on my lap. "And I was little when I started, like eleven or twelve, so I thought it would be like *Zoey 101*."

"I haven't seen that show in ages." Jack shakes his head. Somehow, he manages to make it seem like he's interested in everything everyone has to say. "Was your school actually like that?"

"Uh, no." I unwrap a candy and pop it in my mouth. "It was just girls and we had prayer hour and stuff. No cool motorbikes or lounges or anything."

"I don't know how you did it." Brie sets down her crab, swiping one of the orange Starbursts. Poor misguided soul. "My parents try to drag me to mass all the time, but mostly as punishment. Like that time I tried to steal my dad's car."

"*What?*" Jack's eyes snap up, eyebrows pushed to his hairline. Brie just shrugs again, but I notice the way the corners of her mouth turn up. Scaring boys with stories of theft is a nice way to flirt; I won't deny her that.

"It wasn't a punishment, really," I say around a blob of candy. "I don't know. They asked me if I wanted to go and my dad said it was really important to him, so I did it. It's not like they made me."

"*Okay.*" Brie rolls her eyes. "And you're telling me that it was completely fine? That you just spent, like, all of middle school there and no one found out about your parents?"

I bite my lip. No one found out about my parents while I was at Our Lady of Lourdes, but they found out about me being positive, and I'm not sure which is worse. I don't know what to say, so I start unwrapping another piece of candy.

"It wasn't just middle school." I decide to look at Jack instead of Brie. His face is open and kind. Brie isn't evil or anything, not like Ralph, but she doesn't always come across as the most compassionate. "I actually didn't leave until last year. I go to a different school now."

"Oh," Jack says. At the same time, Brie asks, "Why?"

They lock eyes. I can't tell if they're having a romantic moment or silently sparring each other. Maybe it's a little of both.

"Well, I . . ." My voice trails off. Because, really, what am I going to say?

I could tell them a lie and they'd probably go along with it. It's just that I'm *tired* of keeping secrets. I'm tired of being alone, wading through this shitfest by myself.

"Have you guys ever had trouble at school?" I clear my throat. Maybe this is closer to Julie's original topic than I intended to go. "Like, with people finding out that you're positive or anything?"

It's the first time I've ever seen Brie look sorry.

"Oh shit," Jack says. "I'm so sorry that happened to you."

It's the first time I've ever heard Jack curse.

"It's just . . ." My throat is tightening, making my voice croak out. "It *sucks.*"

Brie scoots her chair over so that her shoulder is pressed against mine. Jack gets up, returning with the entire bag of candy. If I wasn't holding back tears before, I am now. People shouldn't be allowed to be this nice.

"No one's ever found out about me," Brie says as I grab a mini Snickers. "But I get how shitty it can be. Like, in health class, my teacher just spent an entire period ranting about HIV ravaging Africa and how life-threatening it is. No mention of the pills you can take to keep you alive or how doctors can stop it from being transmitted, you know?"

I nod, but I don't feel like talking more. Maybe it's because I don't like to rehash the details of what happened at Our Lady of Lourdes *or* what's happening now. It's comforting enough to just be around people who really, truly *get* it.

"I hate that," Jack says, shaking his head. "I try to correct teachers when they're wrong, but we shouldn't have that sort of responsibility placed on us. If they aren't going to present all the facts, they shouldn't have an HIV unit at all."

"Wait, imagine Dr. Khan talking to my teacher," Brie orders. "She would kick his ass with all twelve of her degrees, I swear to *God*."

I'm giggling so hard I might choke on my candy.

"*Hey*," Jack says in between snickers. "Don't say that around Simone. She's Catholic. It's impolite."

"I don't care," I say, shaking my head. "Seriously."

"Screw polite," Brie says. "Simone doesn't care if I'm polite."

"I don't. You don't have to worry, Jack," I say, popping another Starburst in my mouth. "I'm just using you guys for candy."

Jack's cheeks are red from laughing. Brie's elbow is hard as she jabs it in my side. I laugh anyway. Maybe Group isn't so bad.

CHAPTER 25

By the time sixth period rolls around the next day, I've decided I should go out for lunch with Miles every day and stop trying to get on Claudia's good side. We're standing in the middle of a sidewalk near his house, strawberry ice cream dribbling down my arm, and my chest is filled with the warmest, most pleasant feeling.

"Hey." He nudges me, careful not to drip any of his own cone. "Yours is melting."

Licking streams of melted ice cream off my hand will probably leave a sticky mess, but I do it anyway. Miles shakes his head. There are lots of awesome aspects to the whole *dating* thing—namely, the fact that Miles always pays, even if I pretend that I don't want him to. Maybe it makes me less of a feminist, but whatever. Paying for our dates can be Miles's version of the Pink Tax. Now the relationship is automatically more equal.

But, besides money, the best part of dating is being able to look at him during moments like these: his chest shaking in laughter, eyes crinkled.

I know blowing off my friends for lunch is just making things worse, but I'm not sure what else I'm supposed to do. Claudia doesn't answer my texts and Lydia does, but it's always hours after my first message. Maybe this doesn't exactly count as a fight. But it's the first time we've ever been *weird*.

"Come on," Miles says, tugging at my arm. "You can wash your hands at my place."

We're supposed to stop at his house, so it works out. Apparently, Miles offered to pick up some tools from his garage for the crew to use at rehearsal later today. He didn't need a chaperone, but I ended up taking the bus here anyway.

I still don't know if we're just here to get tools. After all, "grabbing tools" *could* be a euphemism. According to the extremely reliable resource of internet porn, all kinds of situations can lead to sex: making salad, tutoring, playing soccer . . . The possibilities are endless. The question isn't *if* Miles watches porn, but whether or not we watch the same things.

It doesn't take long to get to his house, but I spend the entire time looking over my shoulder. I'm not sure what I'm expecting to see—Eric, recording videos of us on his phone, or maybe one of his friends. Maybe he just hears gossip and leaves letters based on that. I don't know what sets him off.

I want to spend time with Miles, to get ice cream and watch musicals and leave school together. But is that more important than keeping my secret safe?

"God, Simone," Miles says, opening the door. "The point of ice cream is to eat it, not drink it."

Miles's house looks large enough to fit a much bigger family, with a garage and everything. Compared to his place, ours looks more like a bungalow. I guess working in business has some perks.

"You're one to talk." I might have to slurp melted ice cream

195

out of my cone, but streaks of vanilla line Miles's hand like a striped shirt. "Why do we suck at ice cream?"

"*We?*" He shakes his head. "I'm just trying to make you feel better."

I follow him into the kitchen, all stainless steel like the ones on TV. Dad would be jealous of how clean it is. There are only three of us, but between Dad's cooking experiments and Pops's passion for shopping, it doesn't take long for our house to get cluttered. Miles points out some paper towels on the counter, gesturing toward me with his head. I chomp down the last of my cone, reaching for the roll with sticky hands.

"When I first met you," he starts, licking at his cone, "I never would've suspected you ate ice cream like a four-year-old."

As if to prove my maturity, I stick out my tongue. He leans in to kiss me, but he's also a mess, and one of his scoops splats right onto my thigh.

He should be apologizing, but the first thing that comes out of his mouth is a bark of laughter. Miles's happy is so loud that it rings in my ears long after I hear it. It's hard not to laugh along with him. I reach again for the paper towels, but he beats me to it, tearing off a bunch and tossing his cone in the trash.

"You wasted it," I say. He bends down to wipe off my leg. I can feel the heat of his hand through the napkin. Whatever I was about to say dies in my throat. All I can muster is a soft "I can do it."

He glances up at me, something devious in his eyes. By now, most of the ice cream is gone, but his hands, warm and rough, are on both of my thighs.

"It's fine," he says, voice low. "I'm cleaning up after myself."

That's *definitely* a euphemism.

His hands are still pressed against my legs, and instead of crouching down, he's on his knees now. I lean against the counter so I can get a better look. There are so many places to look—at his lips, the long legs folded perfectly, the way he looks at my legs like they're something to be desired. When he catches me staring, neither of us looks away.

Then his mouth is on my thigh, tasting my skin, exploring, leaving sloppy kisses in his wake. It almost tickles. He takes his sweet time reaching for the zipper of my shorts, and my hands shake as I help get them off. His eyes are darker, bigger, when he glances back up.

"Is this okay?"

I nod, blushing so hard that my face burns, but then he's leaning in and my mind goes blank. I'm not thinking about the counter digging into my back or the fact that I'm in Miles's kitchen or how I ditched lunch with my friends. I'm not thinking about anything.

I dig my nails into my thighs, legs trembling. His hand tugs at one of mine, guiding it to his head. I grip his hair between my fingers, letting my own head fall back.

There's heat everywhere: radiating from me and him, burning deep inside my belly. My breathing grows labored, blood rushing through my ears. I know I'm making all sorts of noises, breathing and moaning. I don't care. Miles always makes me happy, but this . . . It's like nothing I've ever felt.

• • •

When I finally come back to my senses, we're sitting on his kitchen floor, slumped against a cabinet.

"Are you okay?" he finally asks. It sounds like he's out of breath, too.

I squeeze his hand, leaning down for my underwear.

"I just—I never knew I could feel like that," I say. It's not what I imagined, alone in my bed at night. It's so much better. It feels like I'm floating, brain clear, eyes blown out of their sockets. I want to share it with him. "But now it's your turn."

I push him against the counter. His eyes are wide.

"You don't have to if you don't feel like it," he says. The corners of his mouth turn up, but his words tumble out. "It's not like you have to pay me back. It's not a business transaction. I just wanted to—"

Before I can say anything else, his lips are on mine. It's different from the first time we kissed. Kissing Miles for the first time was like texting someone for the first time: using proper punctuation and spelling, commenting only on "appropriate" topics.

It's different now. Lazier, a little messier, like we know each other.

"Are you sure?" Miles asks, voice soft.

"I am. It's not about paying you back," I say. "It's because I want to make you feel good, too."

"You already make me feel good."

I roll my eyes, even though I'm smiling.

"Shut up, Miles," I say, pulling at his zipper.

CHAPTER 26

With just two weeks left until opening night, Ms. Klein has gone absolutely batshit. I can't make a single move at rehearsal the next day without her breathing down my neck. Maybe I'd understand the concern if we were further behind, but we're doing pretty well. The sets are all painted, and everyone knows their lines. I'd call that success.

"I think we should try that again," Ms. Klein says, snapping her fingers. The poor kids onstage seem to hate her almost as much as Eric hates me. "You need to have more *emotion* in your voices. Even if you're in the ensemble, you need to accentuate your facial features. Remember, people are looking at you!"

Claire is pouting openly, and it makes her look like a fish. I snicker. Ms. Klein whirls around and I school my features. I can't even breathe without her giving me the stink eye. I'm pretty sure *any* teacher would be better at this than her.

"Do you have any notes, Simone?" Mr. Palumbo asks, turning to me. "You've been quiet."

That's because I'm intent on watching and absorbing every single detail. Once we finish running the show for the thousandth time, I'll start taking notes again. Right now, I need to see what the audience would see if we opened tomorrow. It'll give me a different angle.

"I'm not sure," I say, folding my arms. "The only thing really bothering me is the 'I'll Cover You' reprise, but I don't know if I could get a word in."

As soon as the words leave my mouth, I bite my lip, eyes widening. Sure, no one likes Ms. Klein, but she's still a teacher. Palumbo might think that I'm a disrespectful little shit or something. Turns out, I'm overthinking it.

"You're a riot," he says, belly shaking with laughter. "What's bothering you about it?"

I sigh, digging my hands into my pockets. Part of me still feels weird telling members of the cast what to do, and the whole Eric thing has made it worse. I can't sing, and I don't know how to act, so what do I really know? I think that loving the story as much as I do helps, but sometimes I'm not sure. Being in the show is definitely different from watching it offstage—both sides see different things.

I focus on my side. What do I see? The kids playing Angel and Collins are *good* singers; that's why they got picked. But their delivery of the dialogue is too wooden for such an emotional show. Even when they sing, there isn't enough emotion. Singing is, like, the *original* carrier of emotion. I should feel the grief and sadness and longing just *oozing* out.

"I'm just not feeling the emotion," I explain. "I don't know what it is. Maybe they didn't listen to the original cast recording? No one can listen to that without being hit by a ton of bricks. If they couldn't *feel* it, how am I supposed to explain it to them? You know what I mean?"

"Well," Palumbo sighs, shifting his weight. "I would suggest trying to connect it to something relatable. Not everyone has personal experience with AIDS, but everyone has experienced grief at some point."

"That's true." I could try to talk to them about death. Everyone understands death—wanting to avoid it is basically human nature. But I need something *more* than that. "Why is this so hard?"

"It's only hard because you care so much," Palumbo says, a smile in his voice. "It'll still be hard when you're directing on Broadway, but imagine how fun it'll be."

I've only *dreamed* of that happening, but Palumbo talks about it like it's a fact.

"I mean, we don't know if that'll happen," I say, pulling at my hair. "There aren't a lot of people who make it to a Broadway stage."

"But you would." He doesn't even hesitate. "Don't doubt yourself."

"I'm *not*," I say. "I just—I don't know if it's practical. Maybe I'll study theater, if they don't actually make me get up onstage, but I don't know if I should. I could just become a nurse or something."

"A *nurse*?"

I shrug, not letting myself face him. Teachers who are all supportive and nice sort of freak me out. They start to learn too much about you. In the middle of class, they could watch you daydream and know exactly what you're thinking about. I'd like to keep some things private.

"I don't want to go to school for something that's artistic and hard to do and end up in a sea of debt," I say, folding my arms. "My dad told me he didn't finish paying off his student loans until he was thirty."

He presses his lips together. "It's different for everyone. I say you should go to school for something that you feel attached to, or don't go at all. It is better to be passionate and poor than rich and depressed."

"But what if I'm passionate *and* depressed?" I say. "I wouldn't want to be fifty and living in a shoebox, calling my parents for a cup of ramen."

"That's not going to happen," he says, shaking his head. "Whatever you do—writing or directing or even singing—you'll be successful."

"You can't be sure of that."

My friends think I'll be fine, my parents think I'll be fine—all people who are biased. Mr. Palumbo just met me this year, and he's already so confident about this. I soak it up like a plant desperate for water.

"There are always a few students who really have what it takes," he says, lowering his voice. "You're one of them, Simone. You just have to have confidence in yourself."

I guess he's right. If I can handle switching schools, HIV, and these stupid letters, I can handle anything life throws at me. That's sort of what "I'll Cover You" is about, actually: losing the ability to handle what life throws your way. The characters are telling us about the casualties, physical and emotional, of AIDS, in a time when no one wanted to hear about them. I'm not sure how much that has really changed.

"Hold on," I say to Mr. Palumbo. "I think I have an idea."

Ms. Klein is still onstage when I climb up.

"All right, remember to be quick," Ms. Klein says as I walk past. "We want to get through the entire show before it's time to go home."

I ignore her.

"Guys," I say, motioning for everyone to lean in toward me. "I just figured out how we're going to do this song. It's almost perfect right now, but this will make it better. Do you trust me?"

They share glances. The hardest part of being a director has been getting the cast to trust me. But I'm too invigorated from Mr. Palumbo's pep talk to overanalyze right now.

"What's up?" Rocco asks, turning toward me. He has a game face on. I like that about him. It's probably why I thought he would be so great for the role of Angel. "Let's hear it."

Behind him stands the rest of the cast in varying stages of commitment—more members of an audience. I force myself to take a deep breath.

"I really think we need to tap into the hopelessness of the song," I say. It's difficult to keep all the emotion out of my voice as I describe what it must've been like to have AIDS in the eighties, when it was basically a death sentence. It's difficult not to think of my fathers, who could've died, who lost so many people.

"It was basically genocide. No one released it, no one planned for it, but it was an epidemic that targeted a specific group of people," I say. "Once it started impacting straight people and white people, it started to become important—but only a little bit more. To be in a relationship with someone of the same sex, and to be a person of color with AIDS—it was a hopeless situation because no one cared. So to find someone who *gets* it, who loves you, and to lose them because no one cares about what you're going through—there aren't words for that. The songs are all talking about it, but the words only tell part of the story. That's why we need to hear about it in your voices. Do you know what I mean?"

"Okay," Laila says, a breath of air rushing from her mouth. "I think that we can do that. Right, Eric?"

Eric doesn't say anything. He's chewing on his lip, pensive.

"Are we ready to run it again?" Ms. Klein asks behind us. "I don't mean to rush, but we have to keep going."

I clench my teeth, but don't leave the stage. I'm not sure if I explained it well, if it's even possible for me to share something so close to my heart. That's probably why a song works so well—you don't have to explain emotion when it radiates out of your lungs. It's something you just *get*, even if you can't explain it.

"Yeah." Eric nods. "Let's do it."

As the pit orchestra begins to play, I'm hit with a burst of emotion. Their words are filled with all of it—angst, despair, passion. Maybe they touched on some of it before, but it feels like it's so clear in their voices now. Listening to them, you would think they understand. You would think they lived it.

"Whoa," Jesse breathes, standing beside me. "It's beautiful."

I can't help but smile. Even if I can't sing like them, if I'm not as talented, I helped *make* this. This moment is where I belong. Just being *here*. After all, that's what theater is about.

• • •

I'm not expecting Claudia's car to be the only one in the parking lot when I leave the building. I'm not sure what time it is, but the fading sun tells me that all the other clubs ended a while ago. Was Claudia supposed to pick me up? I don't remember. I pull my backpack over my shoulder, glancing down at my phone. There are two messages from a number that I don't recognize, all zeros. The first message is a picture: Miles and me sitting in his car somewhere. The second is a regular text: *Next week*.

My breath hitches in my throat. No air is getting in or out of my lungs.

It's not just notes now. I knew someone had to be following me, but the pictures make it sickeningly real. But how the *fuck* are they taking pictures without anyone noticing? Eric couldn't just leave school in the middle of the day to watch me, could he? Maybe I was right and he got someone to help him—but who?

I make my way to Claudia's car on shaky legs. She and Lydia will probably tell me to report it to the principal, but this number, 000–000–0000, has to be fake. I doubt the principal would be able to trace it. Maybe Lydia or Claudia would know how. If I can figure out who's helping Eric, I can make them stop.

"Hey," I say, sliding into the back seat. My lungs can't seem to take in any air, and talking doesn't help in the slightest. "I'm sorry I'm late. I totally forgot you were gonna wait, and something happened—"

I catch Claudia rolling her eyes in the rearview mirror. My stomach drops.

"What?" I say, turning to Lydia. My skin is hot, and my chest heaves now that I can suddenly breathe again. I know she's been irritated, but *fuck*, I can't handle it right now. "I said I was sorry."

"I know," she says, turning to look at me. "But you could've texted or something. You know how Claude can get about these things."

I do, but it's not like I did this on purpose. Sometimes we just get caught up in our shit. There are times when I wait for Claudia or Lydia, and it's never this big of a deal. They're hanging me out to dry right when I need the two of them the most.

"What's your problem, Claudia?" I snap. "I'm sorry I haven't been around a lot, okay? We're all busy."

"Of course." Her hands grip the steering wheel. "You hear that, Lydia? She's been ditching us because she's *busy*. Like she's the only one with shit to do."

I glance to Lydia for help, but she just stares at her lap. I want to scream, but I settle for pounding the back of Claudia's seat. She barely flinches.

"What's wrong with you?" I ask. "I'm trying to *talk* to you about this."

"Maybe you could talk to Miles about it. I doubt you're late when *he's* waiting for you."

"Are you *serious*?" I want to force her to look at me. "That's bullshit, Claudia. It's not about Miles."

"*That's* bullshit," she says, turning to face me. "We all know it's about him. All you ever *do* anymore is talk about him or hang out with him. You don't call us anymore. You said you were coming to GSA and fucking *disappeared*. We haven't had dinner at your house in two weeks, and you haven't answered

206

any of my texts about scheduling a sleepover. All because you started dating some *stupid* boy."

"He's not stupid." I hate the way my voice trembles, especially now. Miles doesn't do anything to her, and she doesn't deserve to talk shit. "What, are you pissed that I'm dating a boy and not a girl?"

"Simone, come on," Lydia says, finding her voice. "You know that's not it."

"Maybe she doesn't," Claudia says, shrugging dramatically. "Maybe she's so caught up in herself that she thinks she's somehow oppressed because she's straight."

"What if I'm not straight?"

She freezes for a moment. I'm not breathing.

"You can't just pretend to be queer so that we'll feel bad for you," she finally says, mouth turned down in disgust. "Are you fucking *serious*? You wanna be oppressed so bad that you're making stuff up?"

"Wait," Lydia says, holding out a hand. "Claudia, that's not—"

"Fuck *off*, Claudia." My voice is so high that I sound like Christine's soprano in *The Phantom of the Opera*. "You never listen to anyone besides yourself. You know what? I *am* oppressed. I'm black and probably bisexual, but I've only had one girlfriend, so I guess it doesn't matter, *right*?"

Her eyes are the widest I've ever seen them. I watch her mouth twitch open, but nothing comes out.

"Simone," Lydia says, her voice soft. "Who was it?"

I blink back tears. God, I haven't told *anyone* about what really happened with Sarah, and now is the absolute *worst* way for it to come out. I never told Claudia about it because I assumed she'd be weird. That she would accuse me of lying never crossed my mind.

"Simone." Claudia's voice trembles. "I didn't—"

"Shut up." My voice is hoarse. "Just shut up."

"Claudia didn't mean it. She was just—surprised," Lydia says. She takes a long moment to swallow. "You can tell us who it was. I promise."

"Why should I believe you?" I say, turning to her. "You just sat there and let her scream at me."

"It's because—"

"I don't *care*." It's getting harder to talk with the tears stuck in my throat. "It's like I get a boyfriend and I don't know how to handle it and instead of talking to me, you guys just turn on me. Friends aren't supposed to do that. Friends still act like friends. Claudia is shitty all the fucking time and I never tell her to break up with her girlfriend."

Claudia bites her lip. "It's not . . ."

"And yeah, I *did* have a girlfriend," I say. "Sarah was the first person I met at boarding school, my first kiss, my first girlfriend. . . . I thought I could tell her I have HIV, but she said I was selfish for keeping it a secret and texted five different girls all about it. By the next day, everyone knew. It was all over those stupid parent Facebook groups. None of my friends would talk to me."

I take a deep breath, but my chin is trembling. This is not how I wanted them to find out about Sarah. I still don't understand what it means; does kissing her and liking it make me bisexual or pansexual or still straight? Do I have to wait to be attracted to another girl before I can declare myself anything besides straight? Do I only have to like girls? Can I like people who are feminine and not girls and still be queer? They're all questions I used to want answers to, but now I just wish I could forget all of it.

Why can't I have a boyfriend, a girlfriend, a *person*, like everyone else? The first girl who kissed me was disgusted by me. The first boy I dated was a dick. Then there's Miles—Miles, who touches me all the time because he isn't afraid, who kisses me on my mouth and my neck and my legs, who makes all the second-guessing go away—and I don't even get to have him. Not with someone following us around. Not once everyone at school finds out that I have HIV.

This is how I expected my friends to act after they knew. I thought Claudia and Lydia understood, but maybe things have changed. It was okay when I was alone and pining after celebrities, but now that there's a chance that I could actually have *sex*, they have to sabotage it.

A horrible thought enters my mind.

"How do I know," I start, squeezing my eyes shut, "that you two haven't been sending those notes?"

There's a sharp intake of breath. I open my eyes to see Lydia's lip trembling. Claudia's face is pale.

"You guys don't want me to hang out with him," I say, wrapping my arms around my stomach. The words come out faster and faster, stumbling over each other. "It has to be you. You're the only ones who could've done it, and no one else cares that I'm dating him. You're the ones screaming at me like I tried to kill one of you and calling me a liar who begs for attention and—"

"I can't fucking believe this." Claudia shakes her head, stunned. "We're your *best friends*, Simone. Why would we do that?"

"I don't know," I say, holding my hands over my eyes. I don't want to look at them. I don't even want to be in this car. "You aren't telling me the truth anymore. You're keeping things from me. You've been talking about me behind my back."

"We wouldn't do that," Lydia says, shaking her head frantically. "Simone, I *swear*—"

Claudia is crying now, but I can't look at her. I push myself out of the car and stumble to the closest bench. Only then do I stop fighting the aching in my throat. I pull my legs to my chest and cry into my arms.

CHAPTER 27

The week of Thanksgiving passes by in a blur. I move on auto-pilot, sitting through classes and turning in homework and staying after for rehearsal. Miles gives me rides in the morning and drops me home after school. If Dad's home, he invites Miles in, plying him with snacks and asking questions about school or lacrosse. When Pops asks where Claudia and Lydia are, I don't know what to tell him.

I'm so used to pulling out my phone and texting them. Everything feels different now that I can't, like frayed electrical cords have cut me off from the rest of the world. I still have my phone and the internet, but without my friends, those things don't really matter. Thinking about Claudia and Lydia stings almost as badly as my thoughts of Sarah do. Every time I get a text from one of them, it hurts to ignore it.

Thanksgiving isn't even enough to make me feel better. I usually love having so many people around. We only have one guest room (thanks a lot, crazy San Francisco housing prices), and the house gets so full that I'm sure it'll burst.

But this year, I'm not thinking about Abuela's tamales or what stories Tía Camila will bring to share. All I can think about is Claudia and Lydia, and whether they could actually be behind these notes. It makes sense in a way that Eric never did. Abuela doesn't let me stay in my head for long, though. She never does.

"You don't have to worry about giving up the bed," Abuela says, tossing her coat on the coatrack. "I can sleep on the couch this time. You're a growing girl, and you don't need me to take over your room."

"She's young," Abuelo says, pulling in the suitcases. "I'm sure that one night on the floor isn't going to kill her."

"It's great to have you all back," Pops says, sticking his tongue out at me when their heads are turned. "I have the guest room set up. Camila, you can stay in the office—we have an air mattress up there. And Dave can sleep in Simone's room."

"I don't need to sleep. I think I'm still jet-lagged," Tía Camila says, shuffling in. She's wearing a trench coat, probably something she bought in Paris. I swear, she's always on a different business trip. "Mony, I'm going to tell you absolutely everything about England. You'd love the West End. I'll have to take you one day."

"Maybe this year," I say, forcing a smile for her. "I'll have to beg, but the parental units might let me do it. You never know."

Tía Camila is the coolest person in this family—besides me. Every time she comes over, I feel shy around her, like she's a celebrity I'm finally getting the chance to meet. She tucks a strand of hair behind her ear, pulling me to her side.

As if on cue, Dad and Dave stumble in. Looking at the two of them, standing side by side, is like a before-and-after photo. Dave is Dad's spitting image. Same darkly colored big eyes, same studious air, even without the glasses. The only difference is the hint of a beard growing on my half-brother's face. I don't remember what his mother looks like—I guess I met her once, maybe a long time ago—but it must be weird for her to look at a replica of Dad all the time.

God, that whole relationship is a mess.

"Hey," I say, wrapping my arms around him. Abuelo and Abuela always say something if they notice that we aren't spending time together, so I usually get it over with early. "How are you doing?"

"I'm good," Dave murmurs, his touch light. "How's school?"

"Good," I say. "How's college?"

"It's nice," he says, glancing over at Dad. "Lots of intellectuals."

It's not just my dad, but *our* dad, which always trips me up. Most of the time, I don't have to share him, except for a couple of times a year—summer vacations and the holidays.

"You two should stop yapping and come set the table," Abuelo calls, already in the dining room. "I didn't come all the way to California just to miss Thanksgiving with my grandchildren."

"Don't forget my show, Abuelo," I say, pressing a kiss to his cheek as I set out plates. "Even if you miss everything else and the Golden Gate Bridge, you have to stay to see the show. It'll be worth it."

"I love how modest you are," Tía Camila says, sliding into her own seat. "It's your best feature."

"Don't be jeaaaaalouuuuus."

Dave glances around aimlessly. It takes me a second to remember that he doesn't know where anything is. I leave the plates on the table, gesturing at him to stay put. I'll grab the utensils so he doesn't get lost.

In the kitchen, Abuela speaks rapid-fire Spanish to Dad while jabbing a finger at her tamales. Pops settles everything else on the counters: turkey, sweet potatoes, chorizo stuffing, collard greens, macaroni and cheese, rice and beans. Pecan and apple pies rest on cooling racks. I watch as Pops kicks open the fridge and pulls out an aluminum foil–covered container. Flan's my favorite, but Dad only makes it on special occasions. My mouth waters.

"I bet your Papi's flan isn't as good as mine, eh, mi amor?" Abuela pulls me into her chest. I lean into the warmth, feeling five years old again. "But we love him for trying, don't we?"

"Thanks a lot," Dad says, rolling his eyes. "I appreciate the encouragement."

"We'll be out soon," Pops says, tossing off his oven mitts. "Just give us a minute."

Translation: Please leave. Abuela seems to get the message, pulling me toward the dining room with her.

"Did you get the forks and knives?" Dave asks, hovering near a chair. He's the only one standing.

I glance down at my empty hands, give a sheepish shrug, and turn back toward the kitchen. As I pad down the hall, I can hear loud voices. My steps start to slow. Of course, my parents argue like normal people, but they're always quiet when they do it. Today is the exception. They're fighting and they're loud and they're not even *joking* with each other. What's up?

"This isn't exactly new," Pops says. There's the sound of clanking. "You knew they weren't going to be supportive when you married me, Javier. Things aren't going to change just because our daughter is getting older."

"I just *wished*," Dad says, his voice sharper than I've heard in a while. "I thought you would keep trying to contact them. You know how important family is. Simone has my family, but I don't want her to only see people who don't look like her."

"She doesn't, and you know that," Pops says. "She has me, her friends, that *boy*. It isn't like we're raising her in the middle of a cornfield. Besides, I don't want her main exposure to black people to be with my family. They aren't the type she should be learning from."

I can guess what they're talking about. I have an Uncle Omar and a pair of grandparents on Pops's side, but I haven't seen them since I was little. The only thing I really remember is sitting in a corner while other kids played and ran through fresh summer grass without any shoes on. The parents steered their kids away when they took pity on me and invited me to play.

I don't miss any of that, but I do wish that Pops had his family around us like Dad. Dad has a son from a previous marriage, for crying out loud. It's like he has all of these ties, strong as cement, while Pops has burned all his bridges to the ground.

"Guys?" I say, sticking my head in the doorway. "I think it's time to eat."

"Of course." Dad blanches, turning to Pops. "It's time for us to bring out the food, Paul."

Pops turns to the counter in silence.

• • •

My parents are always a little weird when Dave is around, which I get, but that doesn't make it any less awkward. We pass dishes around the table and start dinner in silence. Abuela, never one to accept quiet, launches into a story.

"These kids these days, they stand outside our house and they just make the loudest noise," she says, shaking her head. "I saw these boys with a flip-and-go the other day, riding around on scooters."

"Abuela, *what*?"

I can't speak to her in Spanish, but understanding her English is almost as hard.

"You know what I mean. The camera that's always flipping." She waves a hand in my direction. "None of them had helmets. I was so sure that one of them would end up dead, and I'd have to clean up their brains on our driveway."

"That's not disgusting at all," Dave mutters under his breath.

Abuelo makes a face, like he can hear him, but I'm not sure. He tries to fool us all into thinking he's losing his hearing, but I think that's his sharpest skill. He catches my eye, winking.

The silence successfully broken, conversation flows naturally for a while. Pops laughs at something Abuelo says. Dad stares at him, something tender in his expression. The knot in my stomach untangles a bit.

"If you have a boyfriend, you should buy him flowers," Dave whispers into my ear. There's a turkey leg hanging out of my mouth. I glance up, but no one else is paying attention to him.

"I'm telling you, London is worse than here," Tía Camila is saying. Abuelo shakes his head. "There's so much smog, *way* different than fog, and it's always dark. You should've seen the apartment that the company put me up in. It was actually ridiculous."

"Don't be such a snob, Cami," Dad says, a teasing note to his voice. "We all can't go jet-setting around the world at the drop of a dime."

I glance at Dave out of the corner of my eye. "Who says I have a boyfriend?"

"Dad was talking on the way back from the airport," he says, rolling his eyes like I'm stupid. "I hear things. But anyway, boys like flowers sometimes. If he doesn't, you should do it just to get rid of him."

I snort, and Abuela glances over at me.

"What happened to the braids, mi amor?" she asks, running her nails through my curls. I can feel them getting stuck, even though she pretends they aren't. "I thought they were stylish."

"Abuela—" Dave starts. That's the cool thing about Dave: I don't always have to say things for him to understand.

"Leave Simone alone," Abuelo says, clucking his tongue. "She doesn't want your hands in her hair while we're eating."

Don't get me wrong; I love both of my grandparents. But there are some things they don't understand. Abuela is weird about my hair, while Abuelo is weird about me having HIV. He still hesitates before he kisses me. It's probably something he thinks I won't notice, but it's hard not to. He holds my head in his hands and stares at me, almost like he's not sure he should be doing it.

The doorbell rings. Dad turns to me expectantly.

"What?" I say, glancing around the table. "Everyone is already here."

"Miles is supposed to come over for dessert," Pops says, speaking slowly. "Don't you remember?"

Shit. In all my wallowing, I forgot our plan. It was Dad's idea in the first place, but Miles was all for it. I don't mind seeing him.

It's just that doing it today feels like bad luck. With a sigh, I push myself away from the table.

"Simone has a *boyfriend*?" I hear Abuela say behind me. "But she's just a *baby*."

I grin, swinging the door open.

"Hey." Miles stands on the porch. He's wearing a white button-down shirt and holds a bouquet of lilies. "I'm not too early, am I?"

His eyes are wide as he glances into the house. I think it's the first time I've ever seen him nervous.

"You're fine." I glance back inside. There's no doubt that the rest of my family is staring, waiting for me to move aside so they can get a good look at him. I step outside, pulling the door behind me so it's open just a crack. Miles freezes, even as I lean forward. "You're perfect. Don't worry about it."

No one should be able to see us on the porch, not if we make this quick. I kiss him softly, the flowers crinkling between us. He tastes like gravy. His hand is on my neck, stroking up and down. After that afternoon in his kitchen, I figured I'd calm down, but now I just want more. More of him on his knees and more time in his room and more time touching, long strokes and hazy eyes, figuring out what works and what doesn't.

"I still can't believe I get to do that," I whisper, pulling away. He has a hickey from the last time we hung out. I pull up his collar, my hand lingering near his neck. "I really like kissing you."

"Yeah, I guess kissing you isn't so bad," he says, making me shove him. His mouth twitches, eyes scanning my face. "Simone—"

"Get in here, you two!" Tía Camila calls. "We need you here for dessert!"

I sigh, gesturing for him to follow me. "Okay, you know my parents. My abuela talks all the time, so don't bother trying to get a word in. Tía Camila is really posh, like Victoria Beckham, but less mean. My abuelo is who you have to watch out for, and maybe Dave."

"That's your brother?"

"Right." I pat his shoulder. "You catch on fast."

Inside, everyone has migrated into the living room, where all the photo albums are pulled out. The smell of coffee mixes with pecan, caramel, and apples. Tía Camila holds a plate of flan, smirking in my direction.

"You're the boyfriend," Dave deadpans.

Abuelo narrows his eyes.

"Uh, yeah." Miles clears his throat. "I'm Miles Austin. It's nice to meet you."

"Are those flowers for us?" Dad asks, rising to his feet. He takes the bouquet, clapping Miles on the back. "That's so thoughtful of you."

"I hope you treat Simone well," Abuelo says, stirring his cup of coffee. "I have many stories of what we used to do to Camila's boyfriends when she was young."

"Strung them up by their toes." Tía Camila nods, tapping her fork against her plate. "Right up with the Mexican flag, so everyone in the neighborhood knew we meant business."

Miles swallows. If he were any other boy, I wouldn't mind watching him squirm. But it's Miles, so I swing my arm around his waist and stick out my tongue at Tía Camila.

"If Simone likes him, I'm sure he's a fine young man," Abuela says, tutting. "Come, come sit down. We're looking at pictures of Javier."

"That's my dad," I say to Miles, sitting next to Abuela. He sits on the arm of the couch, peering over my shoulder. "Pops is Paul."

"Mr. Hampton," Pops says, narrowing his eyes. "That's still my name."

Abuela is too caught up in her photo albums to comment. She points at a picture of Dad when he was a baby, drowning in a white baptism gown.

"He was such a cute little thing," she says, shaking her head. "To think that he could've been Valeria."

I raise a brow. "What?"

"We all thought your dad was going to be a girl," Tía Camila says, glancing over at Dad. He doesn't say anything, but takes a sip of his brandy. "I was so excited about having a little sister. Mama had a name picked out and everything."

"I loved the name Valeria, but your abuelo named Camila," Abuela says, glaring at him. "And I got the second baby. I thought it would be another girl, but we got Javier."

"You sound so disappointed," Dave says, the ghost of a smile on his lips.

"Well, we love him anyway," Abuelo says, picking up his own drink. "And not just because we're obligated to."

Pops chuckles, flipping to the next page. It's a picture of my dads, but they look young enough to be around my age. Okay, maybe that's a little dramatic, but they were definitely young. Dad is wearing a blazer, and Pops has a big old Afro. Nicer than mine.

"Look at the Wonder Years," Tía Camila says, a soft smile on her lips. "I can't believe you two were that young."

"Is this when you first met?" I ask. I've seen the pictures before, but they sometimes get blurred in my memory. It's crazy to see how much they've grown, how long they've known each other. They're leaning against a wall, just like bros. Not sure how long *that* period lasted.

"Well, I came up to New York back when Javier was there," Pops says, stroking his chin. "It was my first time out of North Carolina, and I didn't know anyone. These folks were my second family during school, and the rest is history."

"You were already like our son back then," Abuela says. "I knew that you fit in as soon as you got here."

"Well, nothing happened at first," Dad says, seeming almost uncomfortable. "We were friends for a while, and then I met Miriam."

I glance at Dave. When his mom comes up in conversation, it's usually because *he* mentions her, not someone else. It's hard to guess what he's thinking now. His face is made of stone. Pops flips to the next page. It's Dad and Pops on the day of their wedding. I'm so *little*—maybe three or four years old, but I don't remember exactly.

"Wow," Miles says, glancing at me like he's read my mind. "You were so small. Look at your hair."

It's the hairstyle every black girl has at one point: cornrows with multicolored beads attached at the end. I can still hear the *click-clack* that accompanied each of my footsteps.

"She was," Pops says, smiling at me. "I don't know what happened."

I give him a teasing shove.

"*Dios mío*, the wedding," Abuela says. "What a day. I saw it coming from the moment you two met. Even when you weren't together, it was always clear that you were meant to be."

Dave slams his glass down so hard that it cracks. I freeze in place. Silence echoes around the living room. His jaw moves up and down as he balls his hands into fists. I've seen him pissed and irritated, but not *this* angry.

"I don't need to hear about this," he says, his voice low. "And I don't need to hear you talk about me and my mother like we were just mistakes on your road to *happily ever after*."

He gets up, turning out of the room. I blink as he walks out, but all my words are gone.

"I'll be back," Dad grumbles. "Give me a minute."

He rolls up his sleeves, footsteps heavy as he leaves the room. Miles nudges my shoulder, but I don't look at him. I find my eyes drawn to the broken glass on the table. We only use these glasses when guests come over. Dave was drinking out of one of them.

"*No me mientas,*" Dave says from the other room. His voice is loud enough to vibrate the walls; I guess he was barely able to hold it in. "Am I supposed to think you aren't happier with this new life of yours?"

I can't hear what Dad is saying, but there's a murmuring that must be him. I don't know what he could say to make this situation any better. This will be hanging over us all weekend.

"I did *not* cheat on your mother," Dad snaps. "And I will not have you speak to me without any respect—"

"Why should I have respect for someone who disrespects *me*?"

222

"Who wants seconds on dessert," Abuela says, rubbing her hands together. "So that we don't have to listen to this."

Abuelo grinds his teeth, the same way Dave and Dad do. It's weird to see the same mouth on three different people.

"It's all right for him to be upset," Pops says, his voice so quiet that I almost can't hear it. "It can be hard."

All I can think about is how he would never take any of this shit from me. Then again, I'm *his* kid. Dave isn't. To Dave, Pops is the guy who strolled in and messed up his family. I don't want to think about how our house, the house where fights don't feel so loud and I don't get in trouble, exists because Dave had to grow up without Dad.

Part of me wants to punch Dave for making everyone feel bad. But at the same time, it's not fair. I know it isn't. I just wish they wouldn't fight, especially with Miles here.

I pull my phone out of my pocket, eager for the distraction. Jesse's calling me. I frown. We've been texting more lately, but it still feels weird for him to call on Thanksgiving. I excuse myself to the hall. By then, the phone has stopped ringing, but there's a text from him on the home screen: *Is Miles at your house?* Below the text are notifications for four missed calls. All from Jesse.

Did something happen? I call Jesse's number back, leaning against the wall.

"Hey." His voice is short, blunt. "Is Miles there?"

"Uh, why?" I glance back at the dining room. Tía Camila gestures with her fork while Miles listens intently to something she's saying. Abuelo shakes his head. "Is something wrong?"

"Oh, it's just that I went over to his house to hang out," Jesse says. "And he just left a little while ago, and that doesn't make any sense, since it's Thanksgiving. So I figured he must be there."

My spine tingles. Creepy.

"Look," I say, resting an arm on my stomach. "It's none of your business if he *is* here, Jesse."

"But it actually is." Another heavy breath. "*Someone* has to look out for Miles."

"What?" He isn't making any sense. "Jesse, what are you talking about?"

"You walk around pretending all the time," he says, words rushed. "You can't just *lie* to him, Simone. It's not fair. He could get *sick*."

Fuck. Out of all the people I considered, I never focused on Jesse. We were supposed to be friends. New friends, but still, I never would've expected this from him. Bile rises in my throat.

"It's none of your business," I repeat. My ears are ringing. "Jesse, we're in the show together. If you wanted to know more about me, I don't know why you didn't—"

"It's not all about you," he snaps. "If you really cared about him, you wouldn't even—"

"*Oh.*" My hand clenches as it dawns on me. "I'm not the only one who likes him, am I?"

The other end of the line is silent, but I know I'm right. Jesse was there when Miles and I kissed outside the auditorium and in the hallway. He lives next door to Miles, so he always sees when I'm there. *That's* why he left the notes. He cares about Miles. All the times I talked to him during rehearsal, he wasn't interested in what I had to say. He just wanted to know more. He wants to protect Miles from *me*.

"It doesn't matter." He sighs like this is a huge weight on him. "It's Thanksgiving, and you're out of time."

"What does that mean?"

The line goes dead.

Fuck.

CHAPTER 28

After Jesse hangs up, I fumble with my phone, checking my texts for any sign of trouble. My notifications are suspiciously blank. I guess it makes sense, since I'm not talking to Claudia and Lydia and Miles is in the living room, but it's eerie, like a digital ghost town.

Come on, Simone, think. If you were Jesse, how would you spread something like this to as many people as possible? Sarah texted everyone she knew when she found out about my status, but that doesn't seem like Jesse's style.

I scroll through the apps on my phone. Instagram? No, everything is out of order. Not enough people would see it at the same time. He could've used Snapchat, but when I open the app, it's just videos of people singing at parties or sitting with their families for dinner.

Where else could he reach a bunch of people at once?

Oh shit. I hit the Twitter icon, but the blue opening screen takes longer to go away than usual. It *never* takes this long to load. I jab at the screen with my thumb. Come on, come on, come—

The tweet at the top of my timeline is from the Sacred Heart Drama Department account.

New student director, Simone Garcia-Hampton, has HIV.
I've seen her getting treatment from St. Mary's Hospital,
so I know it's true. Consider yourself warned.

There are a hundred mentions underneath the original tweet,
stretching on and on.

@MattlegQuagga: [GIF of Steve Carell grimacing]

@Purebob7777: Oh my god, do I need to get tested?????

@TinyAngel: It could just be a rumor but I don't know

@Heydayfix_97: Oh boo hoo!! Are we supposed to care
that she made bad decisions?

@Bellswas: this is what happens when you sleep around i
mean we dont even know where she came from

My phone shakes in my hands, tears blurring my vision. I kept
pretending this wouldn't happen until it did. I thought I could
stop it by being—what, *proud* of myself for kissing a boy? God,
I'm such an *idiot*.

Somehow, my feet lead me toward the living room. I can't
look at anyone's face. I can't give myself away. I don't need to
cry in front of Abuela, who will hold me until every last tear is
squeezed out.

"Simone?" Miles reaches for me, but I jerk away. I don't know how to explain something like this to him. He wouldn't get it. No one here would. *I* don't even get it.

Dave and Dad are still yelling in the next room. I can hear someone talking to me, though I'm not sure what they're trying to say. It's like everything is inside out. My feet lead me out the door, into the brisk night. I wrap my arms around my torso, trying not to bawl the way I want to. My eyes already burn; tears already roll down my cheeks.

I'm so *stupid*. Stupid, stupid, stupid. This is going to be just like Our Lady of Lourdes, and there's nothing I can even do about it. Where do I go now? I'm gonna have to finish out junior year, probably, because it's too late to start anywhere else. And *next* year— Where else is there?

"Simone," Pops says, voice exasperated. He must've followed me outside. "We're already dealing with Dave here. I can't handle you running around throwing tantrums, too."

Throwing a tantrum? Part of me wants to snap back at him, but the rest of me—the bigger part—is just tired.

I turn to see him rubbing his forehead, a hand on his hip. I don't say anything, just run a sleeve over my eyes. I can't deal with him, either, not if he's mad at me. Not right now. I don't even know what I'm going to do. How could Jesse do something so *horrible*, all because I dared to like Miles?

"Pops," I say, sniffling. "They know."

"They? Who is *they*?" His eyes go hard. "And *what* is it they know?"

"I . . . There's this boy, from Drama Club." My throat feels like it's burning. "He—he tweeted about it. About me. Now everyone knows that I'm positive and they all think I'm disgusting."

I can barely make it through the story between my tears, and I feel even smaller standing outside with a short-sleeve shirt on. HIV could've killed me, but it didn't get the chance. I'm stronger than HIV, but I can't even handle a few tweets from kids I don't know.

Pops's face goes slack, emotionless, for half a moment. Then, "I'm calling that fucking school."

He stomps into the house, not waiting for me to follow behind.

Maybe if I were younger, I could believe that he would fix this. When I was little, I thought Pops could do anything. Out of all the things I hold on to from my childhood—my memories, my hopes, my fears—I wish I held on to that belief. Maybe then it wouldn't feel like the world is ending.

CHAPTER 29

Needless to say, this year's Thanksgiving strays from tradition. Abuelo tells me that it took forever to get Miles to leave after Pops and I disappeared upstairs. Pops spent most of the weekend talking on the phone and speaking with Dad in hushed tones downstairs. It seemed like everyone wanted to talk to me—Tía Camila, Abuelo, Abuela—but they weren't sure what to say. Even though Tía Camila reported the tweet, she couldn't get Twitter to take it down. It wouldn't even help. I'm sure screenshots are being passed around like gum in the middle of a boring class.

I toy with the idea of turning off my phone. It's exploding with texts from kids from Drama and kids I've borrowed homework from, saying stupid things like *is it time for me to get tested???* and some oddly nice things, like *My prayers are with you <3.* Even Mr. Palumbo texts, *Here if you need to talk, champ.*

Whenever I see Miles's name, I turn away. All I can think about is how I cried in the bathroom on Thanksgiving while Abuelo asked him to leave because I wasn't feeling well. How fucking embarrassing.

I don't want to know what he thinks about this. I don't want more of him being endlessly kind, especially when people will treat him differently after we go back to school. I don't want him to be isolated like I'll be.

I sneak a look at one of his texts, almost hoping that he's said something ugly that would make this easier, but the first thing I see has a heart emoji. I toss my phone in my drawer.

I'm not sure which is worse: the texts from him or the ones from Claudia and Lydia, who offer to come over like I didn't scream at them before break. Either way, I refuse to read any more of them. Thinking of my friends is like touching an open wound. It hasn't even scabbed over, and messing around with it will only make things worse.

To my surprise, Dave makes things feel at least a tiny bit normal. Dad lets us take leftovers to his and Pops's room and we sit together on the great big bed, watching both versions of *Hairspray* and *Mamma Mia!* and *Billy Elliot*. I doubt it's all that entertaining for Dave, but he doesn't say anything. Sometimes I randomly feel the urge to cry, like I do on my period. Dave just finds more movies—*West Side Story* and *Singin' in the Rain* and even *The Rocky Horror Picture Show*. He stands in front of the bed, dancing horribly to the Time Warp with his arms and legs flailing in all directions, until I'm laughing so hard that my face overheats.

"If you tell *anyone*," he says, tossing himself back onto the bed, "I'll deny it and no one will believe you."

When I throw my arms around his neck, he stiffens, but still returns the hug. It must suck for him to be here, especially now, but he doesn't fight with Dad after Thursday. For once, we're more than Holiday Siblings.

On Sunday, I'm ambushed.

"What are you guys doing here?" I ask, turning to see Ralph, Brie, and Jack entering my parents' room. They must feel really bad if they're letting random kids in here. "How did you even get my address?"

"Twitter," Brie says simply, bouncing on the bed. "And Julie gave us your address. It was probably against policy or something."

The thought of Julie giving out my address should make me upset, but the feelings are just added to the "to-be-processed" pile at the bottom of my stomach. There's so much shit going on that I'm running out of emotional bandwidth.

"We thought you could use some company." Jack drops a plastic bag on the bed, pulling out a bag of Doritos and Double Stuf Oreos. "And we brought some snacks for you."

It doesn't make sense for a teenage boy to be so thoughtful. Jack must be a mutant or something. Miles, too. I sit up, pulling the snacks toward me. Brie pats the spot next to her, but Jack tosses himself on her lap. They collapse into a fit of giggles.

My mouth twitches into a smile, but my brain jumps to Miles. Laughing with him over Eddie Redmayne's funny faces in *Les Mis* and making fun of each other for our complete inability to eat ice cream and the sunny feeling I get in my chest when I'm around him.

I feel a sharp stab of pain, too much for me to handle.

I turn my attention to the Doritos.

"I brought my laptop," Brie says, giggles lingering. "So we can watch whatever you want, as long as it's not horrible."

"Then it's not whatever she wants," Jack points out. "And you hate everything."

"Not *everything*."

Oh God. I might puke.

Ralph has the decency to stand away from the bed. He just looks so pitiful, standing in the corner all by himself. I sigh, patting the spot next to me. Sure, he's an annoying jerk, but he came here and hasn't gloated about anything. It's more than I would've expected from him.

For once, I'm all musical-ed out, so I tell Brie to put on *A Different World*.

"What is that?" Jack asks, peering over Brie's shoulder.

"I don't know." She swats at him. "And I don't care, as long as it's good."

"Wait, wait, *wait*," I say, holding up a hand. "Are you guys telling me that you haven't seen *A Different World*? The classic television show that is available for streaming in its entirety, easily accessible to watch?"

"You can't expect everyone to know about your retro interests," Ralph says, shrugging.

I fix him with a glare. That shuts him up.

"I can't believe this," I say, tossing my head back. "I need more black friends."

"Come on, Simone. It was on before we were all *born*." Brie rolls her eyes, pulling the show up on her screen. "Sadly, we don't all have your extensive knowledge of eighties culture."

"It's the nineties!" I smack my hands against my lap. "And it's a black classic. I'm sure all of you have seen at least *one* black classic, probably *Fresh Prince* or something."

"*Fresh Prince* is different," Ralph says. "It was syndicated."

A Different World was syndicated, too. Probably.

"I mean." Jack nervously glances at Brie. "If it's a black thing, that would explain why none of us—"

"Oh my *God*." I toss my head back. "It's just a general classic. I'm sure you guys have seen *Friends*, and *that* was on before we were born."

"That's not fair," Jack says. "*Friends* is always on."

"And it started, like, a few years before we were born," Brie says. "So it doesn't really count."

Ralph nods. "It's a false equivalency."

"*Friends* sucks ass," I say, crossing my arms. "How did they live in New York for all of those years and only meet one black person? It was probably the whitest show on TV. Annnnnnd Ross was such a jerk. Rachel should've ended up with Joey. He was actually nice to her."

Silence. Ralph has this *look*—raised eyebrows and a frown—but he doesn't argue with me. Jack's eyes are wide.

"Well," Brie says, pointing a finger at me. "You're not wrong there."

"We're not saying we *won't* watch your show," Jack says, reaching for the Doritos. "We just don't know what it is."

"It's a spin-off of *The Cosby Show*," I say. "So it's like Cosby's daughter goes off to an HBCU, Hillman, but it was Lisa Bonet, and she got pregnant with Zoë Kravitz and they got rid of Lisa and focused on Dwayne and Whitley and—"

"Wait, Cosby?" Brie wrinkles her nose. "He's *horrible* and—"

"I *know*, I know," I sigh. "But he's not in the show and all our faves are problematic."

Ralph raises a brow. "*He's* your fave?"

"No, no." I shake my head. "*This* show is my fave, but there are obviously things wrong with it. There's something wrong with everything. Come on, put on the first episode."

We hover around the computer screen, passing snacks. Ralph complains about the lack of napkins, and Brie fawns over Lisa Bonet (same, obviously). Around the third episode, my phone starts buzzing. Most people have stopped calling by now, so I grab it, frowning at the caller ID. Lydia.

I drop the phone next to my knee as Jack glances over.

"Everything okay?" he whispers. I nod, grabbing at the Oreos. It took *this* long for me to get my mind off things, or at least push them to the back of my brain. I'm not letting Lydia ruin that.

The thing is, Lydia makes it her mission to wear me down. I kid you not; she calls me almost twenty times. I stare down at the stupid screen. It goes dark for a moment before it lights up again. Even seeing her contact picture makes my heart clench. Part of me wants to talk to her, but the other part can only think of her silence when Claudia yelled at me.

Screw it. I accept the call, holding the phone to my ear.

"Simone?" There's noise in the background, like she's in a cafeteria or restaurant. "Simone, are you okay?"

The sound of her voice brings tears to my eyes. I missed her, but I didn't realize I would start crying before I even saw her again. I've missed her voice and her hugs and her worried eyebrows. Everything that's happened is already so close to spilling out of me, but I hold it in, hurrying into the bathroom and locking the door.

"Yeah, I'm okay." My voice is wobbly when I hold the phone back to my ear. "I just—a lot of stuff has happened."

That's the understatement of the year.

"I hope you're all right. We've been so worried. Claudia—" She stops, clearing her throat. "Can you meet us somewhere? So we can talk?"

"Oh." I bite my lip. I'm actually having something close to fun with my Group friends. Who knew that could happen? "I'm actually hanging out with a couple people, so I can't. But that's the whole problem, right?"

"What do you mean?"

"We started fighting because I was always ditching you guys," I say, running a hand through my curls. "And I made it worse by accusing you. I'm sorry for being such a bitch."

"You're not a *bitch*," she says. I can tell that she means it. "Listen, we were all upset with each other. We thought you were ignoring us because of Miles, but you were dealing with so much. You still *are* dealing with a lot, and I don't wanna stomp on your feelings. It just . . . It hurt that you thought we could be the ones leaving those notes."

"I know," I say, leaning against the sink. "It's just, when Sarah told last time, I never would've thought—" I swallow, tears clogging my throat.

"You trusted her," she says, voice soft. "She was your first."

"Yeah. She was." I swallow. "I guess I just . . . I figured that if she could do something like that, maybe you guys would. I don't know. It's . . ."

"It's a lot," she says, quiet. "I get it."

"Yeah." I nod once, forgetting that she can't see me. "But you're right. We *should* talk about it. You can come over, if you want."

"Can I bring Claudia?"

I pause. All I can think about is Claudia accusing me of faking.

"She really wants to apologize," Lydia says, like she's reading my mind. "But I can come by myself, if you want."

"No, it's okay," I say. My entire family is here, along with Brie and Jack, still absorbed in the show. I guess Ralph counts, too. If Claudia has something negative to say, I can turn to the rest of them. "You should both come."

"Oh? Okay. That's good!" I can hear her smiling through the speaker. "I'll see you soon, yeah?"

"Yeah." My voice cracks. "I'll open the door for you."

I'm expecting both of them to be out on the porch when the bell rings fifteen minutes later, but I open the door to see Claudia standing alone. Her eyes lock on me. She swallows. Even I'm nervous, wiping sweaty hands on my jeans. She glances back toward her car, probably at Lydia, before turning back to me.

"Why'd you let me come?" she asks, shoving her hands in her pockets. "I didn't think you would."

My eyes are focused on her hair. It's shorter, almost like Anne Hathaway's in *Les Mis*. She must've cut it recently. I'm sure her parents gave her hell once they saw. There's a pang in my chest at the thought, but I force myself not to look away.

"I honestly don't know," I say, shrugging. "I'm surprised you came."

She stares at me for a long minute. If she's expecting me to say anything else, she's out of luck.

"I really missed you," she finally croaks. "And I can't believe that I was so messed up to you when you were trying to tell me something important. I know how hard it can be when you come out for the first time. I shouldn't have jumped on you like that. It was such bullshit and I don't expect you to forgive me. I . . . I'm sorry."

Worry creases her forehead. At least it means she's been thinking about this, about me, as much as I've been thinking about her. I open the door wider, stepping outside with her.

"I wanted to tell you sooner," I say, biting the inside of my cheek. "But I sort of figured—"

"That I'd act like that." She sighs, grabbing at her hair. "I suck."

My face softens.

"Only a little," I admit, hooking an arm around her shoulder. She blinks, surprised. "And anyway, I don't really know if I count as bi."

"You do," she says with authority. I raise a brow, and she pauses for a second. "I don't . . . I know I was really shitty about it, but you definitely do, if that's how you feel. Lydia had a lot of weird feelings when she first came out, too. Maybe you guys can talk about it."

It's hard to imagine Lydia going through a sexuality crisis. She's told me about other boys she's dated—notably, some kid named Kevin, freshman year, before I transferred over. She also talks about girls she's crushing on all the time.

Maybe it's part of the reason why we became friends so quickly. Lydia and Claudia are here and queer and don't think twice about it. They're sort of like my dads in that way. Maybe, even before we started talking about bisexuality, I already knew we were alike.

"I'm really sorry," Claudia says again. "And I get it if you're still pissed, but I'm glad you let me come over."

I knock my shoulder against hers. It's the first time she's apologized for anything, at least to me. I'll take it.

"Wanna go inside?" I ask, gesturing toward the door with my head. "If we keep talking like this, I might cry."

She laughs. I'm not joking.

Claudia waves at the car, which Lydia promptly jumps out of. It doesn't take long for her to run over or snake her arms around my neck. I hug her into my other side. If my throat weren't full of tears, I'd tell them how much I missed them.

. . .

I'm sure Brie and Claudia would be married to each other by now if they were single. I barely got through introductions before they started giggling in the corner. *Giggling. Brie and Claudia.*

"Wait, she made you watch *A Different World*?" Claudia shakes her head, chest shaking with laughter. "No way. I think I fell asleep when she first showed me. At least she didn't make you watch that depressing French musical."

"*Les Mis* is a classic!"

Brie raises a brow. "You sure do know a lot about *classics*."

"I didn't know you liked musicals," Jack says, turning to me. "That's so cool!"

"Likes them?" Claudia cackles. "That's the understatement of the century."

"Simone is a director," Lydia says, squeezing my shoulder. "Our school is doing *Rent* at the beginning of December. You should come."

I haven't thought about the play in *ages*. Who even knows what's gonna happen with that?

"Well," I start. "I don't know about *amazing*—"

"No, that's so cool," Brie says, head whipping toward me. "I love that movie."

The *movie*? Not the original, groundbreaking Broadway musical that started it all? Okay, girl . . .

"We all should go," Ralph says, his voice soft. "I know I would love to."

I almost groan. He's not allowed to be nice to me. I can't cry in front of *Ralph*.

"Ugh, that shit stain who outed you is working on the play, right?" Claudia wrinkles her nose, grabbing the Doritos bag. "I hope the school administration rips him apart."

My stomach flips. I hadn't even thought about how the administration would respond. It's one of the things I've been shoving to the back of my brain.

"Wait," Lydia says, leaning into me. "I'm gonna need you to tell me every single thing that happened since Thursday."

"Oh yeah," Brie says, glancing over. "Do you wanna talk about it?"

Not particularly. Thinking about Twitter and everyone knowing—even *if* they think it's just a rumor—makes me want to throw up. But with Claudia and Lydia on one side and my Group friends on the other, I feel safe enough to talk about it. I don't feel like I have to handle it all on my own.

I sigh, plopping on the bed.

"Sure," I say, anger rising in my throat. "Let me tell you guys all about that little fucker Jesse."

CHAPTER 30

Between all the people arguing and moving around the house, I barely got any sleep Sunday night. Dad and Dave aren't fighting anymore, but there are other fights: Dad and Pops arguing about me, Abuela and Abuelo chiming in, Tía Camila telling them all to be quiet. Still, even if my extended family weren't in town, I probably wouldn't have slept well anyway.

Picking up my homework before our Monday meeting with the principal was my idea. I figured it would be easiest—staying at home and coming in after school is better than secretaries in the office gossiping as they gather my work for me. Obviously, I was wrong.

It only takes a few minutes for me to walk into school, but that's still enough time for a million eyes to land on me. The hallway goes silent as I pass through, Lydia and Claudia at my sides like bodyguards. Normally, no one looks at me. Normally, people are talking and laughing and interested in their own lives. This is anything *but* normal.

"Maybe you don't need to go to your locker," Claudia says, sharing a look with Lydia. "There might just be more people there. We can get your stuff for you."

"No, it's fine. I just want to get my shit and get out," I say, shaking my head. I don't want to come back after this. I'm sure there are already parents who wish I would leave. I'll just be doing them a favor.

My theory is confirmed when we reach my locker. There, in bright red marker, someone has scrawled the words NO SLUTS AT THIS SCHOOL. I don't know if I should scream or cry, but neither option comes readily. I just blink. Honestly, I expected as much. It's no different from what I saw on Twitter.

"Simone," Lydia starts. "Maybe—"

I just shake my head, turning down the hallway. It was a stupid idea to show up. Maybe part of me believed it wouldn't be as bad as I imagined, that people wouldn't think it was such a big deal. Maybe I thought they'd all write it off as a hoax. Clearly, I was wrong.

The auditorium doors are open as I walk past. In-school rehearsals—I forgot. The show is this weekend, after all. I peer inside. Ms. Klein is on the stage, in the middle of a speech. Mr. Palumbo stands behind her with his hands folded. I should be relieved that the crew isn't here, but it doesn't change the numbness in my chest. I walk in on autopilot, drawn by the cast on-stage.

Ms. Klein glances in my direction and stops abruptly, staring at me like I'm a ghost.

"Simone," she says, voice soft. "Can I speak with you privately?"

At her words, heads turn and whispers start. I want to groan. If she hadn't said anything, I could've walked out of here without being noticed.

Ms. Klein walks offstage, heading toward the hallway. I hurry behind her. There are eyes on me during the entire walk of shame.

"Look," she says once we're outside. "I know this is probably a really hard time for you. I want you to know that we took the tweets down and suspended the account."

"Oh," I say. It doesn't do much for me now, but it's the nicest she's been to me all year. "Thank you."

"You aren't alone," she says, placing a hand on my shoulder. "We're all behind you."

I give her a closed-lip smile.

"But," she says, "you don't have to think of this as a bad thing."

"What?" I can't tell if I'm misunderstanding or if she's trying to be deep. "I don't even know how that would—"

"I'm sure other people would feel bad if they knew what happened," she says, lowering her voice even more, like she's giving me a hint about a birthday present. "Especially some of the judges at the High School Theater Awards."

I blink. For a second, I'm speechless.

"You know what?" I snap. "Screw you."

She has the nerve to look offended. "Simone—"

"Ms. Klein," thunders Mr. Palumbo. We both turn to look at him. He's in front of us, blocking the door so no one else can see. He must've followed us out here. "I'm going to ask you to leave rehearsal for today. This is a safe space, and that rule applies to *all* students."

"You're not my superior," she says, red traveling up her neck and into her cheeks. "I still have so much to tend to here, and I don't appreciate being spoken to like I'm one of the children."

243

"We can take it up with the principal, if you'd like," Mr. Palumbo says. Some of the kids murmur *ooooh*. Even from over here, a swift look from him shuts them up. "I don't mind cancelling the rest of the rehearsal."

"Fine, let's go," Ms. Klein says curtly, marching down the hall. He moves to follow her but then stops in front of me.

"You're very brave, Simone," he says.

I don't get the chance to reply before he's gone, leaving everyone to stare at me. I feel like a goldfish trapped in its bowl. But goldfish never have *this* many people watching them. Some kids jump offstage and walk closer. God, I almost feel like a Kardashian.

"Simone," Eric starts. "You don't have to—"

"Just . . ." My voice stops. I don't know what to say to any of them. I don't know how I'm supposed to talk to them when I'm not even sure what to think myself. "I need to be alone for a little while."

I walk out the door. It's only a few seconds before I hear footsteps, so I speed up. There are the deliberate footsteps of Lydia and the stomps of Claudia. I shouldn't have expected them to give me more than a few minutes alone.

I settle inside one of the bathrooms. It smells like perfume and hairspray and deodorant but it doesn't seem like there's anyone around. Even so, I lock myself in a stall. It's easier to cry in here. That's something every high school has in common.

I don't think I've ever felt so stupid before. My legs bunch against my chin as I crouch on top of the toilet, trying to avoid the water.

Seriously, how did people handle this during the initial AIDS outbreak? When people were actually dying and everyone else ignored it? I scrunch my eyes shut. Ryan White was basically the country's poster child for HIV and AIDS, and he was diagnosed way back in the eighties. He had to fight to go to school because of the stigma. His mom had to tell people that she wasn't afraid to touch her child. There wasn't even an option of hiding it, because there weren't meds that kept it under control the way there are now. Being so upset almost feels stupid, because none of this stuff is impacting me like *that*.

"Simone? Are you in here?"

Miles. I hold a hand over my eyes. It feels like *forever* since I last saw him.

"What are you doing in here?" I say, coughing to keep the quiver out of my voice. "This is the girls' room. Someone is going to give you a hard time if they see you."

"Your friends said you'd be in here," he says, voice quiet. "I told them I'd try to talk to you."

Of course.

"I—I didn't think you'd show up to school today. You weren't in AP US History."

"I was supposed to be picking stuff up."

"In the bathroom?"

With a huff, I sit up and kick the door open. His face looks bleak, probably because the lighting sucks in here. Only a little bit of sunlight streams in through the window and the ceiling lights are flickering.

"I don't think it was a good idea," I say, my voice quiet. "But I don't want to go back outside. I have to wait for that meeting. Are you going?"

"I'm supposed to." His hands are in his pockets. "My parents say the principal thinks I started it."

"No." My eyes snap up. "I'll tell them you didn't."

"That's not the point." He presses his lips together. "Simone, I'm so sorry about this whole thing. It wouldn't have happened if you weren't hanging out with me."

"That's not true," I say, running a hand through my hair. I don't want to hear him apologize for things that aren't his fault. "It probably would've happened no matter what. The guy who told everyone—he hates me."

Maybe not *me*, exactly, but the idea of Miles and me together.

"You know who it is?" He steps closer. "Who?"

I don't want to say his name. He and Jesse have worked together since the beginning of the year, and if I tell him, I'll have to deal with all the emotions he might have—anger or sadness or shock. Hell, I'm too exhausted to deal with my *own* emotions.

Still, now that he's here, I don't want him to go. Like with Claudia and Lydia, I didn't realize how much I missed him.

"I don't want to talk about it." I shrug. "I'll just have to find a way to deal."

"How?"

"Probably changing schools again," I say, staring at the floor. He's wearing cleats. My eyes snap up in shock. "You were playing lacrosse?"

"Just messing around." He shakes his head. "What do you mean, change schools?"

"Something like this happened at my last school," I say, still focused on his shoes. I can't help but wonder what he looks like when he plays, even if this is a weird time to think about it.

"That's why I came here. But junior year is almost over, so maybe I'll just apply to college earlier."

"So that's it? You're just gonna run away?"

If I go to a bigger school, there will be different types of people, maybe even other positive people. Somehow, positive people exist out in the real world. They deal with high school and go on to have jobs and families.

It's like the guy who played *Hamilton*, the one Jesse hates so much—Javier Muñoz. I don't understand how he could go around telling everyone he's positive without spontaneously combusting. People still went to the show, still lined up for miles to meet him—to shake his hand, to *touch* him—because they *knew* he was so talented. I blink back tears.

The people who went see Javier Muñoz on Broadway aren't like Jesse or the other kids here. I hope this is just something that happens in high school, in buildings full of kids who haven't experienced much outside of themselves. I hope it gets better. But I don't *know*.

Maybe I can go to New York and shed all of this like a dirty coat. I could be like Pops—he left North Carolina, where all his friends and family were pissed about him being gay, and moved to a place where no one would bat an eye if he kissed his boyfriend on the sidewalk. I wouldn't tell *everyone* about being positive, but maybe I wouldn't have to hide. That's different. It's not *running away*.

"You don't get it," I say, stepping away from him. "You don't know what it's like at all."

"Come on," he says, shaking his head. "All I'm saying is, you shouldn't give up just because some people are being horrible."

"Of course it's that simple for you." I roll my eyes, walking toward the door.

"Hey, wait," he says, pulling at my arm. "Come on, talk to me."

"It's not giving up," I say, glaring at him. "I'm trying to protect myself. Did you see my locker? They don't want me in their school, and I'm not staying in a place where I'm not wanted. I'm not going to stay here and have people stare at me every time I walk into a room like I'm a pariah. I'm not—"

My voice catches in my throat, and I shut my eyes.

"You weren't there," I say. I've spent so much time trying to stuff the memories back into my gut. Now they're all rising back up. "After—after everyone found out at my old school, I hid in the bathroom the whole day. These parents started a petition to put me in separate classes. No one would talk to me. I didn't have anyone."

I'm not Ryan White, or Javier Muñoz. I'm just me. I just want to be normal.

"I—I don't even know what to say," he says, hands coming up like he's going to touch me. He settles on my shoulders. "I'll kick their asses."

"Everyone?"

"All of them," he says, nodding. "Every single one. I'll—I don't know. I'll take care of them. I don't want you to worry. I'll make it go away."

"You can't," I say, giving him a small smile. "You can't just change the way everyone thinks."

"Maybe I can't, but *you* can." His eyes roam over my face. "I don't think anyone could hate you if they knew you."

Oh, man. I'm definitely going to cry. "Miles—"

248

"Can I hug you?"

I place my head on his chest before he finishes. He smells like sweat and laundry detergent. His arms slip around my back, and I let him pull me closer.

"I'm sorry," he says. "I wish I knew what to do."

"Me too."

I'm not sure how long we stay like that, my heart slowing down and my breathing evening out, until it's ruined.

"*Simone Garcia-Hampton, please report to the principal's office. Please report to the principal's office.*"

I tense. Why would they *announce* that?

"Don't worry. We're gonna go together," he says, squeezing me closer to his chest. "And I'll get the sweatshirt from my locker for good luck. It won't be that bad. I promise."

I try to force myself to believe it.

CHAPTER 31

Miles and I walk into the principal's office together, my arms swimming in his lucky sweatshirt. Instead of leaving us in the lobby, a secretary ushers us into a conference room. This is probably where the teachers meet to talk about the problem kids, or plan the drug assemblies. Now I'm a school-wide problem. Just *me*.

There's an oval-shaped wooden table filling most of the room. My eyes land on my parents first, holding hands and sitting closest to the door. On the other side of the table sit Miles's parents, who are here for some reason, and it makes me want to throw up. They look like him—I guess *he* looks like *them*—but they also look kind of like each other, with the same brown hair and dark eyes. They sit straight, his mom's fingers folded together, his dad's face resting in a frown.

"Hey, sweetie," Dad says, patting the chair next to him. "Come sit down."

Principal Decker sits at the head of the table. She has a light blue shirt on, and glasses perched atop her nose.

"As you know, it is the goal of the faculty here at Sacred Heart to provide a rich learning environment for *all* students," she begins. "I called you here today because an unacceptable incident has occurred, threatening the chance for students like Ms. Garcia-Hampton to reach their full potential." She folds her hands together, placing them on the table. "Now, I'm not sure if you're aware of what's at play here, Mr. and Mrs. Austin, but we're afraid that your son might be implicated in these events."

It's so messed up that she brought in *Miles*, of all people. We should be talking about Jesse's punishment.

"Wait," I say, voice hoarse. His mother's head swivels around as she meets my eyes for the first time, but his father won't even look my way. "How many people know? And why are *they* here?"

This isn't at all how I imagined meeting Miles's parents. Then again, I guess none of it really matters if I'm just going to leave.

"Simone." Dad's voice is soft. "Principal Decker says that screenshots of the tweets were also posted in a Facebook group for parents of students. She believes Miles might have had something to do with it."

"He definitely didn't—" I say firmly.

"I can assure you that my son would never do something like this," Mr. Austin says, cutting me off. He sounds like an announcer on ESPN. "He isn't nearly so—"

"Vile," Mrs. Austin finishes. "I don't know who would make up a lie like this."

Pops bites his lip. He and Dad share a glance.

"It's not a lie," I say. I'm already leaving, so I might as well go out with a bang. "I actually do have HIV. And Miles didn't tell anyone. I know who did."

Mrs. Austin blinks at me multiple times. Miles stares at her, almost as if he's willing her to look at him, but I don't think he knows what to say. She looks like I've told her I'm a baby snatcher. At least she doesn't know what we did in her kitchen. I can picture her tying Miles up in his bedroom to keep him away, like Penny's mom in *Hairspray*.

"Simone," Principal Decker says. "You're saying you know who posted this message?"

"I mean, I have an idea." I rub my hands together. "There's this guy that knew about my HIV, and he kept threatening to tell unless I—unless Miles and I stopped hanging out. He said I wasn't *safe*."

"Wait," Mr. Austin says, holding up a hand. "You're HIV positive, and you've been seeing my *son*? Miles, how irresponsible could you be?"

He could've smacked me and it would have hurt less.

"*Excuse* me?" Dad shoots to his feet, the fury in his voice barely contained. "Listen, pal. Why don't you go and—"

"Dr. Garcia, Mr. Austin," Principal Decker snaps. "I will not tolerate this type of behavior in my office. But to calm your mind, Mr. Austin, I'll have you know that there isn't any way for Simone to transfer the virus to students—"

"What if she bleeds?" Mrs. Austin interrupts. "And kids fall. They hurt themselves. She could give it to anyone."

"I don't run around *smearing* my blood on anyone," I say, trying to keep my voice firm. "And if I have a cut, I'm the one who takes care of it. In case you didn't know, soap inactivates the virus."

"What about sex?" Mr. Austin says, looking over at Dad. "They're teenagers after all."

"We're not here to discuss our daughter's sex life," Pops snaps. "We're here to see if your son is the one who spread this *extremely* personal information on the internet."

252

"Pops, he didn't—"

"Why would I do that?" Miles asks. It's weird to hear how much he sounds like his dad, especially as his voice gets louder. "I don't—I care about her."

I bite my lip. I can't let Miles get yelled at for something he didn't do, especially since I'm the only one here who knows the full story.

"It wasn't him," I say again, hoping my voice is loud enough. "It was this kid from Drama, Jesse Harris. He told me that he saw me at the hospital, and he's been leaving threatening notes in my locker for weeks now."

"Why didn't you tell us?" Dad asks. "Simone, *why*—"

"Because I didn't think he'd *do this*," I say. "He told me I should stay away from Miles so I figured Jesse would tell *him*, but I didn't think he'd be this heartless."

The room is silent. This is why I could never be an actress; I can't stand people looking at me.

"*Jesse?*" Miles finally repeats. "Like, Jesse-who-lives-next-door-to-me Jesse?"

"Yeah," I say. "He's the one."

Principal Decker furiously scribbles on her clipboard.

"Jesse Harris?" Mrs. Austin shakes her head. "He couldn't have done this. He's a good boy."

"Simone wouldn't *lie*," Pops says. "If she says he threatened her, he did it."

"But she didn't tell anyone about it until now," Mr. Austin points out. "Why not? Who's to say she's not lying about other things? Now, it's Miles's fault that he didn't tell us about this situation—"

"Situation?" I repeat. My eyes dart toward Miles, but he won't look at me.

"Come on, Miles," his mother says, lowering her voice. She leans over toward him, like they're the only two people here. "You know how hard we've worked to get to where we are. You know better than this."

I'm not expecting Miles to jump up on the table and make a speech in my defense. I'm not expecting him to yell at his parents. But his silence takes me by surprise—the way he just sits there between his mom and dad, letting them say these horrible things. I swallow, but it feels like marbles are stuck in my throat.

"Better than *what*?" Dad barks. I jump. That's probably the fourth time I've heard him yell in my life. "The medication and treatment for HIV have come so far, but the public opinion hasn't moved at all. Do you know why? Because of blind ignorance. Because of people like *you*."

"Dad, please just *stop*. I didn't tell anyone, because I didn't want *this* to happen," I say. "I didn't want people to know, and I didn't want people to fight."

"So you decided to lie?" Mrs. Austin turns her iron gaze on me. "You decided to put my son at risk?"

"This isn't even *about* him," I say. My voice is quieter than hers, but it cuts through the room. The principal lets me speak, even though this probably isn't what she had in mind. "I care about Miles a lot, and I wouldn't want to hurt him. That's why I told him about my HIV. But this is about me. Me and Jesse."

The silence in the room is suffocating. I glance over at Miles, just for a second. He gives me a small smile. I look away. His parents turn their gazes onto him, and it's somehow more intense than when they were shouting.

"I can assure you that our staff is committed to Simone's health and safety," Principal Decker says. "We are going to find Jesse Harris and get to the bottom of this. Mr. and Mrs. Austin, thank you for coming in."

His parents are already getting up, but Miles lingers behind. Part of me wishes he would stay. The other part wants to scream at him. I stood up for him. I made sure everyone in this room knew he didn't write the notes. But he didn't stand up for me, not in the end. I stare at the edge of the table, watching as his jeans shuffle out the door.

"So," Principal Decker says, pad and pen before her. "Simone, why don't you tell me the whole story? From the beginning?"

I take a deep breath.

CHAPTER 32

When I get home, all I can think about is how my room hasn't changed since I started talking to Miles. It's been maybe two months and I still haven't cleaned it. If we weren't dealing with so much shit, Pops would've come in here and lectured me about it a long time ago.

Honestly, I'm surprised I'm not grounded. Keeping something this big from my parents usually leads to some sort of punishment. But I started crying when we got in the car, and I'm sure that helped. That and the fact that the whole family is still in town.

Dave and Dad seem to be talking again, and Abuela is frying *plátanos* with Tía Camila. I can hear them laughing tipsily all the way up here. I'll miss them when they leave after the show. Still, I can't bring myself to join them downstairs. The mood will shift, everyone will get quiet, unsure of how to act around me.

Staying up in my room feels like the best option.

I scroll through the group chat with the girls. They offered to come over, but it wouldn't be fair for them to miss their after-school clubs because of me.

I send a text: *Are you guys still coming to the show on Friday?*

Claudia texts me back right away: *The question is, are YOU?*

I tap my fingers on the screen. If I lie, she'll be able to tell. It's

256

the reason I've been avoiding their Google Hangouts. I turned off notifications on all my apps, mostly because Miles keeps texting me stupid apologies. I don't want to think about him. And yet here I am, doing exactly that.

I don't know how this works. I'm not sure if we're broken up, if I can just keep ignoring him, or if we actually have to *talk* about this. Maybe I'll just switch schools and won't have to deal with it at all.

I sigh into my pillow. Breaking up sounds so *final*. There will be other people, of course, but there will never be another Miles. Dave has told me about the girls he's dated, but he talks about them the way adults talk about high school girlfriends: with the knowledge that they were just a way to bide time.

I don't want Miles to be someone I forget about. I don't want to lose his smile or the way he live-texts musicals or his stupid lacrosse obsession. I'd miss the way he looks so serious when we watch movies together and the tenor of his voice when he speaks. But every time I think of him, there's this pang in my chest. He was so cool when I told him about having HIV. He acted like it wasn't a big deal at all. But then his parents got involved, and some kind of switch flipped. It was like he couldn't even talk. Maybe he just didn't want to. Maybe he didn't feel like I was worth it in the end.

"Everything all right in here?"

I freeze, glancing at the door. Dad is standing with Pops, which is weird. He must've gotten someone to cover for him at work, and that takes a lot of string-pulling.

"Yeah," I say, gesturing to my phone. "I was just watching something funny."

"So," Pops says, walking in. "Jesse Harris."

"Yeah." I pick at my fingernails. "Him."

"He wrote you an apology." Pops holds up an envelope. "Principal Decker suggested it."

"Wait, so she spoke to him?" I ask. "How did he even find out? Was he lying about the hospital?"

"Well," Dad says. "I think he wrote about that."

"Oh." I stare down at my bedspread, blinking. "That's—wow."

I don't know what I was expecting, but it wasn't this.

"It doesn't make any sense, trying to piece it together," Pops says, sitting down on my bed. "That kid must be really troubled."

Jesse *likes* Miles. Maybe, if he weren't so horrible, I could feel bad for him. I guess I could tell Miles, but it would just make me feel worse. It would be super weird, for one thing. And it's—I don't know. It seems private. I respect that sort of thing.

"Yeah." I run a finger along my bedspread. "I guess so."

"It's true," Dad says, settling beside him. "Emotionally healthy people don't do things like this."

They're taking their science-based, levelheaded approach to this, like they usually do. I can't remember what they said to me about Sarah—I think Dad tried to say that she was jealous of me, which just made things worse. All I could think about was that I could've stopped it if I just kept my mouth shut.

I'm not sure what I could've done to make this situation better. Going to the principal at the first sign of trouble would've been best, for sure. I'd also skip over the part where I accused my best friends of being manipulative traitors.

"You don't have to worry about him, even though I know it doesn't help," Pops says, sliding the letter toward me. "He's suspended for the rest of the school year, and even then, the principal says they're thinking of not inviting him back."

"That's good." I stare down at the letter. By January of next year, I'll know where I'm going to college. "Would—would it be weird if I wanted to study theater in college?"

I can't believe I just asked that. Right *now*, of all times.

"Of course not," Pops says, surprise clear in his voice. I glance up to see the same emotion in his eyes. "Why would it be?"

"I just . . ." I don't know how to explain myself. Why *would* it be weird? "Because I'd be trying to follow this path that doesn't have a clear start and the two of you have such *good* jobs and San Francisco is so expensive and so is New York—"

"*Cariño*," Dad says. He doesn't say anything else, so I look up at him. It looks like his eyes are watering. Damn, I *hate* when they cry around me. "Do you know that I wasn't always going to be a doctor?"

"No." I bite my lip. "I thought you knew you wanted to be a doctor after Tía Camila almost got pregnant? That's what she told me."

"What?" His brows furrow. "No. I—well, I was going to be a contractor. Your abuelo wanted me to work with him. I knew that it was expected of me ever since I was young. But as I started working, I noticed something. Business wasn't always great. We borrowed a lot of money to stay afloat."

"Well, yeah, that makes sense," I say. "Nothing's *always* great."

"That's the point," he says, taking my hand. "That was the moment I realized that I could fail at something I didn't even like. It would be so much better to fail at something I love than something that already makes me miserable."

It makes so much sense that it makes my throat ache. I glance down at my lap. Could it really be that simple? It seems like most adults have jobs that make them miserable. Spending my life wishing for something else almost seems like a rite of passage. But I guess it doesn't have to be. Dr. Khan doesn't seem miserable. Neither does Mr. Palumbo, or Auntie Jackie.

"Simone," Pops says. "You're the strongest person I know. And that's saying something, since I was in the *army*."

I snort. "And . . . ," Dad says. He hesitates, glancing at Pops. "Your birth mother would be proud of you, too. I wish we could tell you more about her, but we just don't know."

"We do know that she loved you," Pops says. "Anyone could tell. We tried to stay in contact for as long as we could."

"I remember you talking about her," I say. They're dim memories, but still there. "She really liked the name Simone, right? When you told her, she said it reminded her of—"

"—of Nina Simone," they finish together. It's a little spooky. They share another glance before Dad clears his throat.

"We're *so* proud of you," Dad says, squeezing my hand. "You know that, don't you? We don't say it all the time, but you have to know."

I stare at the two of them, the people I don't look like, but who love me and raised me and taught me how to feel.

"I know," I say, giving them a small smile. "I love you guys."

I wait until they leave to read it.

Dear Simone,

    I don't know what I can say to make this better, but they told me that writing a letter was one of the things I had to do. So look, I'm sorry. I didn't mean to hurt you. Actually, I kind of wanted you to hurt a little bit. My dad died last year, but I used to go to all his doctor's appointments with him. I used to see you around the hospital all the time. When Palumbo introduced you the first day of rehearsal, I knew I recognized you from somewhere. I used to walk around when I was waiting for my dad, and I would see you a lot. I don't know why it made me so pissed that you were laughing with other kids, but it just did.

I don't know. When my dad told me he had HIV, I didn't think he was going to die, but he never took any of his pills. It happened so fast. Ever since he died, things have been a mess. My mom has a second job and the house feels empty without my dad. Nothing is the same, no matter how hard I pretend.

I guess it just felt like you were pretending. I would see you in the hallway with your friends or whatever and it didn't feel fair that you were just acting so normal. It's like, people with HIV are sick. You're supposed to act sick. And everyone is miserable when they're positive—at least my dad was—so I figured you would be.

It didn't seem fair. I don't know how else to describe it.

I've known Miles for a long time. He's always lived next door, but I really got the chance to know him better this year. It doesn't help that, you know, I like guys and he obviously doesn't feel the same way. They're telling me I should write that it isn't your fault, and it isn't. I guess none of this stuff is your fault. I don't know why I'm telling you so much, either, but I guess you deserve answers.

I don't really know what I can say to make any of this better, like I said before. I'm sorry that things got so messed up for you. I can't say that I didn't know this stuff would happen, because I didn't really think about what would happen. I just— I couldn't believe that you were positive and everything was working out so well for you—so different from my dad. It didn't feel fair.

So anyway. I'm getting kicked out of school, and you'll probably leave. It's like the balancing at the end of Hamlet that we talked about in English.

                                        I'm sorry again,
                                        Jesse

CHAPTER 33

Friday comes before I'm ready. I've spent three months imagining how I would react on opening night. I know this isn't Broadway, but it's the first time I've been trusted to direct an *entire* show. I owe it to everyone to show up. That's what I told myself on the ride over, anyway.

I take a deep breath, pulling my bag over my shoulder. All students involved with the play are supposed to enter through the side door to the auditorium. But as I walk over, my pace slows. There's a gigantic crowd clustered near the main door. I'm far enough that I can't see every face, but there are too many people there to just be parents.

"I can't believe they're continuing with the play," a woman says. She's practically yelling, so loud the strained pitch of her voice can be heard above the crowd's murmuring. "It was an inappropriate choice in the first place, but now, with that student director? Are they trying to make some sort of *statement*?"

My stomach flips. Forget it. I can't do this. Nothing like this should be happening. Not today, not at this school.

I dart in through the side door, keeping my head down as I walk to the end of the hallway. My best option for a hiding spot is the prop closet. Everything we need is already backstage, so no one will bother me there. I make a beeline for it, cracking the door open and slipping inside.

As legs shuffle past, I pull myself deeper into the closet. The door doesn't lock, but there's enough room for me to curl up out of sight.

"Some of them are complaining about Simone," a nearby voice says. It might be the new crew chief, a girl named Katie. "I'm not sure if anyone should sit outside and take tickets. They're being so rude."

"They're not being violent, are they?" That's Mr. Palumbo. His deep, gentle voice always reminds me of Mr. Feeny from *Boy Meets World*, but I can hear stress underneath it. I can't imagine how he's dealing right now, especially since he and Ms. Klein aren't on speaking terms.

"No, I don't think so," Katie says. "That would be a little extreme."

"I've never seen something like this happen," Mr. Palumbo admits. Then he catches himself. "Listen, go get Ms. Klein and tell her to ask some of the teacher volunteers to stand outside to hand out the pamphlets. I'll try to handle some of their concerns."

"All right," Katie says. "Are we still starting on time?"

"We should be," he says. "Have you seen Simone?"

I grip the door handle. I can't bear to talk to Mr. Palumbo right now. Last time was painful enough, and it was barely a conversation.

I sigh, glancing around my hiding place. There are different hats all over the closet. A sparkly pink cowboy hat and a wedding veil are the closest two things I can see. Piles of half-opened boxes take up the rest of the space.

"I'm going to look for her," I hear Mr. Palumbo say. "Worst-case scenario, we can start the show without her. But I just don't think that would be fair. Are you sure you saw her come in?"

"Definitely," Katie says. "She walked right past me and didn't say anything."

Shit. I guess I wasn't as sneaky as I thought.

"All right," Mr. Palumbo says. "I'll look for her."

I know I'm letting him down. Palumbo picked me because he believed in me. Kids have spent hours memorizing lines and learning songs, painting sets, and learning where props get placed during the few seconds of darkness onstage. This show is the result of a bunch of hard work from all sorts of different people—including Palumbo. I can't just leave him hanging.

And I can't let myself down, the girl who wanted to direct *The Lion King* or *Phantom of the Opera* one day, whose ultimate dream was to direct a production of *Hamilton*. But I'll never do any of that if I hide. I can't even hide the thought I've been trying to control for the longest time—that my biological mother would be disappointed in me. She never got to know me, but I think she would be disappointed if I sat this one out.

I would be disappointed in me.

Someone knocks on the door of the prop closet. I freeze. No one would knock if they didn't think someone was in here. It's a fucking *closet*.

"Simone?" Miles says, voice a question. "Are you there?"

I bite my lip. There's silence on the other side of the door. He might leave if I just stay quiet long enough.

"I can see your shoes," he says after a few moments. "So I know you're there."

265

"Maybe I don't *want* to talk."

He doesn't answer. Instead, he nudges the door open. He's wearing all black underneath a lacrosse jersey. It's weird to see him looking so awkward. I've seen him nervous before, but never like this.

"Are you crying?" His voice drops several octaves.

"No," I say, scrubbing at my face just to prove it. Maybe my eyes were watering before, but I swear there weren't any tears. "I'm just trying to avoid everyone. That's all."

He gives a slow nod, shoving his hands into his pockets.

Right now, liking him isn't as simple as it was when we were watching Netflix together or hanging out on park benches. It wasn't simple when we were hanging out in his kitchen, either, but it felt that way. Now everyone else has become part of this *thing* that was just supposed to be between us.

"So," he says, walking into the closet. I don't move to make room for him, but he scrunches himself between two of the shelves anyway. "I totally get if you don't want to see me again. But I wanted to see you."

"Even though I'm a pariah?" I snort. "Everyone hates me, and most of them don't even know me—including your parents. You didn't even stand up for me."

"That's not fair." He bites his lip. "I tried to."

"Not fair?" I shake my head. "You know what's not fair? What I have to deal with right now. You've never had to deal with this. It's like . . . there's this abyss, and I'm on one side with my family and the few other people who actually get it, and then everyone else is on the other side. I thought you were on my side. I *need* people on my side. It's hard right now, but it's so much harder when it's just me, and I felt totally alone when you sat there and didn't say anything."

"Simone. God, I . . ." He opens his mouth, floundering, before it closes. "I never wanted to make you feel like that. It wasn't . . . It probably doesn't help, but I didn't . . . I just froze. I'm not used to fighting with my parents."

I stare at my knees. I don't know what to say.

"But I did," he says. "As soon as we were in the parking lot. I told them everything they said was bullshit and you acted a million times better than they did, even though you're still just a kid."

My eyes snap up. "You said that?"

"Yeah," he says. "And some other things. They weren't happy— I'm totally grounded now—but it was the truth. I should've said it during the actual meeting. I'm so sorry."

I can't picture him cursing at his parents. Because of *me*.

"Thanks," I say softly. "That was pretty decent of you."

He stares at me for a second, like he's waiting for something else, but I just stare back at him. I'm impressed at what he did, but it's not like we're going to make out now.

"Are you just gonna stay here?" he asks, changing the subject. "You're not going to go out and see the awesome play you've spent all of this time directing? Why'd you even come?"

He's right. I came because I wanted to see it. I know it's going to be amazing. I wanted to be proud of everyone in front of my family, in front of my friends, but also in front of people I don't know. I wanted to watch their faces when they saw these kids singing about things that a lot of us can't even understand, even though we all connect to love and fear and death. But that's a really long answer.

"I don't know . . . ," I say, staring at the door. "I thought I wanted to see the show, but . . . They're all angry because of me, not because of what anyone else did. They're angry because of something I can't even control."

"But it's not your fault," he presses. "You can't—I know it has to be hard, but you worked so hard on this. You can't let them take it away from you."

"So what am I supposed to do?" I ask, looking over at him. "Am I supposed to ignore them? What if they see me? What if they disrupt the show? That means I've ruined the show for everyone."

"You don't have to be alone, though," he says, voice earnest. "That's what I'm trying to tell you. I'm here, and your teachers and your friends and your family. You're not going to be alone. If they want to scream at you, they have to come through me."

"You don't mean that."

"No, I do," he says, sliding closer to me. "I definitely mean it. I'm not letting you down again. Especially because I'm pretty sure I'm in love with you."

My eyes snap up. He smiles, soft.

He can't just *do* that. He can't just spring that on me *now*.

My mouth opens. Nothing comes out. Part of me wants to tell him that he doesn't love anyone, that he's seventeen and doesn't even know what love is. But I know that's not fair, because I'm *also* seventeen and I love lots of people and lots of things. The other part of me is a bundle of nerves. "I'm in love with you" is one of the scariest sentences in the English language. It's like holding out your heart to someone and asking them not to trample on it.

But Miles did it first. He's holding his heart out to me.

"Oh Miles," I croak.

He smiles. He's so close; I'd barely have to move to kiss him. But he seems to read my mind and pulls backs.

"The show starts pretty soon," he says. "Are you going?"

For a second, I wish I had the lucky sweatshirt. But I have Miles here instead, pressed against me, willing to come outside with me. And to think I was afraid that this would make him want to run.

I lean my head back, staring at the hallway through the crack under the door. It's wide enough that I can see some of the people standing outside, still hear them speaking over each other. It's almost like they're in a different world. But this is *my* world, and I'm going to decide what happens in it.

"Okay." I grab his hand, squeezing it. "Let's do it."

CHAPTER 34

It takes a moment for everyone to realize I'm outside.

"But don't you think this will be an *authentic* portrayal of life with AIDS?" The man looks like a professor who just got out of class, with round glasses and a brown corduroy jacket over a blue shirt. "Surely, a student director with HIV could enlighten us *and* all the students by sharing her experiences."

"Not a chance," a white, middle-aged woman cuts in, speaking over him. "I've been saying the same thing since Mikey came home from school talking about this show. It's supposed to be a school musical, but you'd never be able to tell with all the filth in it. I objected *before* I knew about that girl."

So this is Mike Davidson's mom. She's like a comments section in human form. I didn't realize people actually talked that way.

I take a step closer. The noise from the crowd fades as recognition sets in.

Mrs. Davidson's mouth drops open. I wonder if she's ever read about HIV, or if she's just angry because that's her natural state. I can't see all the people out here, but I have a feeling that they'll be able to fill the auditorium nicely—that is, if they still want to come inside.

"You know," Mr. Palumbo starts, putting a hand on my shoulder. "You don't have to do this. We can go back inside. This isn't your responsibility."

My dads are probably out here with Tía Camila, though I can't see them. I'm sure Abuelo and Abuela are here, ready to tackle someone, like Claudia and Lydia said they would. Maybe even Dave decided to come. I force myself to take a breath, squeezing Miles's hand. I'm not alone.

"Hi, everyone," I say, raising my voice. It's just like making a speech in class. "I wanted to come outside and talk to you, because I know you're upset."

The noise doesn't pick back up like I expected. Some of the people in the front won't look at me, instead choosing to focus on the ground or behind my head. Of course, they won't talk about me once I'm actually *here*. Even the professor guy won't meet my eye.

"And I'm not going to pretend that I don't know what you're upset about," I say. Miles squeezes my hand. "So I'm going to tell you a few things I think you need to hear. Number one, I'm adopted. My parents weren't afraid to adopt me, because they knew so many gay men who died from AIDS in their community. You might remember *that* period of history."

More silence. Light from the cars coming into the parking lot is getting in my eyes, but I focus on Mrs. Davidson, in front of me. She keeps avoiding my gaze. I keep my eyes on her anyway.

"For those of you who don't know, HIV is a virus that infects my blood," I say, lifting up my chin. "You can't see it on my skin or in my eyes or hair. I look just as normal as anyone else."

More people are staring at me, some of them with serious expressions. They don't look like people ready to pick a fight, at least not now. I take another breath.

"My medication is what keeps me alive," I say. "It keeps me healthy enough to direct this play, and it kept me healthy for most of my life. It lowers the amount of virus in my blood until my doctor isn't able to detect it."

Miles squeezes my hand again, but I don't allow myself to look at him. I'll get too distracted.

"Even though my viral count is really low, I still have HIV. I just can't transmit the virus to anyone else."

It's absolutely silent now. No leaves moving, no birds chirping. Mr. Palumbo hasn't stepped in to say anything, so I guess he's listening, too.

"Now, none of this is actually your business," I say, trying—and failing—to keep the bitterness out of my voice. "And you probably could've found any of this out if you did some research. My HIV isn't a threat to you, but your ignorance is a threat to me. I've been bullied, harassed, and told that I'm unwanted at this school. Do you know why HIV-positive people don't disclose? Because it's dangerous. People have been injured and even murdered for disclosing. It should be my choice, but you've taken it away from me. But I'm not losing the show, too. I *deserve* to be here."

I pause, glancing at Palumbo. He smiles.

"The other kids in the cast and crew, plus the advisors and staff, have put so much work into this production," I say, my voice even firmer. "I'm incredibly proud of all that we've achieved."

I pause. I don't know what else to say without snapping at

them. They're staring at me now like I'm giving a TED Talk. Bringing up how angry I am probably isn't going to help; maybe another time.

"If you really care about your kids being exposed to good influences, you'll start with yourself and your own behavior," I continue. "Don't let ignorance ruin your chance to enjoy this show we worked so hard on. When it comes down to it, everyone who worked on this musical is part of a team—one you should be rooting for."

The silence is unnerving. I usually don't like silence, and it's even worse now. I'm not sure if I should tell them to come inside, or just lead by example. I don't really think that there's anything else I can say. After all, I'm not going to *apologize*.

"That was good," Miles says, leaning close to my ear. His voice is soft, like we're sharing a secret. "Like, *really* good."

I could wait for one of them to start apologizing, but something tells me that it's not going to happen. Instead, I kiss him. It's soft and quick, but it lasts long enough for a collective low gasp.

He's the one who got me to come out here, and now I don't feel so scared. I don't care if other people know. I *want* them to know that Miles and I kiss. Not just to prove a point, but because he's *Miles*. I want to kiss him everywhere, in front of everyone.

No one has anything to say. I'm guessing they're quiet because they're embarrassed, because they know they treated me like shit. I *want* them to be upset with themselves. All of them were jerks together, but it's like none of them want to admit to it, choosing to share uncomfortable glances with each other instead.

Mr. Palumbo clears his throat. I pull away, winking at Miles. His grin makes me want to kiss him again. How am I supposed to look at him and *not* want sex? There are so many feelings exploding inside my chest. It's so much more than what I expected.

"The doors will be opening now," Mr. Palumbo announces. "You can go to the crew members wearing all black to take your seats. If you decide not to come, however, we can't offer a refund for your ticket."

Those tickets are fifteen dollars apiece. I want to hug him so hard that I crush his bones.

A girl steps forward, pushing through the back of the group and dragging someone behind her. I don't know why people aren't moving aside for her, since they seem like they don't want to get inside, anyway. I recognize the hazel eyes as soon as I see them. *Brie.*

"Oh my *God*." I'm five seconds away from squealing. "You guys *came?*"

Jack is behind her—they're actually holding hands like complete nerds, but whatever—and he has *flowers*. I have to force myself to blink back tears.

"Of course we did." I've never been so happy to see Jack's dimples. "Hope it isn't too late to buy tickets. We sort of brought friends."

He gestures behind him. Ralph's actually here, wearing a button-down shirt like this is the opera, and Julie is talking to some kids I don't recognize. Alicia stands next to them, bouncing a little kid in her arms. She catches my eye and winks.

"Well," I say. My voice is all choked up. "Thank you for—for all of *this*. You really didn't have to. *Really*."

"Thank *you*." Brie grabs my arm. "You don't owe anyone *anything*, but you still came out here. You're so badass."

Shit, I'm crying now. She and Jack head toward the door, the rest of the group trailing behind them. Julie and Alicia pull me into hugs, promising to catch me after the show, and Mr. Palumbo opens the door for them. They're loud, laughing and talking like they're *excited* to be here. I can see the crew kids rushing toward them with pamphlets, racing to be the first to give one out.

"Well said," a gruff voice comes from behind me.

I turn to see Mr. Austin, standing *way* too close. I take a step back, glancing up at him. He's tall, even taller than Miles. It's weird to see him without dress clothes on; he's just wearing a school jersey. He and Miles look like they're matching. It's some *Twilight Zone* shit.

"Thanks," I say, scrunching my mouth to the side. "I didn't know you were going to be here."

He glances at Miles, not even bothering to hide it.

"Oh," I say, blinking a few times. "That makes sense."

He walks into the building without saying anything else. I don't know what I expected, but it wasn't that. It makes me wonder how many more people Miles asked to come. At least his dad would do that much for him.

"I didn't think he'd act like that," Miles says apologetically as he glances back. "I just told him to show up."

I would say something else, but there are more people walking toward the entrance. Even Auntie Jackie appears, pulling me in for a long hug. Not everyone in the crowd is coming inside— I can see some people walking back to their cars—but I don't even care. They could throw tomatoes at me and I wouldn't care now.

More and more people file in, either awkwardly acknowledging me or just pretending I'm not standing here. I'm not sure how much of this is because of what I said and how much is because they already spent money on tickets.

"Are they just going to pretend they weren't, like, demanding my expulsion?" I ask, turning toward Mr. Palumbo. "That happened, right? And they're just ignoring it."

"People don't like to admit their mistakes." He presses his lips together. "When that seemed like the general goal, more people supported it. Now *this* seems like the right thing to do."

"Because you basically told them that they were being stupid assholes," Miles steps in. "And they could've yelled at you about it, but they would've looked even worse. So they went with it."

"Do you think any of them actually *heard* what I said, though?" I ask, resisting the urge to claw my hands through my hair. "Because I really thought that out."

"If even one person learned something, you succeeded," Mr. Palumbo says. "And I learned a lot. Now we'll see the show through different eyes."

"Same," Miles says. "I mean, I already knew a lot of that stuff, because you told me. And because I know how to use Google."

"Shut up." I shove him. "You don't count."

"Oh my goodness, Simone." I don't get the chance to respond before I'm wrapped up in Pops's arms. "I was looking for you earlier. Where did you go?"

"I sort of hid in the closet," I say into his chest. "Something you're familiar with, right?"

I'm expecting him to lecture me, at least to save face in front of other people, but he just laughs. My feet aren't touching the ground, and for a second, I think of his bad back. He's probably going to crack it.

"I don't think I've ever been prouder," Dad says, appearing behind him. "It's really important that you know that, Mony."

"I do," I say, blinking back tears. Pops puts me down, and I gesture behind me. "Guys, this is Mr. Palumbo. He's the reason I'm doing this tonight."

They shake hands, and Miles nudges me again.

"Do I get to sit with you backstage?"

If he sits with me, we're not going to be watching, and he *knows* that. I roll my eyes.

"Come on," I say, pulling at my parents' hands. "I want you to see the show."

"As long as we can find seats." Pops grins.

• • •

It's pretty hard not to cry. Part of it is because of how beautiful the sets look—like this could actually be a Broadway stage. Maybe I'm biased, but so what? Laila completely knocks her solo out of the park and Rocco dazzles the audience, as predicted. But my favorite part is when everyone is out onstage at the end for bows. I stand backstage, screaming until my throat is sore as members of the crew, pit orchestra, and ensemble run onstage. Members of the cast go out one by one, but Eric surprises me with a crooked smile before his turn. Maybe the thrill of opening

277

night has unlocked a secret pool of empathy in his heart or some-thing.

"And last," Palumbo's voice calls out, "but *certainly* not least, is our wonderful student director, Simone Garcia-Hampton!"

I freeze. Directors don't go onstage for bows. I never went onstage when we rehearsed. I glance behind me, but there's no one left backstage to urge me on. Slowly, I shuffle onstage. The lights are blinding. I can barely see anyone in the crowd, but I do make out Claudia's new haircut, which means Lydia must be here, too. Everyone's smiling and clapping, probably because they're onstage, but it definitely doesn't make me feel *bad*. Palumbo waves me forward, Ms. Klein standing on the other side of him.

And up there, standing center stage with everyone clapping and cheering all around me? That's the best part of the entire night.

CHAPTER 35

The High School Theater Awards don't quite live up to opening night.

"Do you think taking too many pictures is just a dad thing?"

"Probably," Lydia says. "My dad does the same thing, but I thought it was just because he's always unbearable."

"Come on, girls," Dad says, looking up from behind his camera. "Don't make this harder than it has to be. Is it really that bad that I want pictures of your special night? Just a few more."

I don't even hide my groan. I've been wearing heels for about thirty minutes, and my feet already hurt. Tía Camila's gonna get an earful later since it was her idea for me to wear them.

"I'm sort of glad my father ignores me," Claudia mumbles, shuffling toward me. "Because I never have to deal with any of this."

"Smile!"

I blink on purpose.

"If you keep taking pictures, you'll run out of memory," Lydia says, ever the supportive friend. She looks better than I do, as always, with a red dress and her hair in a bun that makes her look like a princess. "You won't be able to take pictures at the actual ceremony if you waste them all here, Dr. Garcia."

"Don't encourage him," I grumble, smoothing my hands over my dress. I haven't worn a dress since eighth grade, so this feels unnatural. "I was trying to get him to leave it here."

"No way," Pops calls from the other room. "You're going to win all the awards, and we're going to capture every minute of it."

"Make sure you clear the camera after today," I say, walking down the stairs and toward Dad. "Knowing you, you'll forget and we'll meet Lin-Manuel Miranda and you'll miss it because your camera is full."

It'll be the first summer we spend in New York in the *longest* time. The idea is that we're "spending time with family," but I'm pretty sure I can get Dave to take me wherever I want. I'm looking forward to dragging him to Broadway.

"Don't joke like that," Dad says, frowning. "I can use my phone."

"But will your phone capture the moment in high definition?"

"*Simone*," Claudia says. She's wearing a tuxedo-looking top and a pair of pants. I almost wish I'd followed her lead. "Your dad deals with all *your* foolishness, give him a break."

"Thank you, Claudia," Dad says, pausing. "I think."

The doorbell rings, echoing throughout the house. Dad moves to answer it, but I grab his arm, smiling up at him.

"I can get it, Dad," I say. "You should take more pictures of Claudia and Lydia."

"Nice," Claudia calls. "Already abandoning us."

"I'm *not*," I argue, pulling open the door. Miles is there, wearing his lacrosse jersey again. "Dude, if you were going to wear that, I wouldn't have worn this."

"I was gonna change, actually," he says, giving me his stupid grin. He tugs at the strap on his shoulder, and I glance down at the gigantic bag hanging off his side. "Is that okay, Madam Director?"

"Yeah, whatever." I roll my eyes, but when Dad's head is turned, I kiss his cheek. "You can change in my room. I have something for you, anyway."

"Wait, don't you have a policy for boys coming over?" Lydia asks, folding her arms. "I don't think that the two of you should be alone."

"I hate you," I say, brushing past her. "I should remind *your* dad to take pictures of you when prom comes around. We'll call him."

"You wouldn't," she says, glaring at me.

"Lydia is right," Dad says, raising a brow. "Door open, Simone."

"He's *changing*, Dad."

"So you don't need to be in there, do you?"

I sigh, pulling Miles up the stairs with me. He laughs as I drag him into my room, keeping the door open just a crack.

"Do you actually want me to change?" he asks. "Because I can make it interesting, if you wanna watch."

I try not to blush—it's probably no use—and cross my arms.

"Yeah, you definitely can't wear that to the award ceremony." I turn toward my drawers, trying to find the gift I got for him. "My dad will be up here in a minute, probably."

"Wait, what is this?"

I turn back to see him holding my vibrator. My eyes widen. I leave it under my pillow, but never figured he'd go snooping. I'm pretty sure my cheeks are burning.

"*Miles.*" I dive for it, but he just holds it higher. "That's not yours. It's private."

"Obviously." He glances at it with a grin. "How many settings does this thing have?"

"*Ugh.*" I smack my hands against my thighs. "I was gonna give you something before my parents show up, but now you don't get it."

"A present?" His eyebrows rise, but he still holds the vibrator above my head. "What for?"

"I don't know." I step back, turning toward my drawers. "I'm pretty sure today is important."

"Really? I think I forgot."

I glance back at him. He's smirking.

"Whatever, you don't need your gift," I say, turning away. "Anniversaries are for old people, anyway, and it's only been three months."

"I was just joking." He leans against my back. "You look pretty."

"Thank you," I say, pulling out the box. "You look pretty sometimes, too."

He plops on my bed, the vibrator resting on my pillow, which is so weird. There have been many nights where I've sat here and talked to him, thought of him. "Um, maybe you shouldn't sit on my bed. I just—I do stuff there."

"Really?" He snickers. "With the vibrator?"

"I don't have to talk about this."

"Wait," he says, pulling his bag open. "I have something for you, too. Even though anniversaries are for old people. It's for good luck."

He tosses a maroon bundle at me, and the box in my hands topples to the floor. I glare at him, but his face doesn't change at all.

"You're a pain," I mutter, unwrapping the bundle. It's a black sweatshirt with a golden *Hamilton* logo in the center. "Okay, I actually really love this. Now I have my own lucky sweatshirt and it's *awesome.*"

I pull it over my head and get stuck halfway before wriggling through.

"Ugh," I say. "Now my hair's all messed up."

"It's fine," Miles says. "It's always fine."

"You're such a sap," I say, even though I am, too.

"Maybe," he says. "What'd you drop on the floor?"

I glance down at the box. Giggles escape my lips.

"You okay there?"

"Oh yeah," I say. "They're condoms. I got, like, four different kinds and put them all in here. There's ordinary latex and glow-in-the-dark and blueberry and 'intensified orgasm,' which sounds fun."

His eyes widen. For a second, I'm sure that this is going to be an intense moment, but then he starts to laugh. Not just normal laughing, either, but the way I figure people laughed when Eddie Murphy was still on *SNL.*

"Okay, I didn't tell you that to be *funny.*" I sit down next to him, pulling at the sweatshirt. "I just mean—you know. Three more months. It's not supposed to be funny."

"I'm not—I'm not laughing *at* you," he says, turning toward me. "Okay, maybe I am, a little bit."

"You don't get any condoms," I say, reaching for the box. "They're for people who are nice to me, okay?"

He kisses me. I was going to say something about a lacrosse team in New York, but it's sort of hard to think when I'm kissing Miles. Then I feel something hit my cheek. I push Miles away as he starts to laugh.

"You did *not* throw a condom in my face."

"Maybe I did." God, I like his smile. "But don't take it the wrong way. I only give condoms to cute girls who are being a pain."

I grab a handful out of the box, tossing them in his face.

"There are a ton for you, then," I say, grinning. "Because you're the biggest pain."

"Okay, so—" He lunges for the box, and I jump off the bed. Since he has all the ammo, he just keeps tossing it in my face. I lunge for the box, doubling over in laughter, but he jerks out of the way.

"I bet you wish you played lacrosse *now*," he says, tossing a condom in my face. "Because I have more stamina than you."

"I *bought* the condoms," I say, grabbing a handful off the floor. "So at least I can do something right."

"In what world are blueberry condoms *right*?"

"Hey!"

I pelt him with condoms. He puts his hands up, laughing as I back him into a corner. There are so many on the floor that my room looks like there's about to be a really large orgy.

"Come on," I say. "You can do better than that."

"Oh, *shut up*." He throws a blueberry condom in my face.

"Prepare to meet your fate," I say, ripping open one condom, then another. "Do you have any last words?"

"You think about me when you masturbate," he sings. "And I'm always going to remember that."

"Not the right words," I say, throwing them in his face. "Dude, you're going to be in trouble if someone ever holds you at gunpoint."

"Simone?" The door swings open, and I freeze. "We have to go now, or we're going to be late. Is Miles ready?"

Dad and Pops are both standing in the doorway. I see their eyes move from the vibrator on the bed to the condoms in my hands and on the floor. Miles stands up, his jersey decorated with blue condoms. This is what happens when I'm left alone with boys.

"Whoa," Claudia says, running into the room. "Is this what straight boys do? Is this, like, a mating call?"

"I don't *think* so," Lydia says, squinting. "I never did any of this with Ethan."

"Who the hell is Ethan?" I ask, raising a brow. "You're dating *Ian*."

"I've had *other* boyfriends, Simone."

"I just . . ." Pops's voice trails off. He rubs his temples and looks at Dad. "Why didn't we get a normal child? Everyone *else* has normal kids."

"This is *not* sex," I say, dropping the condoms. "I promise."

"*Definitely* not sex," Miles agrees. "We were, uh—"

"I don't need to know," Dad says, sighing. "I definitely don't need to know. Just do me a favor and get ready, all right? And take off that sweatshirt for the ceremony."

"Remember when you two said you were really proud of me?" I say, giving them a smile. "Remember when you said I'd win all the awards? Hold on to that pride."

"Well, you didn't have a condom in your hair then," Dad says, crossing his arms. "But I guess I'm still proud."

"You *guys*," I say, feeling around in my hair. "Come on."

Miles pulls a condom from the back of my head. I have to bite my lip to keep from laughing. The idea of using that specific condom makes me laugh.

"I've always been proud, Simone," Dad says, gripping the doorknob in his hand. "And I'm always going to be."

I smile at him. It's not the first time that he's said it, but maybe it's the first time I've been just as proud of myself. I survived the play and the kid who outed me in front of everyone. I survived coming out to my best friends as bisexual. I can survive a lot more.

"So, you're proud of me for buying condoms?"

Pops glares at me. "Don't push it."

Miles laughs into my shoulder.

"I love you all the time," he whispers. "Especially when you buy condoms."

I freeze, unable to hide my smile. He grips my hand, and I hold it closer to my heart.

"I'm changing my mind," I say, leaning back into him. "I think that I love you in the super-dramatic way. If that's okay."

"It's more than okay." He kisses my neck. "Maybe later, I can show you how okay I am with it."

"I think I'm gonna throw up," Claudia says, rolling her eyes. "This is disgusting."

"Aw, come on." I hold my hand out for the girls. "I love you guys in the super-dramatic way, too. I always will."

We're all pressed together, the people that I love with me. And so what if I don't win Best Director at the ceremony tonight? I don't need acceptance from some random judges, not when I have this: heaps of condoms, and excellent people.

EPILOGUE

The next time I have a gynecologist appointment, Dad wants to listen to Aretha in the car, and before long, Pops is belting out the lyrics to "(You Make Me Feel Like a) Natural Woman" so loud I'm surprised it doesn't stop traffic.

These are the moments I secretly love.

It's just that I'd rather see my doctor by myself.

"So," I say, tapping on my knee as Dad pulls into a parking spot. "What would you say if I asked you two to drop me off?"

They pause, sharing one of their *looks*. I can't read their expressions from the back seat. Aretha continues singing in the background.

"I mean, I love you and everything," I say, biting my lip. "It's just—I'll be eighteen soon. You're my parents, but *I'm* the one responsible for me, especially when it comes to—you know. Sex and stuff."

This definitely sounded less awkward in my head.

"Why don't we go outside?" Pops clears his throat. "It'll be easier to talk."

I bite back a groan, unbuckling my seat belt and sliding out the door. Pops and Dad stand next to each other. It's just like the first day they dropped me off at Our Lady of Lourdes, when Dad wouldn't stop hugging me and Pops made me take the blanket from the end of their bed. It smelled like clean soap and mint. Like them.

Fuck. I don't need to get all emotional now. This is *important*.

"I'm old enough to go by myself," I say, rushing out the words so they can't interrupt me. "I get that you're worried and that's fine and everything, but you don't have to baby me or freak out about me and sex. I've researched and talked to people and I'm going to make good choices. I just need you to trust me to do that."

Dad smiles. "We know."

"I *know* I'm still your kid, but—"

Wait. I close my mouth. Did he say what I think he said?

"We know that you understand the risks of sex," Pops says, heaving a deep breath. "And it's important that you manage your own sexuality."

"*Really?*" I raise a brow, folding my arms. "Are you serious?"

"Is it such a surprise?" Dad asks, leaning against the car. Pops leans against him, and I follow suit. The three of us look like we're posing for a car magazine. "You're obviously a responsible young lady."

"It's true." Pops nods, but he looks a lot more reluctant. "You're not a little girl anymore."

"But we want to be here to support you," Dad continues, snaking an arm around my shoulders. "Whether that's out here or in the waiting room."

"Preferably in the waiting room," Pops interrupts. I snort, but he keeps going. "What your dad is trying to say is that we know you can do this on your own, but that doesn't mean you have to. We're always here."

Shit. I might cry. And if I cry, one of them will cry, and we'll have a crying fest.

"We want to help," Dad says, pulling me close. "However we can."

I suck in a breath, forcing tears back. It's weird to think of them on the sidelines instead of front and center. They've always given me freedom—at Our Lady of Lourdes, at Sacred Heart, with my friends. But this is a new step. A big step. Even though I'm glad to take it, I'm glad that they aren't completely gone.

"Could you come inside?" I ask. "And, like, wait in there?"

Dad smiles. "Of course, *cariño*."

"We're right behind you." Pops knocks his shoulder with mine. "Lead the way, Simone."

AUTHOR'S NOTE

My interest in HIV and AIDS existed long before Simone did. We spoke briefly about HIV and AIDS in my high school health class, but it wasn't until I started reading blogs written by parents of kids with HIV that my education truly began. It was while researching and learning that Simone's character came to life.

Once I had a basic idea of who Simone was, I took my research to the next level to figure out the details of her story. This led me down several different avenues: I watched movies and read blogs, shared early drafts of the manuscript with readers who were HIV-positive, and followed people on social media. At first, I just wanted to know what life was like for a teen with HIV, but I soon found myself interested in the AIDS epidemic in the United States and the ways different communities responded. I'm still shocked I didn't learn any of this in school.

The resources listed below were extremely useful to me, not just in ensuring Simone's story was true-to-life, but because they taught me a wealth of information. I'm still learning and always will be. I hope these resources will teach you something new as well.

DOCUMENTARIES:

The Battle of amfAR, directed by Rob Epstein and Jeffrey Friedman (HBO, 2013)

Blood Brother, directed by John Pogue (2018)

How to Survive a Plague, directed by David France (2012)

We Were Here, directed by David Weismann (2011)

FICTIONAL MOVIES:

Angels in America, various directors (TV miniseries, 2003)

BPM (Beats per Minute), directed by Robin Campillo (2017)

Rent, directed by Chris Columbus (Sony Pictures, 2015)

BOOKS:

Angels in America: A Gay Fantasy on National Themes by Tony Kushner, rev. ed. (New York: Theatre Communications Group, Inc., 2013)

The Great Believers by Rebecca Makkai (New York: Viking, 2018)

How to Write an Autobiographical Novel by Alexander Chee (New York: Mariner Books, 2018)

The Normal Heart by Larry Kramer (New York: Samuel French, Inc., 1985)

Reports from the Holocaust: The Making of an AIDS Activist
   by Larry Kramer (New York: St. Martin's Press, 1989)

ARTICLES:

"American Woman Who Adopted HIV-Positive Child
   Tells Parents There Is 'Nothing to Be Afraid Of,'" by
   Lizzie Dearden. Published September 22, 2014, in *The
   Independent*.

"HIV Did Not Stop Me from Having a Biological Child," by
   Ben Banks. Published June 25, 2014, in *Time*.

"I Feel Blessed to Be HIV+ in the Age of PrEP and TasP," by
   Jeff Leavell. Published March 7, 2018, in *Them*.

"Odd Blood: Serodiscordancy, or, Life with an HIV-Positive
   Partner," by John Fram. Published March 29, 2012, in
   The Atlantic.

"Telling JJ: A year after learning she has HIV, an 11-year-old
   has a breakthrough," by John Woodrow Cox. Published
   August 27, 2016, in *The Washington Post*.

WEBSITES:

AdvocatesForYouth.org

Advocates for Youth is a nonprofit that works with young
people and other organizations to champion sexual health
and rights. They have a bunch of programs, including ECHO,
which trains HIV-positive youth to become leaders in the
movement to combat the stigma against HIV/AIDS. They

also coordinate National Youth HIV and AIDS Awareness Day, and the hashtag #MyStoryOutLoud, which is an online storytelling project for HIV-positive youth and LGBTQ+ youth of color.

tht.org.uk
The Terence Higgins Trust is the UK's leading HIV and sexual health charity. It supports people living with HIV and amplifies their voices, and helps the people using its services to achieve good sexual health.

PedAIDS.org
This is the website for the Elizabeth Glaser Pediatric AIDS Foundation, a nonprofit that works to prevent HIV and stop AIDS around the world, specifically in children.

POZ.com
An online magazine for people with or impacted by HIV/AIDS. There are columns and first-person accounts and all kinds of other information. I turned to this website a lot when I was writing my book. It shows how vast the experience of having HIV is and also how different HIV-positive people can be from each other.

UNAIDS.org
This United Nations program is committed to raising awareness and fighting AIDS on a global scale. Its website includes data and resources from around the world.

Even though Simone is very real to me, she isn't actually a real person. But all of her great qualities—her determination, perseverance, you name it—are reflected in these activists I drew inspiration from. The five activists included below all have HIV and use their voices to advocate for themselves and others. You can read their work, listen to their talks, or follow them on social media (I recommend doing all three).

ACTIVISTS:

Ashley Murphy is a young woman who was born with HIV and gives speeches and writes columns about her experiences. You can follow her on Twitter at @TheAshleyRose_ or watch her TED Talk, "How to Be Extraordinary" (July 2, 2015).

Ben Banks has written and spoken a lot about how having HIV hasn't stopped him from having children (which is something Simone worries about). He's written for *Time* and was commended for his work by President Obama.

Shawn Decker and his partner, Gwenn, are a sero-diverse couple who use their relationship as a jumping-off point to talk about sexual health. Visit them at shawnandgwenn.com or follow Shawn at @shawndecker.

George M. Johnson is a queer black man with HIV who writes about his experiences, including in his YA memoir, *All Boys Aren't Blue* (New York: Farrar, Straus & Giroux, 2020).

Visit him at iamgmjohnson.com or follow him at @iamgmjohnson.

Rae Lewis-Thornton is a black woman who has had HIV for over thirty years. She blogs about her experiences at raelewisthornton.com, and you can also follow her on Twitter at @raelt.

ACKNOWLEDGMENTS

I've been on my publishing journey ever since I was thirteen, so my acknowledgments are long and very dramatic. I apologize in advance.

The first person I have to thank is my mother, because this book wouldn't exist without her. Mom: I read the dedication to you and you didn't "get it." So "for Mom, always," means I'm able to do all of this because of you. All of your love and support and everything you've sacrificed. For never once doubting me, even though I do it all the time. I love you more than anything, even though you don't read.

Bri: I don't even know where to start. Thank you for pulling me out of the slush and seeing something there. For taking a chance on me. For teaching me more about writing than I thought I could possibly learn with one book. For your editor's eye, your business sense, and the fact you don't take any shit. For being honest. For answering all my random emails and all the brainstorming sessions. For coming up with the sex-store scene. For laughing at all my jokes. For making my dreams come true. I couldn't ask for a better agent.

Allie: I just want to leave you a bunch of exclamation points, but that's not fair. Thank you for answering emails with weird questions and reassuring me every time I freaked out (which was often). For listening to me talk about college. For freaking out about the cover of this book with me. For your notes and your attention and your hard work. For your support. You're the best.

Thank you to Katherine for offering on this book after a day like a maniac and giving me an asthma attack. For your excitement, dedication, and your vision for this project. For believing in Simone and her story. For believing in me. For making my dreams come true. Thank you to the rest of the publishing team, specifically Melanie Nolan, Kerry Johnson, Janet Renard, Jazzmine Walker, Sylvia Al-Mateen, Artie Bennett, Jake Eldred, Mary McCue, Andrea Comerford, and Emily DuVal. It's been such a pleasure working with you all.

Thank you to Theodore Samuels, Rhesa Smith, Jen Heuer, and Alison Impey for the cover of my dreams, and to Stephanie Moss for the beautiful interior design. I always fantasized about having a book published, but never could imagine what it would actually look like, and now I feel like the luckiest writer in the world every time I look at this book. Thank you all for your work on this gorgeous package.

Thank you to the entire UK team, including Naomi Colthurst, Amanda Punter, Simon Armstrong, Ruth Knowles, Ben Horslen, Amy Wilkerson, Francesca Dow, and Michael Bedo. You've all had so much enthusiasm throughout this entire process. Thank you for your notes and your positivity and the pamphlet you made me before the deal (which is saved on my desktop). It's been so great working with you. A very special thanks to Emma Jones, who is the absolute best.

Thank you to Dad for all the hours in the bookstore. For never refusing to buy me a book, even when I was only supposed to get two. For all the hours I hung out on the computer next to you in your office and typed on my diary. For your old computer. For all the memories.

Jayden: I doubt you'll read this, but thank you for being my sister.

Thank you to Aunt Jessica for never thinking anything I wanted to do was weird. Thank you for never telling me to slow down. Thank you for being the coolest, in general.

Thank you to Mark for being more excited than me about this book sometimes. For tweeting my Goodreads link and reading my work and sending me memes. For your friendship, even when I'm a pain. For sharing yourself and your words with me. For being you. I love you, and those black shoes.

To Michael: You once said you think the "best friend" thing is stupid, but you're one of my best friends, so you have to deal with it. I feel like we've grown up with each other, even though we live in different places. I'm so grateful to have you in my life. I'm grateful for Teens Can Write, Too!, which let me believe I could be a writer. I'm grateful for every complaint you listened to, for every time you somehow found a way to help me hang on. Thank you for making me feel like you were in the next room when you were farther away. For believing in me and being gentle and also ruthlessly funny at the same time. For everything. You're amazing and I love you.

To Aisha, thank you for stalking me on Twitter and starting our friendship; thank you for reading Drew's story and believing so much in it, even though it didn't work out. For introducing me to different viewpoints and making stupid jokes.

To Maliha: For taking pictures of me when I signed the contract. For coming up to middle school and telling me you liked my shirt; for the framed picture of me staring dramatically out a window that's still on my nightstand. For shipping Stucky with me. For naming Ren, even though his book didn't get published. For your friendship.

To Natalia, Gabi, Abi: Thank you for making high school bearable. Thank you for being the friends I could talk to about literally anything. Thank you for answering odd questions about sex at lunch or via the group chat. Thank you for inspiring Simone, Claudia, and Lydia. You're the first group of girlfriends I felt especially close to. I love your makeup skills and how great you are at making art. I love that none of you know what you're doing. I love that you know everything and nothing all at once. I love that there's always one of you awake at two in the morning. I love the memes from Tumblr and the characters you think up. Thank you for listening to me talk about imaginary people. Thank you for loving me for who I am. I love you.

Thank you, Chey, because you'd probably torture me if I didn't include you here. Thank you for being one of my first friends at college. I'm so excited to see what we create together in the future.

Thank you, thank you, thank you, Miss Kalter. You were excited for me when I couldn't process anything and I love you for it. Thank you for being proud and happy and so awesome, even before I got this deal. For introducing me to different sides of storytelling. For listening to me ramble at the beginning of the school day and during random periods. For everything.

Thank you to every English teacher I've ever had. Thanks for letting me hang out in your classrooms and talk about books, even when I was supposed to be somewhere else. Specific thanks to Dr. Johnson for being visible and making sure all the other black kids were, too.

To Jenni Walsh: For being my first substantial critique partner. For reading my really bad writing, somehow getting through it, and giving me important notes that I took with me when writing my next books. For letting me know it was okay to slow down, that I didn't need a book by the time I was sixteen. For your guidance.

To Shveta: For your warmth. For listening to me complain about writing and everything that frustrated me about it. For sharing your knowledge and your own journey with me. For your words and your presence. For generally being great.

To Lana Wood Johnson, who said, "You won't ever be the Oprah of daytime television. Or Shonda of nighttime TV. You'll be the Camryn of . . ." I've been thinking about it ever since you said it, and I'll continue to think about it long after this book is published. Thank you for saying it.

To my Wakanda Ladies: Adrienne, Elle, Angie, and Cara. Thank you for the safe space to complain about things only you-all would understand. Thank you for the guidance and for acting as honorary aunties. For paving the way for me.

To Mason, Cody, Ava: For letting me freak out over the smallest parts of the journey. For reading the book early on and falling in love with it. Thank you to Cody, for coming up with the title. For your encouragement and your excitement. For your advice. For your friendship.

To Courtney Milan: For your generosity. For giving me advice about things no one I know really understands. For taking it upon yourself to help me in ways no one (literally no one, at all) would expect you to. For looking at me, seeing I needed help, and saying, "Yeah, I'll do this myself." For being a resource and a person I could go to with questions. For your Twitter feed in general. Thank you.

To Nita: For being one of the best critique partners! For all the complaints we've shared about everything related to publishing. For sharing stories about your girls falling in love. For your soft, lyrical writing. For your friendship.

To Kaye: For your warm spirit. Your smiles and kindness shine through tweets, even back when they were only 140 characters long. Thank you for lifting me up before I thought I deserved it. Thank you for believing in me. Thank you for consistently being such a lovely person. You are the best.

To Kacen Callender: For giving me an R&R on the book of my heart. It wasn't ready, but I loved it (and I still do) and I think you loved it—or at least really liked it—too. Thank you for giving me that chance. Thank you for working with me and teaching me. Thank you for letting me know I still had work to do. To Rebecca Podos for your lovely rejection/ offer letter. It gave me the ammunition to keep querying. And to Alexandra Machinist for the nicest rejection letter in the history of queries. It's still favorited in my email account. It meant so much to me when I first read it and still does.

To Nic Stone: For reading one of my earlier books and giving me notes. For the help you gave me, even when I wasn't exactly ready for it. For paving the way with your own work. To Becky Albertalli for being generally amazing and so, so kind. To Justina Ireland: For showing me I'm allowed to speak up about what's important. For being a badass. For welcoming me into the community when I was fifteen. For inspiring me.

To Wendy Xu: For being a protective Twitter auntie. For the talk we had about success and how it doesn't need to happen when you're so young. I needed to hear it.

To Sierra Elmore and Phil Stamper: For staying in the group chat, even though no one is making you. For listening to me talk about who and what I'm attracted to and answering embarrassing questions. I'm not thankful for all the times you dragged me, but I am thankful for all the times you listened.

To Dahlia Adler: For the amount of work you do for the YA community in general, but specifically for queer books. I'm in awe of you. For reminding me that f/f YA books exist, even when I didn't think they did. For recommending the best books. For the Figgy pictures whenever I'm sad. You're the best.

To Rachel Strolle: For all you do for the YA book community. For the little mock-up version of the cover you made when the book was first announced. For your excitement. You're the best.

To Taylor and Liz: For being two of the first people to publish me on the Internet. For the community you created at *HuffPost Teen*. For staying in touch after that awesome moment ended. For your tweets and your help and every time you guys congratulated me. For being young and hip and cool. For hooking me up with opportunities after you were no longer obligated to. For creating more than one space where my voice mattered.

To all my *HuffPost Teen* people: Bekah, Leo, Sam, Erin, Lauren, Taylor, Emma (who snuck in somehow without us realizing it). You were all older cool kids and I wanted to be just like you. I'm pretty sure that's why I started writing books. Okay, it's part of it, anyway.

Thank you to those I wrote with at MTV Founders. Thank you to *Rookie*, specifically Tavi Gevinson, Diamond Sharp, and Derica Shields. It was the first (and so far only) experience I had where only black women were editing my work. I loved it and was extremely proud to be published by *Rookie*.

Thank you to Julie Zeilinger for running the WMC FBomb and giving me opportunities to rant about *Stranger Things* and interview people about herpes.

Thank you, especially, to the *TIME for Kids* Kid Reporter Contest, which was the first step in my journey as a published author. I was edited by a real editor and interviewed people who wrote actual books and were in movies. For the first time, I wasn't so shy. For the first time, I thought my words could make me a big deal. Thank you for that experience. I'll always cherish it.

Thank you so much to Shawn Decker, Sakhile Moyo, Vic

Vela, Nina Martinez, and Nick Cady for sharing your expertise and making this book as real and authentic as possible. Thank you so much for your time and your knowledge.

I also have to thank the people who have been following me and cheering me on via Twitter since I was fifteen, including, but not limited to: Molli, Leah, Chasia, Gabe, Saba, Summer, Kelley, Anne, Katherine, Hannah, Justine, Gwenda, Brandon, Tehlor, Marieke, Meagan, Ellen, Julie, Rebekah, Angie M., Nafiza, Samira, Jessie, Ami, Alyssa, Sarah, Katie. Thank you to everyone who follows me and has to deal with my ramblings at all times of the day. The people who engage in conversation with me over random things and teach me about subjects I know nothing about. For making Twitter a community, even when the rest of the website is a garbage fire. Specifically, thank you to all the teens on Twitter. Some of you aren't under the same usernames and some of you are still here. Thank you for all your thoughts. Thank you for holding the YA community accountable and forcing us to be better. Thank you for the work you do. Thank you just for being there.

I also need to shout out to the queer community, especially the black queer community. You were hit the hardest with HIV and AIDS, and this community survived. Thank you to the elders and those who continue to keep the memories of those who passed alive. Thank you to everyone who was out on the streets at the height of the AIDS crisis, protesting and demanding. Thank you to groups like ACT UP for fighting, always fighting. I wasn't even there and I feel so indebted to all of you. Thank you. I'm so glad this community exists and I'm so grateful to be part of it.

Finally, I have to thank you, dear reader, for picking up this book. For making it to the end, even if you skipped. Not every book is for everyone. But thank you for giving me a chance.

Camryn Garrett was born and raised in New York. When she was thirteen, she was selected as a TIME for Kids reporter, where she interviewed celebrities like Warren Buffett and Kristen Bell. Her writing has appeared in the *Huffington Post*, MTV, and *Rookie Magazine*. In 2015, she was named as one of MTV's 8 Inspiring Teens Using Social Media to Change the World. Camryn is also interested in film and is a freshman at NYU's Tisch School of the Arts. She is a proud advocate of diverse stories and writers.

You can find her on Twitter @dancingofpens, tweeting from a laptop named Stevie.